Raves for *Alone With the Dead* and Robert J. Randisi!

"Randisi power-shifts this work from the start, slowing only to provide procedural detail before resuming speed. As one killer comes to the surface, the other's rage intensifies. This is top-notch suspense, right from the chilling prologue to the brutal conclusion."
—*Publisher Weekly* (Starred Review)

"Forget comparing him with Ed McBain and Joseph Wambaugh. From now on Robert J. Randisi is the yardstick against which all books of this type must be measured."
—Loren D. Estleman, Author of *Edsel*

"I've been telling people for years that Bob Randisi will someday be a name to reckon with. *Alone With the Dead* marks that day. Randisi has arrived!"
—Ed Gorman, Author of *Black River Falls*

"Randisi deftly creates characters, gets the reader hooked by the third paragraph, and fashions a plot that encourages readers this highly recommended book in one sitting."
—*The Armchair Detective*

"Bob Randisi keeps on getting better. This one's a pip—lean, tough-minded. and right on target."
—Lawrence Block, Author of *Eight Million Ways to Die*

More Critical praise for *Alone With the Dead*

"This is a major step forward in a career that's been paid too little attention. Randisi is now a contender."

—*Mystery Scene*

"*Alone With the Dead* is tough, gritty and grippingly realistic. Randisi knows which button to press—and how to press them. This one hits hard and on target."

—John Lutz, Author of *Single White Female*

"Robert J. Randisi successfully combines dry humor and suspense to come up with one heckuva read.

—*Rave Reviews*

"This is an entertaining, well-written novel that stands out on the basis of its shifting points of view, sharp dialogue, and bang-up conclusion."

—*Booklist*

"Brooklyn is one of America's most famous regions, and Randisi is one of its best chroniclers."

—*Rocky Mountain News*

THERE COULD BE ONLY ONE

The Lover read the *Post* over his morning coffee and roll. He chewed vigorously, but the roll was tasteless in his mouth. Somebody was encroaching on his territory, and even though this second killer—and only *he* knew there was a second killer—seemed to be plying his trade in Brooklyn, the Lover didn't like it.

There was something in particular, though, that the Lover was actually offended by. After the women he had loved, how could anyone—the newspapers, the readers, and especially the police—believe that he would stoop to . . . to touching underage girls, high school girls, like the two who had been found in Brooklyn. Wasn't it obvious to the police that these were not his doing? Couldn't they see the difference?

He had already decided what he was going to do if this bogus killer struck again, and when he got to his office for this morning's summer session he would put his plan into effect. If the police couldn't see for themselves that what was happening in Brooklyn was *not* his doing, it fell to him to set them straight.

The city had to know there was only one Lover.

Other *Leisure* books by Robert J. Randisi:
TARGETT

ALONE WITH THE DEAD

ROBERT J. RANDISI

LEISURE BOOKS ⊔ NEW YORK CITY

To Marthayn.
Thanks for the best two years of my life.

A LEISURE BOOK®

September, 1999

Published by

Dorchester Publishing Co., Inc.
276 Fifth Avenue
New York, NY 10001

ISBN 0-8439-4641-5

Prologue

Kopykat opened the album.

It had been meant for use as a photo album, but instead it held fairly recent newspaper clippings, which had been Scotch-taped into the book.

From down the hall, he heard his mother's cries and the sound of creaking bedsprings. . . .

The first clipping was from a page-three story in the *New York Daily News*, dated March 5. The girl had been raped and strangled, then laid out with a rose protruding from her vagina. (He'd had to look up the word *vagina*.) She had been discovered in her own apartment that way. From the moment Kopykat had first read the story, he knew that it was something special.

He could hear the man now, a deep voice, shouting unintelligibly, bellowing. . . .

The second clipping was dated a month later. This time, it made page one of the *New York Post*. A second girl, raped and strangled and laid out with a rose. This time, the body had been found in Central Park.

Kopykat had known, even before anyone else did—even before the newspapers made the connection.

His mother had started shouting, things like "Yes, oh yes" and "Now, now" over and over again. . . .

It was with the third clipping, from a *New York Post* issue dated three weeks later, that the killer was first called "the Lover." The third girl had been found exactly the same way, roses and all, in the laundry room of her Manhattan apartment building. It was because of the roses that the *Post* dubbed him "the Lover."

His mother and the man were still rutting as he looked at the fourth clipping—again from the *Post*, which was Kopykat's favorite newspaper. This one had a headline that read LOVER CLAIMS FOURTH VICTIM. This was eleven weeks after the first victim had been found.

The headline on the fifth clipping—the fourth from the *Post*—read LOVER TAKES NUMBER FIVE!

The five women were killed within a four-month period.

As Kopykat closed the album, feeling all warm inside just from reading the clippings again, the door to his mother's room opened and the man came staggering out. He was wearing nothing but a pair of dirty Jockey briefs, and his hairy bare belly hung down like a swollen balloon. The man stopped when he saw Kopykat sitting there.

"Hey, where's your ol' lady keep the beer, kid?" he asked.

"It's in the refrigerator," he replied, pointing toward the kitchen.

The man walked into the small kitchen, scratching his belly, digging lint out of his navel with one hand while opening the refrigerator with the other. He reached in and took out a cold can of Meister Bräu.

"Jesus, this shit," he muttered, but that didn't stop him from popping the tab and draining half the can. He was *still* digging into his navel with the index finger of his other hand. Kopykat hoped that the man would push his navel all the way in. He wondered idly if that would cause the air to escape from the man's swollen belly.

He walked out of the kitchen carrying the can and looked over at Kopykat, sitting on the sofa. His eyes fell on the closed album.

"Whatcha lookin' at?" he asked. "Pitchers?"

Kopykat nodded.

The man leered and asked, "*Dirty* pitchers?"

Kopykat shook his head. If the man tried to look at the album, Kopykat would hurt him. He didn't try, though. He burped, scratched his belly, and said, "M'gonna go give yer ol' lady nother ride."

Kopykat didn't say anything. The man went back into his mother's room, closing the door behind him. Kopykat picked up the album and cradled it in both arms, holding it against his chest. He almost wished the man *had* tried to look at the book.

Others took clippings from the careers of movie

stars or sports figures. For Kopykat, "the Lover" was the ultimate celebrity.

It was time, however, to do more than just sit back, cut clippings, and admire.

It was time for Kopykat to step forward and take action.

July

Chapter One

The kite swooped, caught an updraft, soared, swooped again, coming perilously close to crashing, then suddenly caught a good strong updraft, soared, higher, higher, and then stayed up.

It was a box variety, not Keough's favorite, but he'd wanted to try it out. Here, along the Belt Parkway in Brooklyn, right off the water, was where you saw kite fliers every day—*serious* fliers, not your weekend variety. Even in the middle of the summer, there was enough of a breeze coming off the water to accommodate a true enthusiast. Keough was just one of a dozen people flying kites, but most of the others were kids, either in a group or with a parent or parents. Joe Keough, all thirty-seven years of him, went there alone, every month, to fly a kite.

He hadn't liked flying kites when he was a kid. Back then, his interest had been sports, but sports—almost *any* sport—involve other people, and when Keough reached his thirties, he suddenly found that he needed some solitude. So once a month—sometimes more—he went out and flew a kite.

Keough worked the string gently, looking around at the joggers, the bike riders, the picnickers. One of the joggers was a particularly fetching-looking blonde wearing black and orange. She was tall, rangy almost, built like a long-distance runner rather than a casual jogger. Keough generally liked his women a little more padded, but he had no problem watching this young lady until she was out of sight before turning his attention back to the kite.

He watched it fly, every so often letting out more string, for almost an hour and then started to reel it in. As he did so, he looked down and saw a young boy about eight or nine standing next to him, watching the kite. He stopped reeling in the kite and watched the boy for about ten minutes. The youngster never took his eyes from it.

Keough checked his watch. If he was going to get some sleep before he went to work, he was going to have to get going now. He still had some errands that needed taking care of.

"What do you think?" he asked the boy.

"Huh?" the boy said, without taking his eyes from the kite.

"What do you think of the kite?"

"It's *fresh!*" the boy said enthusiastically.

Fresh. Keough assumed that meant *neat*, which was what he would have said when he was eight or nine.

"What's your name?" he asked.

"Kyle."

"Are you here alone, Kyle?"

"With my brother," Kyle said. "He flying a kite with his friends."

"Why aren't you with them?"

Kyle wrinkled his nose and said, "They're *teen-agers*!"

Keough looked around and saw three boys nearby, about fifteen or so, flying one kite, a colorful, swooping thing that resembled a dragon.

"Kyle, I have to leave now, and I really don't have time to reel this sucker in. Would you like to fly it for a while?"

Finally, the boy looked at *him*.

"Really?"

"Sure," Keough said. "Here, take it."

The boy took the string from Keough and stared up at the kite.

"I have to go, Kyle."

"Okay."

"Make sure you stay close to your brother, huh?"

"Okay."

Keough started to walk away, toward his car, when he heard Kyle shout, "Hey, mister."

"Yeah?"

"W-what do I do with it after I bring it in?"

"Keep it," Joe Keough said. "It's yours."

"Really?"

Keough nodded, but the boy wasn't looking at him, so he said, "Yeah, really."

"All right!" Kyle said. "Fresh!"

"Yeah," Keough said, smiling at the boy's enthusiasm, "fresh."

He hadn't felt that kind of innocent enthusiasm about anything in a long time.

He missed it.

Detective Joseph Sean Keough was working the night watch that week—second week in a row. He was regularly assigned to the Six-Seven Precinct in Flatbush, which had become known as a dumping ground for misfits, fuckups, and assholes.

The night watch was usually worked by three detectives from three different commands. They worked out of an office in the Borough Headquarters, which was right upstairs from the Six-Seven, on the second floor of the Snyder Avenue building. That is, the Borough *Headquarters* was on the third floor, but the actual office the night watch used was on the second. It wasn't usual that one man would work the watch two weeks in a row, but it wasn't unprecedented, either.

The night watch covered all of the precincts in the Brooklyn South Area, which pretty much covered Brooklyn from Eastern Parkway to Sheepshead Bay.

Keough was actually working a second week in a row because he had switched with a married detective whose bliss was under a strain. Keough, single and living alone, didn't much care *which* tour he worked, so he'd readily switched with the man.

He was working this night with Johnson, from the Six-Nine, and Adair, from the Six-Three. Both men were out getting something to eat, leaving Keough alone with the radio and his thoughts—which was always a danger these days.

Keough had a lined yellow legal pad on the desk in front of him and he had written three words on it. He was sitting in a borough office, even though the office of his own squad was right across the hall.

The three words were *misfit, asshole, fuckup*. Actually, he'd written *fuck up*, then *fuckup*, and then crossed out the former, finally deciding that *fuckup* was one word.

Which am I? he thought, looking at the three words. He'd been assigned to the Six-Seven Precinct five months ago, following an unfortunate . . . incident. As a result of the incident, he had been labeled one of these three things and dumped into the Six-Seven Detective Squad. He supposed now that he was lucky they hadn't dropped him back into ''the bag''—into uniform again.

He thought about the boy he'd given the kite to that afternoon, Kyle. He realized now that the boy had strongly resembled the other boy, the one he'd seen five months ago in the men's room of the Manhattan Criminal Courts Building, with Eddie Vargas.

Eddie Vargas . . .

In January of that year, Keough had been working Vice in Midtown Manhattan. The funny thing was, he'd liked it—up until Eddie Vargas, that is.

Eddie Vargas was a weenie-wagger, with a long sheet to prove it. Everybody knew what Eddie did, but Eddie was also a snitch. Keough didn't use him, but several other detectives who worked Vice did.

Keough had been taken off the clock to testify in court on a collar he'd made the month before. While waiting to be called, he saw Eddie Vargas in the hallway. As it turned out, Eddie was testifying in a different case, for one of Keough's colleagues. Keough saw Eddie Vargas go into the men's room and then saw a small boy go in moments later. Keough waited a few minutes, and when neither Vargas nor the boy came out, he got a bad feeling.

As he entered the men's room, he saw Eddie Vargas kneeling down in front of the boy, his hands on the boy's shoulders. It was the sick, hungry look on Vargas's face that convinced him, rather than the look on the boy's face, which simply looked confused. Also, the boy's pants were down around his ankles.

"Pull up your pants, son," Keough said, "and go find your parents."

Vargas started to get up, but Keough pointed and said, "Stay there, Eddie."

"Wha—"

"Stay there!"

The boy, who was about eight or nine, pulled up his pants and ran from the room. At that moment, he was more afraid of Keough than he was of Eddie Vargas. Keough was speaking sharply, while Eddie Vargas had spoken to him in soft, soothing tones.

"H-hey, K-Keough," Vargas said, recognizing the detective. He started to get up again.

"Damn it, I *said* stay there, Eddie," Keough said. He moved right up to Vargas, pulled out his .38, and jammed it into the man's ear. Vargas's hair had so much grease in it that it reflected the light from the overheads.

"Jesus, Keough—" Vargas said, bug-eyed and sweaty, "you gotta have a heart—"

"You like little boys, Eddie?" Keough asked him.

18

"Look, Keough, the kid was cute—b-but I wasn't gonna do nothin'—"

"Graduating from weenie-wagging, Eddie?" Keough screwed the .38 into the man's ear even tighter. He felt a rage that frightened him, that was uncharacteristic, and the thing about it that bothered him even more—at that moment *and* later—was that he didn't know where it came from.

But it was there, and he was in the throes of it.

"You like weenies so much, Eddie, I got one for you," he said, and he proceeded to unzip his own fly, remove his penis, and urinate on Eddie Vargas.

Vargas, humiliated by the indignity, started to rise almost involuntarily, stunned by what was happening to him. Keough clubbed him down with the .38. Had he left it at that, maybe things would have been different, but the rage had a firm hold on him and he began to beat Eddie Vargas, not with the gun but with his fists, and with his feet, until the little boy's story to his parents *and* Vargas's screams brought several pairs of hands to pull him off. . . .

The phone rang, jerking him from his reverie.

"Keough, night watch."

"We got one for you, Keough."

"Who's this?"

"Aiello, downstairs."

Aiello was a Six-Seven cop Keough knew personally. He often worked the front desk as the desk officer when there was no lieutenant or sergeant available for that duty—as was often the case on late tours.

"What have you got for me, Jerry?"

"A body," Aiello said, "a girl."

19

"What's it look like?"

"I'll tell you what it looks like to *me*," Aiello said. "It looks like the Lover has moved his dance card to Brooklyn."

Chapter Two

Erasmus High School was once attended by young students who went on to bigger and better things in life. Two in particular who came to mind for Keough were Neil Diamond and Barbra Streisand.

In recent years, however, Erasmus had gone the way of this particular section of Flatbush Avenue in Brooklyn. No longer was it considered one of the finer high schools in Brooklyn, as it had one of the higher crime rates of all the Brooklyn high schools. Keough had often thought, during his short tenure at the Six-Seven Precinct, that it might be a good idea, once school was in session, to bar the doors and windows and keep all of the students inside. He thought that would cause an immediate drop in the neighborhood crime rate. Some

people who lived in the area—and a lot of cops—
called it "Ignoramus High School."

His car had been parked in the precinct parking lot.
He'd pulled out onto Snyder Avenue, turned right, and
driven down the one-way street until he reached Flatbush Avenue. His partners had gone to find their meal
in their unit, so he had to take his own car to the scene.
There he turned right and drove to Erasmus High
School, which was only a block away, on the corner
of Flatbush and Church avenues. There was a blue-
and-white RMP—Radio Motor Patrol—parked in
front, and one officer was leaning against the car, waiting.

Keough parked behind the RMP and got out. It was
a warm night, and he could feel the perspiration starting in his armpits. He approached the officer and recognized him as Neil Bullion, a barrel-chested
ex-Transit Police officer who was having some trouble
making the transition. For one thing, he still wore
three guns—service revolver, off-duty in a belt hol-
ster, and another in an ankle holster—a holdover from
his Transit days, when he was working the subway
stations and tunnels *without* a partner to back him up.

"Anyone else here yet?" he asked.

"No," Bullion said, "just the *squad!*" He pro-
nounced it *squahhhd*, drawing the word out, meaning
that Keough himself had arrived.

There was no love lost between uniformed patrol
and the detective squad. Patrol usually felt that the
"Squahhhd" was of the opinion that their shit didn't
stink. Of course, a uniformed officer who made detective and transferred to the squad often changed his
opinions accordingly.

"Where's the girl?"

"In the schoolyard, by the side door. My partner's with her."

"Thanks."

"Use your flashlight," Bullion said, "or you'll break your fuckin' neck."

"I didn't bring one. Can I borrow yours?"

Bullion stared at Keough for a few minutes, then sighed and removed his metal-cased oversized flashlight from his belt.

"Make sure I get it back, all right?"

"Sure," Keough said, hefting the thing. "What would I keep it for, a baseball bat?"

"Believe me," Bullion said, "I've used it as one a time or two."

Keough was sure that Bullion and his flashlight had cracked quite a few heads in their time.

He walked around to the schoolyard and switched on the light. He noticed that there was no lock on the schoolyard gate, so the gate had not been forced. Somebody in the school would catch hell for that.

He found the side door, which was at the bottom of a set of steep steps. Bullion's partner, Frank Cuccio, was waiting at the top of the steps, smoking a cigarette. Keough saw the tip glow brightly for a moment before it was ground out beneath the man's foot.

"The 'Keyhole' man," Cuccio said, using a nickname Keough had been hearing most of his life. "About fuckin' time you got here." There was no rancor in Cuccio's tone.

"Hey," Keough said, giving it back, "I'm first, ain't I? Where is she?"

"Down there. Watch your step."

Cuccio switched on his flashlight and they used both lights to make it to the bottom of the steps without killing themselves.

The area at the bottom was approximately five feet wide by nine feet long. The girl was lying atop the storm drain. There was still some dampness on the ground, even though it had not rained for three days. The sharp odor that tickled Keough's nose told him that all of the dampness was not plain water.

Keough leaned over the girl and shone his light in her face.

"Fuckin' shame, huh?" Cuccio said.

Keough nodded.

"How come you're alone?" the other man asked.

"My partners are out getting something to eat."

"Sounds good," Cuccio said. "My partner and I were on our way to a meal when we got the call on this."

"Who called it in?"

"Don't know."

The light made her face seem even paler than it was. She looked young, sixteen, or seventeen, probably a student, possibly a student here at this school. Her face was serene and appeared unmarked, but the garish light of the flashlight in the dark area could have been washing out any bruises she might have had. The medical examiner would have to determine whether she was bruised or not. From the position of the body, however, it was clear enough that she hadn't simply been dumped down the steps. She had either been killed there or been carried and placed there after she was dead.

"The ME?"

24

"On his way, or so they say," Cuccio said. "Also the lab, and the duty captain."

"Who is it tonight?"

"Baker."

"Keep your hats on."

Captain Baker was notorious for bawling out officers for being seen in public without their hats on their heads. It had become even worse since a photograph of about half a dozen hatless officers had made it to the pages of the *Post* recently.

The girl was wearing a tight black top with half sleeves, which showed off her shoulders and her flat midriff and deep belly button. Below that was a green skirt that would normally have been short, had it not been hiked up around her hips at the moment. Around her were some remnants of the Fourth of July, some dead bottle rockets and at least one exploded pack of firecrackers, maybe more.

"See the rose?" Cuccio asked.

"I see it."

He had seen it without being told, and it made his stomach jump. There was a single rose protruding from the girl's vagina. She wasn't wearing panties. In the dark, the rose looked red, but when he shone the flashlight on it, he saw that it was instead a white rose with thick red stripes.

Unusual.

"Do roses come in that color naturally?" he asked, just out of curiosity.

"Fucked if I know."

Keough had been speaking to himself and hadn't expected a reply. For that reason, he ignored it.

"Have you seen her panties around?"

"No," Cuccio said, and then he admitted, "but I haven't looked around upstairs."

Keough nodded. He decided not to send Cuccio up to do it now. It would get done, later.

He leaned over and touched her briefly without moving her. There were no visible wounds, but he noticed that her neck had suffered some trauma. He couldn't tell how bruised she was. The yellow light from their flashes was washing her color out.

"Strangled?" Cuccio asked.

"Looks like it."

He noticed that her breasts were pert and taut. While noticing that her inner thighs were bloody, he also noticed that her legs were tan and smooth. A tennis player's legs, an athlete's body. This little girl would never hit a tennis ball again.

"Looks like the Lover's MO, huh?" Cuccio asked.

Keough ignored his comment. He was wondering what color the roses that had been found on the other victims were. He'd assumed they'd been red, and he hadn't read the newspaper accounts closely enough to know differently. He looked up at the door the girl was lying next to.

"Is this locked?"

"Tight."

He tried it anyway and found it locked. He made a mental note to see the custodian about the door.

He stood up, played the light around the area. It was damp but not wet, so there were no footprints. She was barefoot, and her shoes were lying apart, one in a corner, the other near the body. They were white, and while not high heels, the heels were high enough to have shown off her legs. Walking around dressed like that, at this time of night, in this neighborhood . . .

"So?" Cuccio asked. "Who the fuck did it?"

Keough ignored him.

"You'd better go back up and wait for the others."

"Want to be alone with her?" Cuccio asked. A leer was plain in his tone.

Keough stared at the cop and said coldly, "Yes."

Cuccio shrugged and went back up the stairs.

Keough illuminated her face again. She was young and pretty. In Vice, he had witnessed all kinds of abuse being heaped on the human body, but this . . . this was the worst, the most final abuse of all.

This was a true sin.

When the ME and lab arrived, he had to vacate the stairwell to make room for them. The girl's purse had been half under her, and he pulled it free and took it up with him.

Up in the schoolyard, he found the duty captain waiting. Capt. Andrew Baker was the exec at the Six-Seven. It was no secret that he was waiting for Captain Farrell to be promoted to deputy inspector so that he could inherit the command of the Six-Seven. He was a smallish man, perhaps five eight or nine, with red hair and freckles, which he was forever having to live down. Behind his back, the men called him "Howdy Doody." His tough facade was his way of retaliating.

"Who are you?" the man asked.

"Keough, Six-Seven Squad."

"Oh yeah," Baker said, as if he recognized him. "You alone?"

"My partners are on another call."

"Bullshit," Baker said, but he pursued the matter

27

no further. "This officer says we have the Lover's next victim."

Keough looked at Cuccio, who found something else to look at.

"This officer's conclusion may be a little premature," he said dryly.

"Well, is there a rose in her pussy or isn't there, Detective?" Baker asked.

"There is a rose, Captain, yes," Keough said.

"Well," the captain said officiously, "I'll take a look and decide."

Keough didn't bother telling the man that it wasn't his decision to make. Keough was the detective who had responded to the call, he had "caught" the case, and he was in charge of the investigation. He moved aside so that the captain could go down and get in the way.

He leaned against a wall and opened the girl's purse. It was white imitation leather with a gold plated chain. It was filled with the usual paraphernalia, doubled by the fact that the girl had both a woman's and a child's belongings inside. He dug among them and came up with her wallet. Holding the flashlight in the crook of his arm, he went through the wallet. He came up with a program card from Erasmus High School and a library card, both in the name Mindy Carradine. Neither had her address. Didn't kids know anything about carrying proper ID? Now he'd have to wait until morning, when the school opened, to get her address and notify her parents. He put everything back in her bag and tucked it under his arm. He'd submit it to be vouchered when he got back to the Station house.

While Baker was downstairs, Keough instructed

some of the uniforms to search the immediate area with their flashlights.

"What are we lookin' for?" Cuccio asked.

"Panties," Keough said.

"Oh," Cuccio said, "a treasure hunt."

Keough ignored him as the cops fanned out and began searching.

Moments later, the ME, Dr. Ethan Mahbee, came up, muttering to himself. He was a tall, handsome West Indian in his late forties who detested the name many of the detectives in Brooklyn had assigned him: "Dr. Maybe."

"Damned idiot bantam rooster," Keough heard Mahbee mutter. Obviously, the medical examiner did not think anyone could hear him. Keough did not let him know that he was wrong. Besides, the detective agreed with the man completely.

"At least he doesn't yell at you about your hat," Keough said before he realized that the comment might alert the ME that he had heard *his* comment after all.

Mahbee, however, did not seem to mind.

Mahbee looked at Keough and said, "The man's a monumental asshole." There was a thin sheen of perspiration on the man's forehead and he swiped at it with his palms, then wiped the palms on his trousers.

"I know," Keough said. "What have we got, Doc?"

"A dead girl, damn it," Mahbee said. "A child. What a waste."

"Dead how?"

"For now, let's say she was strangled," Mahbee

29

said. "I'll need to examine her where there's some light."

"Raped?"

"Possibly. If she was, judging from the blood, she was probably a virgin." Mahbee shook his head and added, "She probably lied about that to her friends. Most girls do these days."

"You got a daughter?"

"Hell no," Mahbee said, "and thank God for that. You?"

"No."

"You catching this one?"

Keough nodded.

"On the off chance that we've got a Lover victim here," Mahbee said, "I'll try to get it to you as soon as I can."

"I appreciate that, Doc. Off the record, though, what do you think?"

"I *don't* think," Mahbee said. "I haven't seen the other victims. This is going to be for someone else to decide, Detective, not you, not me, and certainly not that asshole down there."

"Well, it's my case, for now."

"For now," Mahbee said. "I wouldn't advise you to get too comfortable with it, though, Detective. The likes of you and me don't usually get involved in things this big, do we?"

Mahbee threw one last disgusted glance down the stairs, then nodded to Keough and left.

Keough was relegated to spectator for the next hour or so. There wouldn't be much he could do now until he received everyone's reports, collated the information, and did his own report.

After awhile, Johnson and Adair showed up. Keough had left a message for them back at the precinct.

"What have we got?" Johnson asked.

"A hungry detective, an irate captain, and a dead girl."

Adair smiled.

"We brought you something, but it's probably cold by now. Why don't you go and get something to eat. We'll stick around here until the party thins out."

At that point, two men from the coroner's office brought the body up the stairs in a body bag. Keough knew that inside the bag the girl's hands and feet would be individually bagged. A forensics man trailing the corpse handed Keough a plastic bag with the rose inside, thorns and all. Keough winced when he saw that.

"That won't be long," Keough said. "The guest of honor just left."

Chapter Three

Keough was allowed to suspend his night-watch duty in order to make his interviews and official notifications on Mindy Carradine and to write his reports. In effect, he was now working a double shift, staying through the eight-to-four shift. At least he'd have that night off, then go into his "swing," his time off between shifts—what civilians would call a weekend, only for cops it didn't always fall on a weekend. Cops didn't know what weekends were. For them, one day was pretty much like another. In this instance, Keough wanted to get as much as he could done on this case *before* he went into his swing.

He thought the notification was going to be the tough part, but Mindy's parents—an aging blond mother who dressed the same way her daughter did and a father who answered the door wearing a dirty T-shirt and holding a can of beer—loudly blamed Mindy for her own death. . . .

"I don't know how many times I've told that girl not to go out dressed like some low-life bimbo," Sam Carradine said. He turned, looking at his wife, Honey—who was dressed like some low-life bimbo—and said, "Haven't I told her that? Why couldn't you get her to dress proper?"

Honey—Keough couldn't tell if that was her name or just what her husband called her—tugged at the hem of her short skirt and said, "Sammy, I can't control her if she won't listen."

"Well, she ain't around to listen anymore, is she?"

Keough and Sam Carradine were about the same age, and he knew that the man was the type who had kept a pack of cigarettes wrapped in the sleeve of his T-shirt when he was a teen. He was the kind who thought he was a real man because he drank and spit and cursed. He was holding an open can of beer now, and when he gestured, some of it slopped onto the floor. Apparently, he had his wife well trained, because although she saw it, she made no comment, just stared at the spill as it soaked into the rug.

Keough had to interrupt their argument to get one or both of them to go down to the morgue and identify their daughter.

"I gotta go to work," Sam Carradine said to Honey. "You do it."

Keough was about to give her credit later when she broke down during the ID, but then she ruined it by muttering, "The little bitch had to wear *my* skirt to get killed in."

* * *

Keough read the coroner's report, which stated that the girl's larynx had practically been crushed and that she had definitely been raped. Whoever had strangled her had exerted incredible pressure with his thumbs, probably *while* he was raping her. Chances were good that by the time *he* came, *she* was gone.

Keough shook his head, scolding himself for that little bit of morbid humor. He wondered idly if Mindy's loving parents would have seen the joke in that.

The ME's report also indicated that the rose had been inserted into her vagina, thorns and all.

Sick fuck.

He talked to the school custodian, who explained that the basement door she had been found by was *always* locked and that *he* was the only one who had the key—except for the spare that hung on the Peg-Board in his office, where almost anyone could have taken it.

Keough wrote up his "five"—DD5, the Supplementary Complaint Report the detectives used to follow up or make changes in their cases—and submitted it. Naturally, it would have to cross the desk of the Six-Seven's executive officer, Captain Baker, but that would happen during Keough's swing.

Keough knew that he would hear about it when he came back.

During Keough's swing, Lt. Henry "Clipboard" Carson read the detective's five on the Carradine girl. Carson was called "Clipboard" because he was never seen without one. Every so often, he'd even been seen writing on the damned thing, but no one could ever figure out what the hell he was writing.

Carson read Keough's report and immediately thought of the Lover Task Force. Since Captain Baker's name was in the report as having responded to the scene, he immediately left his office and headed downstairs to the exec's office—with his clipboard.

Capt. Andrew Baker had also read Joe Keough's five on the Carradine murder, and if Clipboard Carson hadn't come through his door at that moment, he would have sent for him.

"Captain, do you have a minute?"

"Of course, Henry," Baker said. He sat back from his desk, wishing once again that he had an office. All he had was a desk in a room with two other desks, right outside the precinct commander's office. One desk—the one by the door—belonged to the precinct commander's clerk, a pretty civilian named Betty Roland, whom the old man liked having around. It was a bonus that she was also good at her job.

The other desk, which was back-to-back with Baker's, belonged to Lt. John Brady, the administrative lieutenant. Brady was a white-haired man in his sixties who was good for little else at this time in his career than pushing papers around his desk and pressing little colored pins into a precinct map, marking off the locations of this month's burglaries and robberies. It was he, with the help of the female clerk, who kept track of how many of each crime were committed each month, which enabled the command—the precinct— to keep track of whether crime was up or down in the precinct.

Given half a chance, John Brady would downgrade a crime—like changing an "assault" to a "harassment" because the latter was a lesser crime—to keep the precinct figures down.

This kind of thinking usually infected anyone above the rank of lieutenant, which was why Clipboard Carson and "Where's Your Hat" Baker were about to have the conversation they were about to have.

"What's on your mind?" Baker asked, casting a covetous glance at the door to Captain Farrell's office.

"This homicide that Detective Keough caught on his night watch . . . you were at the scene."

"I was."

"Well, sir, it's my opinion that this is another Lover victim. I think we should refer the case to that task force."

"Henry," Baker said, sitting forward, "that's why I like you, because we think alike. Yes, I was there, and yes, I agree with you. It's definitely another Lover killing. Refer it to the task force."

"I'll take care of it, sir."

As Carson was leaving, Betty Roland was coming in. Instead of letting her in first, Carson tried to fit through the doorway with her. They passed so close that her breasts brushed his clipboard, which he was holding against his chest. He wasn't trying to cop a feel; it just never occurred to him to step aside and allow her to enter first. She tried to see what he had on the clipboard, but he kept it too close to his chest.

There was a fifty-dollar reward in the precinct for anyone who could find out what Carson had on that clipboard. A couple of cops broke into his office one night on a late tour, but the clipboard wasn't there.

Everyone was convinced he took the damned thing home with him.

"Betty," Captain Baker called.

She turned around and looked at the red-haired captain. She was sorry that they had an office in common, because she thought Baker was a real asshole.

"Yes, sir?"

"Who is the head of the Lover Task Force?"

"I'll have to look that up, sir."

"Well, do that, will you? And then get him on the phone for me?"

She bit her lip, wanting to tell him that she worked for Captain Farrell, but Baker *was* a captain and she was only a civilian.

"Yes, sir," she said, "I'll do that right away."

"Thank you, sweetheart."

She bit her lip harder and sat down at her desk to look up the information.

Lt. Daniel Slovecky hung up the phone and rubbed his hands together. He'd just finished talking to the exec of the Six-Seven Precinct in Brooklyn, Capt. Andrew Baker. Apparently, the Lover had included Brooklyn in his little crime wave and had killed a girl out there. That made six victims. By the time they caught him, maybe he'd have killed a few more. When Slovecky did catch him, he knew that the more people the Lover had killed, the better he was going to look for catching him.

He had told Baker to send the report right over, then had thanked him effusively.

Dan Slovecky was thirty-four and had twelve years on the job. The job had cost him two marriages and would probably come between him and the woman he was presently living with, as well. Slovecky had graduated from the Academy near the top of his class and had worked his way up to lieutenant fairly quickly. In fact, he'd made the rank just a week after his thirtieth birthday. Since then, however, he had not been able to make any headway toward a promotion to captain. He thought it was a matter of jealousy—higher-ranking officers who had taken longer to get there were trying to slow him down. What he'd never admit to himself was that his personality and failure to play the game might be standing in his way, but that was, in fact, the case.

He had lobbied and fought hard to be the whip of this task force, and he was damned sure there was a captaincy in this for him—as long as nobody fucked it up for him!

The Lover was his own private rainbow *and* pot of gold rolled into one.

When Joe Keough returned from his days off, he was informed that the squad commander wanted to see him. He suspected that he was about to be informed of the fate of the Carradine case.

Keough went to the lieutenant's office and knocked on the door.

"Come!"

"You wanted to see me, Loo?"

"Yeah, Keough," Carson said. His speech pattern was staccato style, with barely a pause between words, sentences, and phrases. When there *was* a pause, it was usually to chew on the piece of gum he always had in his mouth, which he did with a particularly offensive liquid sound. As always when Carson spoke to him, Keough had the urge to wipe the corners of his own mouth with his thumb and forefinger.

"You did some good work on that girl the other night," he said between chews.

"Thanks, Loo—"

"The case has gone to Manhattan, to the Lover Task Force," Carson said, "so you won't have to worry about it anymore."

There was a note of finality in his statement, which irked Keough.

"Uh, Loo, did you read my five on that?"

"Sure, I read it."

"I wasn't finished with the investigation—"

"I told you," Carson said, interrupting him, "it's out of your hands—it's out of *our* hands."

"By whose authority?"

Up to this point, Carson hadn't looked up from his desk. Now he looked up and stared at Keough for a moment.

"Captain Baker went over your five," he said finally, "and he transferred the case to the Lover Task Force. It's somebody else's headache now, Keough. *We* don't need that kind of headache in this command."

"Loo—"

"That's all, Keough." Carson stood up and picked his clipboard up from the desk. "I have to go downstairs and talk to the exec."

He walked past Keough, opened the door, and then looked at the detective wide-eyed and said, "You want me to tell him anything for you?"

"No," Keough said. "No, Loo. Nothing."

Carson left the room for his meeting with Baker, and Keough figured that the two men were made for each other. Baker loved having his ass kissed, and Carson was a brownnoser deluxe. It was a well-known fact in the command that Baker couldn't wipe his ass without first asking Carson to please move his nose.

Keough left Carson's cubicle and sat at his desk. He had no cases at that moment. The Carradine killing had been his only one, and now that was gone. Good riddance. Let the task force handle it.

Now that he was off night watch and back on the chart, he'd be working with his partner again. He and Pete Huff had been partners for five months now, having been put together as soon as Keough arrived, and they still hadn't worked the kinks out of their relationship. Keough was a bit relieved that Huff wasn't in yet.

The phone at his elbow rang.

"Keough, Six-Seven Squad."

"This is PAA Haley," a man's voice said, "down in the one twenty-four room?"

Haley was a civilian, the station-house clerk. The job used to be manned by cops, but more than fifteen years ago, the city began to bring in civilians—calling them PAA's, short for police administrative aide—to cover inside clerical jobs so the cops would be free to patrol the streets. Among other jobs, the station-house clerk interviewed complainants who walked in off the street to report a crime, then referred the proper cases to the squad.

"What can I do for you today, PAA Haley?" Keough asked.

Fuck it, he thought. Mindy Carradine's own parents

didn't give a shit who killed her, and neither did his bosses, so why should he?

"Got a lady down here says she needs to talk to a detective. You catching?"

"Yeah," Keough said with a sigh. "Yeah, I'm catching. Send her up."

Chapter Four

Kopykat pasted the new clipping into his book with unrestrained glee. His eyelids felt heavy and he was aware of the pulsing erection he had as he ran his hands over the article.

It was from page one of the *Post*, and the story was continued on page two.

The headline said:

LOVER EXTENDS HIS REIGN OF TERROR
TO BROOKLYN!

He continued to run his fingers lovingly over the headline, giggling at the fact that he had fooled them all. He had perfectly copied his idol's style, and now they all thought that the Lover had killed again—and it was really *him*!

Abruptly, he closed the book and hugged it tightly to his chest. He held it that way as he walked to the bathroom.

The man the newspapers had begun to call "the Lover" stared at the *Post* headline that morning. What the hell was going on? He knew that he damn well *hadn't* been out last night. Somebody had killed a girl and was trying to blame him. Hell, he didn't mind being blamed for murders he did commit, but he didn't like being blamed for something he *didn't* do. Also, he had come to like the nickname the papers had given him, and he didn't like the idea of someone else being called by it.

"Professor?"

He looked up from his desk and saw one of his male students looking in at him.

"Yes?"

The student looked pointedly at his watch and said, "Lecture time, sir."

"Oh," the Lover said, "right, I'll be along, Ken. You go ahead."

"Yes, sir," the student named Ken said.

The Lover stared at the newspaper for a few moments more, then folded it and left it on his desk. He had a lecture to deliver, and to date he hadn't let his little extracurricular activities interfere with his job. He knew that he had to do something, but he didn't know what. He'd just have to think about this later. . . .

Chapter Five

Keough rushed home from the station house because he had a dinner invitation.

Nancy Valentine was Keough's neighbor. At thirty-two, she was widowed and the mother of a precocious ten-year-old girl whom Keough admitted he was in love with. He also felt that Nancy would have liked to be more than neighbors, but she wasn't pushy about that. Keough didn't quite know why he was so . . . reticent.

When he was transferred to the Six-Seven, he moved out of Manhattan and found an apartment in the Bay Ridge section of Brooklyn, on Oliver Street. That was his way of admitting to himself that his "dumping" was going to last a good long time.

Nancy and her daughter, Cindy, had the apartment

next to his, and from day one Cindy had been very friendly toward him. It had been Cindy who introduced him to her mother, and although Nancy had been friendly, she had also been wary of the stranger. After a few months, though, they were all friends, and after five months, Keough didn't have many friends better than Nancy and Cindy.

He often had dinner at their place, and tonight was one of those nights. He had returned from his first day back at work after the Carradine killing, very unsatisfied with himself. The more he thought about it, the more he became convinced that the Carradine girl was not a Lover victim. To his way of thinking, the differences outweighed the similarities. He had, however, already been overruled by his lieutenant and by Captain Baker, so who was going to listen to him? He had thought about talking to Huff about it, but Huff had spent the whole day talking about his new girlfriend.

At forty-three, Pete Huff was married, but he always had something on the side, and he loved to talk about them. Keough had learned to turn a deaf ear and just let Huff go on and on, but on this particular day, Huff's droning had annoyed him. That, combined with losing the Carradine case—and not having spoken up about his hunch—had put him in such a piss-poor mood that he had forgotten about dinner until Cindy Valentine reminded him in the hall.

"Don't forget, Joey," she said as they passed in the hall, "you're having dinner with us tonight."

Nobody had called him Joey since his mother, when he was little.

"How could I forget, kitten?" he asked, hoping that he was successfully hiding his guilt. They had gotten to the point in their relationship where this beautiful little girl could read him like a book.

"Sure, sure. I'm going to the store for Mommy," Cindy said. "She's making . . . well, I'm not gonna tell you. It's gonna be a surprise."

"I love surprises."

"See ya later," Cindy called, and ran out the front door, her long blond ponytail bouncing behind her. She was probably going to the little deli right on the corner.

Knowing Cindy Valentine made Joe Keough wonder what it would be like to have kids of his own— but he never wondered about that for very long.

It wasn't until after dinner—an Oven Stuffer roast chicken with gravy, stuffing, broccoli, salad, and Italian bread—and Cindy was in her room finishing her homework that Keough started to talk to Nancy about the Carradine girl. Keough had been drinking wine with dinner after more than several beers before dinner.

"I read about that in the paper," Nancy said. "I was wondering if you were involved."

"Well, I am," Keough said, scowling, "for all the good it's going to do that little girl."

"She wasn't so little, Joe," Nancy said.

"She was to me."

"They're all little girls to you, Joe," Nancy said. She put her right elbow on the table and tucked her hand beneath her chin. Her chin rested on the second joint of her fingers. Nancy's eyes were large and brown and would have dominated her face had it not been for her mouth. Her upper and lower lips were of equal fullness, giving them an overripe look. "You know, in the past few months I've come to know you pretty well."

"You have, huh?"

She nodded, bending her fingers as she did so. A lock of dark blond hair had fallen across her forehead, and she left it there.

"Yes. You bleed."

"We all bleed when we get hurt, Nancy."

"Not you," she said. "You bleed even when other people get hurt."

He reached for the bottle of wine and filled his glass again.

"A lot of people do that."

"Policemen?"

"Some."

"Not many though, huh?"

"Some," he said again. "I can't give you a number."

"Well, I only know one. You bled for that little boy in the men's room."

He frowned. He had gotten drunk on wine one night, and Nancy was *such* a good listener, he had told her the Eddie Vargas story.

"That was different—"

"You bled for the children you encountered when you were on the Vice squad," she said. "Hell, you probably even bled for the adults—"

"No," Keough said, cutting her off, shaking his head, "not for the adults. They had a choice; they had control over their own lives. Children do not. The little boy in the men's room didn't, and this little—this girl certainly did not."

47

"That's it, then," Nancy said. "You bleed for children. That's why Cindy likes you so much."

"Is it?"

She nodded, bending her fingers again, and then lowered her hand.

"She sees that in you, Joe," she said, "and she loves you for it."

"Well, I lo—I'm pretty fond of her, too."

"I know," Nancy said, smiling, "I know you do." Love her, she meant.

"Yeah . . ."

An awkward silence followed and Keough tried to fill it by filling Nancy's glass with wine. They both listened to the sound it made flowing into her glass.

"I shouldn't have that," Nancy said.

He put the bottle down and said, "I didn't notice you stopping me from pouring."

She laughed, picked up the glass, sipped the wine, and put the glass back down.

"What are you going to do, Joe?"

He took a deep breath and stared at her.

"Keep my mouth shut, I guess."

"Are you sure?"

His expression became pained and he said, "No, I'm not sure, Nancy. I'm not sure at all."

He picked up his wineglass, filled it, drained it, and filled it again. When he drained that one, Nancy pushed hers across the table to him.

"Here," she said, "drink that, too. Cindy and I will walk you back to your apartment."

As promised, half an hour later, Nancy and Cindy staggered across the hall, trying to support Keough's weight between them.

"This is silly," Keough said. "I can walk."

"We know you can, Joe," Nancy said. "We just want to make sure you know when to *stop* walking."

At Keough's door, Nancy put her hand into his left pocket and felt for his keys.

"The keys aren't on my side, honey," she said to Cindy. "Try yours."

Cindy put her hand into Keough's right pocket and came out with the keys.

"Unlock the door," Nancy said.

"Can you hold him?"

"I'll hold him."

While Cindy unlocked the door, Nancy fought to keep Keough on his feet. His knees kept bending and she kept having to jerk him upright. If Keough had been sober enough to notice, he probably would have been impressed by her strength.

"All right," Cindy said, "it's open."

She backed up and took her share of Keough's weight again.

"He looks so skinny, Mommy," she said. "How can he be so heavy?"

"He's a strong man, honey," Nancy said to her daughter. "It's his strength we're feeling, not his weight."

Cindy frowned, grunted as they started forward, and said, "It sure *feels* like weight to me!"

Chapter Six

It was the beginning of the week, and Det. Len Swann did what he did at the beginning of every week. As the stat man on the Lover Task Force, he went through all the statistics of all of the cases from all the precincts in the city at the start of each week to see if any of them matched the Lover's MO. Since the task force was first formed, copies of UF 61's—the original crime reports—and DD 5's from all the precinct squads were routinely sent to the task force office, no matter what they were about. You never knew if something that was reported as an attempted robbery might actually have been a busted Lover attempt. It was up to Swann to go through the paper trail to look for similarities in the cases, no matter how small.

Statistics were Swann's strong suit. At thirty-three,

he had been a detective for three years, and he always felt that he had been promoted to handle his squad's paperwork. When the Lover Task Force was formed, he was ecstatic at having been picked—until he found that he had been chosen to handle the task force's paperwork and stats. He'd been recommended by his commanding officer, who was friends with the chief of detectives. Every squad needed a good man to handle the paper, and when the chief had asked Swann's CO for a recommendation, the man had given him Swann's name without hesitation.

"Of course," Captain Hedison had said to Swann, "I told him I wanted you back right after this maniac has been caught."

"Yes, sir," Swann had said. He hoped that, as a member of the squad who would eventually catch the Lover, when he did return to his own squad, he'd be put on the chart to catch cases of his own.

That did not seem to be in his future, however. He was doing the same thing here that he had done in his own squad, and he would probably end up doing the same thing when he returned to his squad. Damn it, *he* knew he was a damned good detective. Why couldn't he convince anyone else of that?

That was what the civilians—the police administrative aides—had been brought into the department to do, the damned inside paperwork, and here he was, still doing it.

Frowning, he read the Carradine file again. It had been referred to the squad from the Six-Seven Precinct in Brooklyn during Swann's weekend swing, and this was the first time he was seeing it. He noted that it had been logged in by Lieutenant Slovecky personally.

Robert J. Randisi

After reading the file, Swann stood up and, carrying it with him, walked to Slovecky's office.

The Lover Task Force had been set up in two rooms on the third floor of the old Property building on Twelfth Street, between Broadway and University Place. One room was Slovecky's office, while the five detectives and one sergeant who were assigned to the squad—all transferred in from different commands—shared the second room.

It was early, but Swann knew that Slovecky was usually in his office before anyone else arrived. Swann also knew that they had at least another half hour before any of the others would arrive.

He approached the whip's office door and stopped there. The Lover Task Force had been formed right after the second victim was discovered, one month after the first girl. They had been together, then, for about twelve weeks. During that time, Swann had come to know Lieutenant Slovecky fairly well as a commander. Slovecky did not like to be questioned, and what Swann had to say could only be construed as questioning his commander.

Maybe, he thought, he could phrase it . . . differently.

He took a deep breath and knocked on Slovecky's door.

"Come!" Slovecky's gruff voice commanded. The lieutenant never "invited" anyone to enter his office; it was always a "command."

Swann took another breath and entered.

Slovecky was seated behind his desk. He was a big beefy man who wore his hair in a crew cut and strongly resembled former football great Dick Butkus.

Even though he was sitting, Slovecky's size was still impressive.

Swann was intimidated by the man and that irked him, especially since they were very close in age.

"What is it, Swann?" he asked. Slovecky always seemed to be glowering, even when he wasn't.

"Sir, I just read the report we got from the Six-Seven?"

"Yeah?"

"Well, uh, it came in while I was off, so this was the first time I've read it—"

"Get to the fucking point, Swann," Slovecky said peevishly. "I'm busy."

"Sir, I, uh, see some discrepancies between this and the other cases."

"Is that a fact?"

"Yes, sir. Uh, for one thing—"

"Swann, are you aware that I logged that fucking report in myself?"

Swann looked at Slovecky, who was pointing a huge forefinger at him.

"Yes, sir, I saw that notation—"

"And are you also aware that I spoke to the exec at the Six-Seven on the phone?"

"Yes, sir—"

"Swann, was there a fucking rose?"

"Yes, sir, but it was—"

"And was she strangled?"

"She was, but there was—"

"And was she raped?"

"Of course she was, but—"

"Then screw the discrepancies, Swann!" Slovecky said. "There's enough there to match the Lover's MO, and as of now, the fucking case is ours. Is that understood?"

Swann closed the file folder in his hand, held it down in front of him, and said, "Yes, sir."

"Have you got a pot of coffee going yet?"

"Yes, sir."

"Get me a cup, will you?"

"Yes, sir," Swann said. He hesitated a moment, then turned and left.

He walked back to his desk and laid the file down on top of it. He kept his hand pressed down on it, then almost picked it up again, but finally he viciously pushed himself away from his desk, picked up the coffeepot, and went to fill it with water.

Slovecky stared at the door after Swann had gone through it, closing it behind him. Of course, the lieutenant was aware that there were discrepancies in the case of the latest victim, but another lieutenant and a captain had referred the case to him. Who was he to turn it away?

Besides, six murders were better than five—and if this case had been left in the Six-Seven, it probably never would get solved. Now, when he caught the Lover, the case would be marked "Solved" and "Closed" and be taken off the books.

Everybody's stats would be the better for it.

What the hell was Swann trying to do, fuck it up for everyone? The man was a whiz at paperwork, so why the hell was he trying to act like a real detective?

August

Chapter Seven

"Six-One Adam, 'kay."

"Adam, 'kay."

"Adam, we have a report of a *woman down* in the park at Bedford Avenue and Avenue W. It might be a homeless person sleeping it off, but check it out, 'kay?"

"Adam, we'll have a look, Central."

Police Officers Jeff Sherman and Frankie Adinolfi had been partners for five years. They knew the signs of each other's moods and rarely read them wrong. For instance, Adinolfi knew without being told that Sherman's ulcer was bothering him tonight. Sherman, red-haired and forty, divorced and bankrupt, always had a frown on his face, but the frown deepened when his ulcer was bothering him. Also, he was silent for long periods of time when his stomach was acting up. If it was Friday morning, Adinolfi knew without being told whether Sherman had won or lost at the precinct poker game the night before. The "I couldn't buy a hand to save my life" frown was subtly different from the ulcer frown. These days, his drink of choice alternated between beer and scotch and milk. The milk was in deference to his ulcer. For years, he had drank only beer, which had earned him the nickname "Sudsy."

Adinolfi, dark-haired, mustached, thirty-four, was called "Big Foot" by everyone in the precinct. The reason was obvious. Six foot two and skinny, his size thirteens looked even bigger than that because of his long, rail-thin legs. He rarely took part in the precinct poker games, but he was a regular around the station house in knock rummy—and rarely won.

Sherman and Adinolfi were Six-One Adam, and they responded to the park in question to investigate the report of a woman down.

The park at Bedford, between Avenue W and Gravesend Road, was not actually a park, but a children's playground. At the present time, however, it was a shambles, having been bulldozed and jackhammered into submission and disuse in what was probably an attempt to improve it.

They were working their third of five midnight tours. It was Sherman's turn to drive tonight, but Adinolfi—reading the signs right, of course—knew that his partner couldn't drive when his ulcer was bothering him, so although he was down on the roll call as recorder and Sherman as operator, it was Adinolfi who had taken the wheel when they left the station house.

Adinolfi pulled the car to the curb by the playground and he and his partner got out. They put their hats on, adjusted their belts, and palmed their nightsticks before approaching the fence.

"See anything?" Adinolfi asked.

"Yeah," Sherman said, "lots of dust and dirt and shit." He paused to belch. "Whataya want to do? Split up?"

"What for?" Adinolfi asked. "Let's just walk around the park together."

They started to walk along the fence, squinting their eyes in an effort to see inside.

"When are they gonna finish fixing this fuckin' place up?" Sherman asked.

"You worried about the kids in the neighborhood now?" his partner asked.

"Worried, shit," Sherman said. "If they could play basketball here, maybe they wouldn't be pullin' so many fuckin' burglaries."

"They play basketball during the day, Sudsy," Adinolfi said, "and rob stores at night. You know that."

"See anything?" Sherman asked.

"I can't see shit," Adinolfi said.

"Let's get the fuck out of here," Sherman said. "Who the hell is around at two in the morning to see a fuckin' body?"

"Wait," Adinolfi said, moving closer to the fence. "What's that?"

Sherman moved closer to the fence. All he could see were long-out-of-use swings, seesaws, and monkey bars.

"Where?"

"By the monkey bars," Adinolfi said. "See it?"

Sherman squinted for a moment and then he saw it. It looked like someone lying half in and half out of the monkey bars.

"All right," Sherman said, "how do we get in there to check it out?"

"Gate?" Adinolfi said.

"Let's look."

They found two gates, both padlocked. Adinolfi, the thinner of the two, was *almost* able to squeeze through one of them, but in the end, no luck.

"Hole in the fence?" he asked at that point.

They walked around the entire playground without finding one.

"Sure," Sherman said when they had come full circle, "with the fuckin' place out of use, *that's* what they fix first. What's left?"

Adinolfi looked the fence up and down and then gave his partner a wounded, puppy-dog look.

"Forget it," Sherman said. "I ain't climbin' the fuckin' fence."

"Why do *I* always have to do all the climbing?" Adinolfi complained.

"Well," Sherman said, "it could be because you're younger and more athletic. . . ."

"But?"

"But it ain't," Sherman said. "It's because I'm the senior man."

"Old fart, you mean," Adinolfi grumbled, but Sherman ignored him.

"Gimme your belt," Sherman said.

"Fuck," Adinolfi said, "I ain't going over this fence without my gun."

"The park is empty, Frankie," Sherman said.

"Fuck," Adinolfi said again. He replaced his night-stick into the metal loop on his belt, then removed the belt and handed it to his partner.

"You get your belt stuck on the damned fence and I got to call Emergency Service to get you down," Sherman said. "How would that look?"

"Shit," Adinolfi said, and started to scale the chain-link fence.

"How can you do that," Sherman asked when Adinolfi was halfway up the fence, "with such big feet?"

"Blow me," Adinolfi said over his shoulder, and Sherman chuckled.

The truth of the matter was, Adinolfi couldn't get the tips of his feet inside the chain links, so he simply braced his feet against the wire and pulled himself up, like actually *scaling* the fence rather than climbing.

"Hey," Sherman shouted when Adinolfi was almost to the top, "you could be on that show—whataya call it? *American Gladiators*?"

"Fuck *American Gladiators*," Adinolfi said to himself, then remembered that he wouldn't have minded *really* fucking some of those blond female gladiators.

When he reached the top, Adinolfi swung one leg over the fence and promptly caught his pants on a sharp edge, tearing them.

"Goddamn it!" he shouted.

"Quiet," Sherman said. "You want the neighbors to complain?"

"I tore my pants."

"So you'll buy a new pair."

"Fuck I will," Adinolfi said.

He swung his other leg over and then started down

the other side. When he reached the ground, he felt behind him for the tear.

"How is it?" Sherman asked.

"Not too bad," Adinolfi grumbled, "but it's still got to be sewn."

"Walk over to the gate and I'll give you your belt back," Sherman said.

Adinolfi felt for the tear again, poked his finger in it, cursed under his breath, and then walked along the fence until he and Sherman were at one of the gates.

Through the padlocked gate, Sherman gave his partner back his belt. Adinolfi put it back on and then settled his gun, nightstick, and radio into place. He also had a compartment for extra bullets and a flashlight.

"Okay," Sherman said, "check it out."

Adinolfi took his flashlight in one hand and his nightstick in the other and went to check it out.

"Six-One Adam to central, 'kay."

"Go ahead, Adam."

"Central, we need a sergeant and a duty captain at Bedford Avenue and Avenue W, on that woman down? 'Kay?"

"What have you got there, Adam, 'kay."

"We have a deceased female in the monkey bars, 'kay."

"Say again, Adam, 'kay?"

"We're gonna need the whole crew, Central. Detectives, ME, oh, and would you ask the house to get somebody from the city on the phone? This playground is locked up tight. We're gonna need somebody with a key, 'kay."

"Adam, say again? Did you did say you had a deceased *monkey*, 'kay?"

"A deceased *f*emale, Central, deceased *female!*"

"Was that female, Adam?"

"That's affirmative, Central."

"Okay, Adam, stand by. They're on their way, 'kay."

Chapter Eight

Joe Keough had resigned himself to the fact that there was nothing he could do about the murder of Mindy Carradine. It was now part of the Lover Task Force's caseload. That was why he cursed when he saw the story in the *New York Post* four weeks after Mindy Carradine was killed, on the morning of his first day tour. It was 8:30 A.M.

He had parked his car in the precinct lot, which meant he had to pass the front desk to get to the squad room. As he passed, he saw two things. One, a woman was standing at the desk, complaining loudly to the desk sergeant, Phil Greco, that someone had done something to her daughter, or somebody.

"... kept touching your Rosa Mundi, wouldn't you be upset?"

"Yes, ma'am," Greco said, "I would."

"I keep calling," she complained. Greco looked over her head at Keough and rolled his eyes.

The second thing Keough saw was a newspaper on the desk, with the headline facing up: LOVER STRIKES AGAIN IN BROOKLYN.

"Shit," he muttered. He hadn't bought a paper that day or listened to the radio. This was the first he knew of it. He snatched the paper while Greco wasn't looking and took it upstairs with him.

Keough read about the young woman who had been found in the monkey bars of a playground on Bedford Avenue. She was raped, strangled, and a rose was found inserted into her body. That was enough for anyone to conclude that she was the Lover's latest victim.

"Where are you going?" Pete Huff asked as Keough got up from his desk and headed for the door. He was holding a jelly doughnut as big as a catcher's mitt in his hand, and the powdered sugar was raining down on his pants, tie, and jacket.

Keough stopped in his tracks. Where *was* he going? According to the newspaper, the body had been found at about 2:00 A.M., which was only six and a half hours ago. The investigation would still be going on, with detectives, the duty captain, the medical examiner, lab people all still running around like chickens without heads. He knew some of the detectives in the Six-One Squad, but nobody would be ready to talk to him. In fact, it might not even have been detectives from the Six-One Squad who caught the case, unless one of them had been working the night watch.

"Who worked night watch last night?" he asked, throwing the question out to the room.

"Beats me," Huff said.

Also in the squad room were Detectives Vadala and Goldstein, who turned and gave him, in turn, a blank look and a shoulder shrug.

"I'll be back later, Pete," Keough said.

"Yeah, but *where* are you goin'?" Huff asked. "I mean, if we catch a case or somethin', the sarge is gonna wanna know, ya know?"

"I'll stay in touch," Keough said.

"Hey, Keough," Huff called, but Keough was out the door and on the stairwell, disdaining the elevator.

First he went upstairs to the borough office to talk to one of the clerks he knew, a police administrative aide named Dani Rini. Dani handled the stats for the borough, and if there was any information available, she'd have access to it.

Dani was a young woman in her early twenties, and her tall, full-bodied figure and shoulder-length blond hair made her the object of much lust among the men who worked in the Six-Seven building—and anyone else who happened to visit. She was also very direct and outspoken and wouldn't take shit from anyone unless she wanted to. It was generally known that she was either sweet as sugar or a ball-buster supreme, depending on whether or not she liked you.

Keough wasn't sure what category he fell into. He really didn't spend that much time talking to her beyond saying good morning, and he had never asked for a favor before.

"Good morning, Dani," he said, fronting her desk.

He hoped that using her first name wouldn't be a mistake.

She looked up at him, her face blank for a moment, and then she smiled, which was encouraging.

"Detective Keough, right?"

"That's right," he said, and then added, "Joe."

"What can I do for you, Joe?"

"The *Post* has a story about another Lover murder in Brooklyn last night."

"Yeah, I saw that."

"I was wondering who was working the watch last night?" he said.

She didn't seem to think anything was out of line about the question.

"Let me see," she said. She checked her logs and then said, "Detective Jackson, from the Six-Nine; Detective Carcaterra, from the Six-One; and Detective Godoy, from the Seven-One."

"Carcaterra, huh?" he said. Another coincidence, like him catching the Carradine murder in his own command while working the watch.

"And who had the duty?"

"That was Captain Deutch, the exec from the Seven-Oh."

"Do you, uh, have any information on the case yet?" he asked.

"I don't think an Unusual Report has been forwarded to us yet, Joe. Why are you so interested?"

"Well, I caught a case on the watch a couple of weeks ago. . . ."

"Oh, that other girl," she said, suddenly remembering. "Was that you?"

"Yeah, it was me."

"The case went to the task force, didn't it?"

"That's right."

"Well, they'll probably get this one, too, won't they?" she asked.

"I guess they will," he said. "I was just . . . curious about it, you know?"

"Sure, I can see why," she said. "Tell you what, if I get any information on it during the day, I'll give you a call. How's that?"

"That'd be great, Dani," he said with genuine gratitude. "I'd appreciate it. If I'm out, maybe you could leave a message?"

"Sure," she said, "no problem. I drink tea, lemon, no sugar, no milk."

It was customary to pay off the civilians for favors in coffee—or, in this case, tea.

"I'll remember," he said, and went out.

He bypassed the second floor on the stairwell and went directly to the first. He still had his *New York Post* in his hand as he left the building and went out to his car. There was one other place he could check for information.

Mike O'Donnell was probably the *New York Post*'s top crime reporter. That was why he was the one rousted out of bed and sent out to South Brooklyn at three in the morning to cover the discovery of the latest Lover victim's body.

O'Donnell had been working for the *Post* for six years. He'd made himself a small reputation working for some other, smaller papers in New Jersey, but when he broke a story in Newark that resulted in the federal government's shutdown of a top Mafia family there, and *then* wrote a best-selling true-crime book about it, the *Post* hired him in a minute. Since then, his reputation as a crime reporter and true-crime writer—two other books, which also made the best-seller list—had grown considerably.

O'Donnell was going over his notes, trying to sort them out legibly so that when he started to work on his Lover true-crime book he'd have everything laid out in an orderly fashion, when his phone rang.

"Yeah, O'Donnell," he said, his tone distracted.

"This is downstairs," a man's voice said, "the guard in the lobby?"

"Yeah?"

"There's a man here wants to see you," the guard said.

"Who is he?"

"He said to tell you he's buyin'," the guard said. "Said that would shock the shit out of you."

O'Donnell looked up from his notes. It always shocked the shit out of him when Joe Keough offered to buy.

"Tell him I'll be right down," O'Donnell said.

"He says he'll meet you at Brendan's."

"Tell 'im I'll be there in fifteen minutes," O'Donnell said.

He hung up and started carefully putting away his notes. After all, a free drink is a free drink. . . .

Chapter Nine

The *New York Post* was housed in a huge white building on South Street, near the docks and not far from the South Street Seaport. Keough had always preferred their location to the midtown locations of their competitors, the *Daily News* and *The New York Times*.

About a block from the *Post* building was a dive called Brendan's. Hugh Brendan, the owner, invested not one red cent in ambience, and he served the best Irish coffee in the city. When Keough worked Vice, he spent a lot of time there, shooting the shit over Irish coffee or a beer, many times with Mike O'Donnell.

"Well, as I live and breathe," Brendan said as Keough entered. "Where the hell have you been, me boyo?"

"Got bounced from Vice, Brendan," Keough said.

"So? That don't mean ya can't come a see an ol' friend once in awhile, does it?" Brendan asked. Brendan was in his sixties now and had been in this country for fifty years, but he still hung on to enough of his Irish brogue to please his customers.

"I'm in Brooklyn now, Brendan." Keough took a stool.

It wasn't 9:30 A.M. yet, but more than half the stools were taken, and most of those customers were leaning over an Irish coffee, even in the summer heat.

"Ah," Brendan said, nodding, "that explains it. Would ye still be likin' a taste of my Irish coffee?"

"And quick," Keough said.

"Your buddy still comes in here," Brendan said, setting Keough's coffee in front of him. "O'Donnell."

"I know," Keough said, "I'm meeting him here."

Brendan gave Keough a little salute and then left the detective to his thoughts. One of Brendan's talents was knowing when his customers wanted to talk and when they didn't, and he was greatly appreciated for that ability.

Keough knew he was probably making a mistake in talking to O'Donnell. All he was going to do was get the reporter's curiosity up, but his own curiosity was running pretty high. If he was right, then a second case that shouldn't be transferred would be transferred to the Lover Task Force.

He opened the *Post* and spread it on the bar. The name of the girl who had been killed last night had not yet been released, and neither had her age. In fact, there was precious little information in the paper except that a second Brooklyn murder had occurred and it was being attributed to the Lover.

The first time Keough became aware that O'Donnell had walked through the door was when Hugh Brendan put another Irish coffee on the bar. He turned just as the reporter took the stool to his left.

"Ah . . ." O'Donnell said. He closed his eyes and took a moment to revel in the first sip of the day, then wiped the cream from his lips with a napkin.

O'Donnell was older than Keough by five or six years. His graying hair was cut very short and held two tones of gray—silver and iron. He hadn't shaved that morning, and his stubble was black and gray. His eyes were bloodshot from being dragged out of bed at 3:00 A.M.

Keough knew O'Donnell was unmarried. More than once his friend had said he wouldn't get married unless he could find a woman who would drink Irish Coffee with him at 10:00 A.M., and Irish whiskey at 10:00 P.M.

"You have a fine way of worming your way back into a person's heart, Keyhole man," O'Donnell said finally. He opened his eyes and looked at Keough. "Where the fuck have you been?"

"He's in Brooklyn now," Brendan said, nodding sagely, as if that explained everything.

"Shit," O'Donnell said, "it's just across the fuckin' bridge—and you got *two* bridges to pick from."

"I've just been out of touch, Mike," Keough said.

The sympathy O'Donnell felt for his friend seeped through the banter.

"It's been rough, huh?" he asked.

"I liked Vice, Mike."

"Bullshit," O'Donnell said, "but I'll give you one thing—you were good at it."

"Yeah," Keough said. He finished his coffee and signaled Brendan for another drink. "Beer this time."

"What kind?"

"What else?"

Brendan smiled and set a bottle of Harp on the bar in front of Keough.

"So what finally coaxed you across the bridge— whichever one you took?" O'Donnell asked.

Keough pushed his copy of the *Post* along the bar until it was at O'Donnell's right elbow and pointed to the front page.

"That's right," O'Donnell said, "you found the first victim in Brooklyn, didn't you?"

"I found *a* victim in Brooklyn, yeah," Keough said sourly.

"Ooh," O'Donnell said, "that sounds familiar."

"What does?" Keough asked, looking at him.

"That 'I know something you don't know' tone of voice," O'Donnell said. "Gimme, gimme."

"You first."

"At least some things haven't changed," O'Donnell said. "What do you want to know?"

"What you know about last night's victim," Keough said.

"Not much," O'Donnell said. "The follow-up will have a lot more facts."

"It should," Keough said. He tapped the paper and said, "This had none, except that a girl was killed."

"And found in the monkey bars," O'Donnell said. "That was a nice touch."

"How old was she?"

O'Donnell shrugged and said, "I'll get that on the follow-up. Young, I think."

"How young?"

"I don't know," O'Donnell said. "Why?"

"What did you see, Mike?"

"I didn't see anything," O'Donnell said. "By the time I got there, they were carting her away. I talked to the cops who found her, but they weren't sayin' much. I also talked to the night-watch detectives, but they weren't giving me much, either."

"In the paper, you said there was a rose on her body," Keough said.

"That's what they told me," the reporter said. "A rose in her vagina, like the others. So? That just makes her one of the Lover's victims."

"Mike," Keough said, staring into his beer, "what color was the rose?"

"Whoa," O'Donnell said, "stay with me on this one, partner. That's the first time I've heard anything about the color of the roses."

"Rose," Keough said, "we're talking about one rose, right, Mike?"

"What gives, Keough?" O'Donnell asked, his tone and expression curious.

Keough looked around. Brendan's wasn't exactly a hangout for reporters and cops, but there was still a possibility that there might be some in the place.

Brendan had a few booths in the back and Keough tugged at O'Donnell's elbow so that the reporter followed him to the back.

When they were seated opposite each other in a booth, O'Donnell said, "What's goin' on, Joe?"

"I'm not sure, Mike," Keough said, "and you can't do anything with this, because it's just my theory. Understand?"

"Sure, I understand," O'Donnell said, a hungry look coming into his eyes. "Let me have it."

Keough told O'Donnell what he knew about the Mindy Carradine case and ended by saying that he didn't think Mindy had been killed by the Lover.

"There were too many discrepancies, Mike," he said. "Okay, enough similarities to make it sound like a Lover case, but I don't buy it."

"What, then?" O'Donnell asked. "A copycat?"

"Maybe," Keough said, "I don't know . . . but this one last night . . . I need some more information on it."

"Like the color of the rose?" O'Donnell asked. "What's that about?"

"Mike," Keough said, "I don't want to say any more, but I need your help."

"And in return?"

Keough grinned and said, "You're already planning another bestseller, aren't you?"

O'Donnell scowled and said, "My publisher hopes so. That last book really wasn't a best-seller, you know. I mean, it made some regional best-seller lists, but it didn't make the *Times* or *Publishers Weekly* lists or anything like that. I need whatever I can get, Joe, to make this one a national best-seller."

Keough said, "You know you'll get whatever I know, Mike, but remember I'm not on anyone's *A* list anymore. I've been hung out to dry in Brooklyn."

"But if you can prove that the Brooklyn victims aren't Lover victims, that there's another killer . . . Jesus—"

"How am I going to prove it?" Keough asked. "I might get enough to convince myself, but I have to

75

deal with paper, captains, and lieutenants. . . ." He ended by shaking his head. "Do your follow-up, Mike, and then we'll talk again, but I can't promise anything."

"When did you ever?" O'Donnell asked. "Okay, Joe, I'll let you know what I find out."

"Thanks."

"What are you gonna do meanwhile?"

"I'll try and talk to the night-watch guys," Keough said. "I know Carcaterra from the Six-One. Maybe he'll tell me what I want to know."

"Okay, then," O'Donnell said, "you tell me what you find out."

"Okay, and Mike, you could do me a favor?"

"What's that?"

"I didn't pay much attention to the news articles of the first murders. Could you have someone clip them and send them to me?"

"The *Post* ones I could, yeah."

"Well, what other newspaper would I want them from?"

O'Donnell smiled and said, "Good man."

"And we'll talk about this again, Mike," Keough said, "I promise."

"I've got to get back to work," O'Donnell said. He drained his cup and stood up. "If this pans out, Joe, maybe you can get yourself out of Brooklyn."

"That's assuming I want to get out of Brooklyn, Mike," Keough said.

"Well," O'Donnell said, "only *you* know that. I'll see ya, boy."

"Thanks, Mike."

As O'Donnell left the saloon, Keough unfolded the

Post so he could look at the front page again. There was a picture of the playground at Bedford Avenue, all torn up with dirt and concrete chunks all over the place. A red circle had been drawn where the body had been found, lying half under the monkey bars.

If Keough was right, he wondered what the real Lover was thinking about these two extra murders he was being credited with.

Chapter Ten

When Kopykat was sure that his mother was busy in her room with another boyfriend, he opened his photo album and carefully snipped the pages in that day's *Post* about the newest Lover victim found in the playground.

LOVER STRIKES AGAIN IN BROOKLYN

He ran his fingers lovingly over the headline and imagined that he could feel a thrill through his fingertips. From his mother's room, he heard her cry out, but he knew that the pleasure she was feeling—or that she thought she was feeling—was nothing compared with his. He was glad she had brought another boyfriend home last night. Some nights when she came home alone, she made him go to bed with her, and that disgusted him. He didn't like doing that with her. In fact, he didn't like doing it at all. Women, he had decided long ago, were not for doing it with.

He pasted the headline into his album and smiled.

The Lover read the *Post* over his morning coffee and roll. He chewed vigorously, but the roll was tasteless in his mouth. Somebody was encroaching on his territory, and even though this second killer—and only *he* knew there was a second killer—seemed to be plying his trade in Brooklyn, the Lover didn't like it.

There was something in particular, though, that the Lover was actually offended by. After the women he had loved, how could anyone—the newspapers, the readers, and especially the police—believe that he would stoop to . . . to touching underage girls, high school girls, like the two who had been found in Brooklyn. Wasn't it obvious to the police that these were not his doing? Couldn't they see the difference?

He had already decided what he was going to do if this bogus killer struck again, and when he got to his office for this morning's summer session he would put his plan into effect. If the police couldn't see for themselves that what was happening in Brooklyn was *not* his doing, it fell to him to set them straight.

The city had to know there was only one Lover.

Chapter Eleven

When Keough got to the Six-One house, he presented himself at the desk, identified himself, and asked for Detective Carcaterra.

"You know where the squad is, don't ya?" the desk officer asked.

"I know."

"Go ahead, then," the man said, and turned his attention to one of his uniformed cops, who was complaining about a faulty radio unit. "Whataya want from me? Get another one!"

"They're all faulty . . ."

He went to the second floor, to the office of the squad, where he found Det. Steve Carcaterra seated at a desk, working on a container of coffee and a lethal-looking jelly doughnut.

"Joe Keough," Carcaterra said, "what are you doing here?"

"Came to see you, Steve," Keough said. He sat opposite Carcaterra and studied the man. They had been on the job roughly the same amount of years, but Keough had been a class or two ahead of Carcaterra at the Academy, so they had not met there, but on the job.

"Want some coffee?" Carcaterra asked, looking around. "I think there was an extra container. . . ."

"That's okay, Steve," Keough said. "I'm good."

Carcaterra turned back around to look at Keough and said, "Okay, then what can I do for you?"

"You caught the playground case last night," Keough said.

"That's right," the other man said, pausing to lick some jelly from his thumb, "another Lover murder. We're passing it on to the task force."

"Are you sure it's a Lover murder, Steve?"

Carcaterra shrugged his shoulders and said, "It fits the profile, Joe. Why?"

"Weren't there some . . . differences?"

Another shrug.

"A few maybe, but more similarities than differences," Carcaterra said. "Hey, it's no skin off my nose if the brass want to give it to the task force. I've got enough cases as it is."

"So have I," Keough said, "but I caught the other Brooklyn case."

"A few weeks ago, right?"

"That's right."

"And you gave it to the task force, right?"

"My lieutenant and captain did."

Carcaterra put down his doughnut and wiped his hand with a napkin. He didn't pick it back up, and he moved the coffee aside so he could lean forward and put his forearm on the desk.

"What are you tellin' me, Joe?"

"Steve," Keough said, "I don't think either case was a Lover victim. I think there's another killer."

Carcaterra stared at Keough a little longer, then sat back in his chair.

"Joe, why would you want to rock the boat?"

"What?" Keough asked, frowning.

"This is a theory of yours, right?"

"Right," Keough said, "so . . ."

"So write up a five and send it to the task force. Let them worry about whether it's the Lover or not. You and I, we've got enough to do without forming theories that are gonna give us more work."

Keough stared at Carcaterra for a few moments, then made a quick decision to play it.

"I'm not looking to increase your workload, Steve," Keough said. "I was just hoping you could answer some questions for me."

"What questions?"

"How old was the girl who was killed?"

"Seventeen."

"High school student, right?"

"Right," Carcaterra said. "Sheepshead Bay High."

"Sexually attacked?"

"Yes."

"And the rose," Keough said, "the one found on the body?"

"Oh yeah," Carcaterra said, nodding his head,

"there was a rose. That's what makes it a Lover case, Joe, no matter what you think."

"Where was the rose, Steve?"

"It was in her pussy, Joe," Carcaterra said with a frown. "Like the others."

"Okay," Keough said, then added, "a red one, right?"

"Right."

"It wasn't, like, white, with thick red stripes?"

Carcaterra said, growing somewhat annoyed, "Jesus Christ, Joe, I know a red rose when I see it, don't I? I ain't color-blind."

Again, Keough wondered about the color of the roses found in Manhattan. He cursed himself for *not* having read the newspaper coverage more closely.

"Okay, Steve," Keough said soothingly, "I'm just checking."

Carcaterra hesitated a moment, then frowned and asked, "Is that like the other cases?"

"Yeah, Steve," Keough said, rather than trying to explain about the striped rose. "It is. Thanks."

Keough stood up and said, "Thanks for talking to me, Steve."

"Joe," Carcaterra said as Keough headed for the door, "remember what I said about rocking the boat?"

"I remember, Steve."

"I mean," Carcaterra went on, "ain't that how you ended up in the Six-Seven in the first place?"

"Thanks for your help, Steve," Keough said. "Say hello to Lyn for me."

Keough was disappointed in Carcaterra, but he really couldn't blame the man. "Don't rock the boat" seemed to be a prevailing attitude these days, not only in the department but everywhere. Why make trouble, or extra work, if you didn't have to? The only problem with that was that Joe Keough didn't like the idea of a second murderer going free just because he was committing his murders in the shadow of the first one, the so-called Lover.

Keough wondered if the second man continued to kill, wouldn't he eventually want to get some credit for his own work?

Keough drove back to the Six-Seven Precinct feeling helpless. He was, after all, just a detective with a stigma. He was "unstable" and had been assigned to the Six-Seven so that he could stay out of trouble. If he started running around now, spouting off about his new theory involving a high-profile case like the Lover, what would his superiors think? They would think that he had really gone off the deep end, and he'd end up in Staten Island—or worse, they'd send him away to the farm.

It grated on him to take no action, but if he just let nature takes its course, maybe somebody at the Lover Task Force would notice the striped rose—if, indeed, it was different from the others—and the comparative youth of the two Brooklyn girls and attach some significance to these facts.

Chapter Twelve

Two weeks later, nothing had changed on the Lover case, and the killer—either killer—had not struck again. The papers still had stories, though—stories on the victims, stories on their families, interviews with experts on when or where the killer might strike next. Even if the story was in danger of dying in the minds of the public, the newspapers would see to it that it didn't—not to mention television. All of the special news shows seemed to be doing some sort of feature on the case every night. Keough'd even heard a radio call-in show concentrate on the case. They were asking for callers who might know anything about it, and all they got was a bunch of nuts, some of whom claimed to know the Lover and some who claimed to be the Lover.

During this time, Keough had received the news clippings from the *Post* on all the murders. None of the Manhattan victims were under twenty. Both of the Brooklyn victims were high school girls. Was he the only one who noticed this? Also, while all of the stories told how the roses were inserted into the vaginas of the victims, none of them mentioned the color of the flower.

During the course of the first week, Mike O'Donnell had called Keough to tell him that he couldn't get any information on the color of the roses.

"I can imagine the task force keeping some information to themselves," O'Donnell had said, "you know, so they can weed out the chronic confessors? But the color of the damned roses?"

"That's okay, Mike," Keough had said. Actually, it made sense to Keough. Most people would assume that the roses were red, and that would eliminate the chronic confessors. "Thanks for trying."

"You will remember that I tried, won't you, Joe?" O'Donnell asked.

"Don't worry, Mike," Keough said, "when I find out something, you'll be the first to know."

"Hey, did you see the story in the *News* yesterday. The one by the psychiatrist who says the Lover kills women and inserts the rose in them because he wants to be a woman?"

"I saw it, Mike," Keough said, "I saw it. Thanks again."

He hung up, feeling slightly guilty over not telling O'Donnell about the striped rose in the first Brooklyn killing, but he had decided to keep that to himself for awhile. He didn't know what he was going to do with it, but he was going to keep it quiet, for now at least. He wondered if the red rose in the second Brooklyn case blew his theory? What if the killer had simply run out of red ones with the first Brooklyn girl?

Now, fully two weeks after the second Brooklyn killing, Keough awoke late on a day that he was working four-to-twelve tours. He'd been up late thinking about his two-killer theory, even though nothing had changed over the past two weeks.

Who was the Brooklyn killer?

If he was right and there was a Brooklyn killer, what was he like? What was his motive? All the psychiatrists put this sort of thing down to childhood abuse, mother fixations, and the like. Could there be two killers running around with that kind of background? Or was the Brooklyn killer simply emulating the Manhattan killer for some reason? Hero worship? Trying to hide one of his crimes among the apparently motiveless serial killings?

Why, he wondered, stumbling out of bed, was he even thinking about it?

He staggered to the front door and opened it to see if there was still a newspaper in the hall he could borrow this late in the day.

"Late night?" he heard a voice ask.

He turned and looked at Nancy Valentine. She looked fresh and pretty and smelled wonderful, straight from a bath or a shower. She was wearing jeans and a black short-sleeved blouse, which looked great on her.

He, on the other hand, looked disheveled in an old

robe and he smelled like a goat. Suddenly, and for the first time in a long time, he felt uncomfortable being in her presence . . . and she noticed.

"It was, uh, yeah, pretty late . . ." he said lamely. "You're, uh, getting a late start yourself."

"I took the day off," she said. "Cindy has a play at summer school this afternoon."

"Oh . . . she'll be real good. . . ."

"She, uh, wanted me to ask you if you could come," Nancy said. "I warned her you might be working."

"Oh, I'm sorry . . . I am," he said. "Four to twelves, this week."

"See? I told her."

"I'm sorry, Nancy—"

"She'll understand, Joe," she said. "Don't worry about it. Uh, are you all right?"

"I'm fine, Nancy, really."

"Well, all right."

She started down the hall, then turned and said, "Terrible about the Lover, huh?"

"What?"

She turned and looked at him, surprised.

"I heard it on the radio this morning," she said. "Oh, you just got up. That's right. You don't know."

"No," he said, blinking. "No, I didn't . . . hear."

"He struck again," Nancy said, shaking her head. "Poor girl."

Keough stood stock-still and said, "Where?"

"What?"

"Where, Nancy?" he said too harshly. "Where did he strike?"

"I . . . don't know the address—"

"In Brooklyn, or in Manhattan?" he asked, trying to keep himself under control.

"Oh . . . Manhattan, I think. . . . Yes, I'm sure they said Manhattan. The Village."

"Are you all right, Joe?"

"I'm fine, Nancy. I—I'm fine, really. . . ."

"Well . . . okay . . ." she said, backing away. She eyed him with concern one last time, then turned and went to the elevator.

He shook his head and entered his apartment. He went right to the phone and called the office at Borough Headquarters. The phone was answered by the civilian aide he wanted to talk to, PAA Dani Rini.

"Dani, it's Keough."

"Hello, Joe," she said.

"I heard the Lover hit again last night. Is that right?"

"Gee, I don't know, Joe," she said. "It wasn't in the papers. Was it in Brooklyn?"

"My neighbor told me she heard it on the radio," Keough said. "She's sure it was Manhattan."

"I'm sorry, Joe," she said apologetically, "I don't know anything about it."

"Okay, Dani, thanks," he said, hanging up.

He knew he wasn't thinking right. Nancy had said the murder happened in the Village. All he had to do was call the Sixth Precinct.

He dialed the number and got a Detective Riley.

"Riley, this is Keough, Six-Seven Squad," he said. "Did you have a Lover victim last night?"

There was a pause and then Riley said, "The lid is supposed to be on it."

"Jesus, it was on the radio," Keough said. "All I

89

want to know is whether it's true or not. I'm not asking for any state secrets.''

"Well . . . okay, then, it's true," Riley said.

"You turning it over to the task force?"

"Definitely."

"Anything about it different from the others?"

"Shit, I don't know. It's not my case—well, it's not our case anymore, but I didn't catch it."

"Who did?"

"Bobby Porter."

Keough didn't know the man.

"Is he there?"

"No," Riley said, "he's gone for the day."

"Already?"

There was silence. It was Keough's bet that Porter didn't want to talk to anyone about the case, not even another cop—or someone on the phone claiming to be a cop. At that moment, Keough hoped that Riley wouldn't ask him for the color of the day—the usual code that identified cops to one another on the phone. The color was changed each day, and he didn't know yet what today's color was.

"You got a location on the body?" Keough asked, pushing his luck. "Where it was found, I mean."

"Negative."

Keough decided he'd gotten enough on a pass. Any minute, the cop on the other end was going to ask for ID. In fact, he should have before even talking.

"All right," he said, passing a hand over his tired eyes. "Okay, thanks, Riley."

"Sure," Riley said. "What's your interest, anyway?"

"Just curious," Keough said. "I caught one in

Brooklyn, and I've sort of been following it.''

"Oh," Riley said. "Well, anything else I can do for you?''

"No," Keough said. "No, that's it. Thanks.''

He hung up and rubbed both hands over his eyes. He could call Mike O'Donnell at the *Post*, but his guess was that the press didn't have much on it yet, either.

He needed to talk to someone who was actually on the Lover Task Force. He picked up his phone and dialed his old command, the Vice Squad. When the line was picked up, he asked for Detective Lowell.

"He's not here.''

"Who's this?''

"PAA Corby.''

"Corby," he said, recognizing the name. Pat Corby was a sharp, young black female aide who was the most competent civilian he had ever worked with.

"Joe? How the hell are you?''

"I'm fine, Pat.''

"You don't sound fine, Joey," she said.

"I'm fine, sort of.''

"Lowell's gonna be pissed he missed you," she said. "Can I help?''

"I don't know, Pat," he said. "You tell me. I need to talk to somebody on the Lover Task Force. Do they have a civilian clerical who you might know?''

"Nah," Corby said, "the task forces usually use cops as clericals.''

"You wouldn't happen to know anyone on the squad, would you?''

"No," she said, "but I might know somebody who does. I know a civilian in the C of D's office.''

"Jesus," he said, she had an in to the chief of detective's office? He wondered idly if there was some sort of civilian pipeline running through the whole department.

"I can find out for you, Joe," she said. "What do you want?"

"The names of all the detectives on the task force, Pat. Can you do that for me?"

"Sure I can, Joe," she said. "The way the job shit on you? You deserve a favor, don't you?"

"Hey," he said, "I think so."

"So do I," she said. "I'll see what I can do and get back to you."

"If I'm not home, you can get me at the precinct."

"Six-Seven Squad, right?"

"Yeah."

"Bummer," she said, and hung up.

He hung up and dry-washed his face with his hands again. He needed a shower and a shave.

Chapter Thirteen

The department courier from the Sixth Precinct showed up at the task force office and Len Swann accepted the packet from the uniformed cop. He opened it, scanned it, and then took it straight to Slovecky's office.

"The report's here, Loo," he announced.

There were four men in the room. Slovecky was seated behind his desk, looking like a man who had just gotten up—and he had. He'd only arrived about twenty minutes ago, and he looked as if he hadn't even combed his hair.

Sitting in a chair right in front of the desk was Detective Sgt. Artie Dolan, a pleasant, red-faced man with brown hair who was in his late thirties. He had one leg crossed over the other, and his foot was wiggling up and down. Dolan was the second whip. He was destined to be a lieutenant before he was forty.

Sitting next to Dolan was Eddie Samuelson, a slow-moving man in his fifties who was counting the days until his retirement. He was a detective third grade.

The third man was standing, and he towered over everyone else in the room. Det. Tim Mollica stood about six four and was broad in the shoulders and chest. In his late forties, he had played minor-league ball in the New York Mets organization. A first baseman with good hands, he couldn't hit a curveball, and he couldn't catch a ball that was thrown directly at him. He could field and he could scoop bad throws out of the dirt, but that ball coming directly at him always flustered him. Consequently, he never made it beyond Triple-A ball, where for a while they had been calling him the next Ed Kranepool.

This was half of the field men who comprised the Lover Task Force. There were three other detectives, and then Swann, the clerical man. With Slovecky, it was an eight-man task force.

"Let me have it," Slovecky said, putting out a meaty hand.

Swann handed it over and Slovecky dropped it on the desk in front of him. He looked up at Swann, who hadn't moved.

"That's all, Swann," Slovecky said. "Why don't you make some coffee."

Swann bit his lip and said, "Yes, sir."

He went back into the other room, leaving the door to the boss's office open. He'd be able to hear everything, anyway.

The case was identical to the others, apparently, except for one thing. This time, the killer had left a note. That was why the lid was on. The newspapers didn't know about the note yet.

Slovecky held up a copy of the note, the original of which had already been sent to the lab on the precinct level.

"What's it say, Loo?" Dolan asked.

Slovecky read it aloud: " 'I am the real Lover; there are no others. I would not sully my hands in Brooklyn. Do not look for me there.' "

"It's signed," Slovecky said, " 'the Lover.' "

"Well," Dolan said, "apparently he's accepted the name the press have hung on him."

"Big deal," Mollica said around his pipe. "We've only been calling him that for months. Now we have his permission."

Slovecky wasn't listening. He was on the phone dialing the Sixth Precinct. When the phone was answered, he asked for the duty captain who had shown up at the scene where the body was found. The man was still there, and he came on the line.

"Captain, this is Lieutenant Slovecky, of the Lover Task Force," he said. "Yes, sir, we received the reports. That was very prompt. Yes, sir, I will. Uh, Captain, this note—can you tell me who else read it? Uh-huh . . . uh-huh . . . and that's all? We're talking about three men, counting yourself, right? . . . Okay, good. Captain, I probably don't have to tell you this, but I will anyway. We don't want anyone—and I mean anyone—else to know what that note says. . . . That's right, yes. . . . Uh-huh . . . I knew you'd understand. Would you make it clear to the other two men? Ask them if they want to work in East Flatbush, or the Bronx. Right . . . right . . . I knew I could count on you, sir. Thanks.''

Slovecky hung up the phone and said, ''Asshole!''

''Which asshole are we talking about?'' Dolan asked.

Dolan always spoke to Slovecky with an amused tone. It burned Slovecky's ass, but he let it slide.

''Needleman.''

''Captain Eric Needleman?'' Samuelson asked.

''You know him?'' Slovecky asked.

''I went through the Academy with him.''

''And he's a captain while you're still third grade?'' Dolan asked, urning in his chair to look at the other man.

''The cream rises to the top,'' Samuelson said with a lazy smile, ''slowly.''

''Uh-huh,'' Dolan said.

Slovecky wasn't listening to their banter. He was on the phone again, this time to the lab.

''Yes, hello, this is Lieutenant Slovecky, of the Lover Task Force? Who am I speaking to? Stilwell? Listen, Stilwell . . . what? No, I know you haven't had time to examine it yet. When you do, give me a call. Meanwhile, I want you to know that if the contents of that note make it into the newspapers . . . Uh-huh, I know you know that; I'm just making it crystal-clear. If any of it—stop interrupting!'' Slovecky's voice now got harder and colder. ''If any of that note makes it into the newspapers, I'm gonna hold you personally responsible, Stilwell. You got it? Your ass'll be mine! . . . Yeah, well you better remember it.''

Slovecky slammed the phone down and stared at the note again.

"Why do you think he left a note this time, Loo?" Samuelson asked.

"And what does it mean?" Mollica asked.

"Well, that's fairly obvious," Dolan said.

The others looked at him, particularly Slovecky.

"Tell us, Sergeant," he said slowly. "Tell us the obvious."

Dolan looked at Slovecky and said, "The Brooklyn killings are copycat."

"What?" Mollica asked.

Dolan turned his head and looked at his ex-athlete colleague.

"Sure," he said, as if it made all the sense in the world, "he's telling us he didn't do those two, and he doesn't want whoever did stealing his thunder."

Dolan looked at Slovecky, as did the others.

"Whataya think, Loo?" Samuelson asked. "You agree with Dolan?"

"No," Slovecky said, shaking his head slowly. "No, I don't." He was looking directly at Dolan.

"Why not?" Dolan asked. "What do you think he's tellin' us?"

Slovecky's mind raced for an answer. He couldn't have the Brooklyn murders being taken away from him. He needed those to add to the Lover's list, so that when he caught him, it would make that much more of an impact. This case, when he solved it, had to be so huge that a promotion would be automatic.

"I think . . ." he said slowly, and then it came to him, ". . . that the Lover doesn't want us looking for him in Brooklyn, and he's trying to keep us out of that borough."

Mollica took up the cause, pointing with his pipe.

"And that's why he's disavowing those murders," he said. "It makes sense."

Dolan frowned, but he had to admit that it made as much sense as his assumption. Maybe the Lover was trying to throw them off his trail.

"So what do we do?" Samuelson asked. "Concentrate our search in Brooklyn now?"

"No!" Slovecky said quickly, startling the others. "No, we don't do anything different. We just keep going by the book. That means that you three get over to the Village and start canvassing."

"Right, boss," Dolan said, standing up. "We'll get right on it."

"Stay in touch," Slovecky said as they left their office.

In the outer room, Swann had the coffee ready. He'd prepared it while he was listening to the conversation.

"No time for coffee, Len," Dolan said.

Out of earshot of the others, Swann said, "I agree with you, Artie. I think the Lover's telling us he's not the doer in the Brooklyn killings."

"Yeah, well," Dolan said, jerking his head toward Slovecky's office, "he don't agree, and he's the boss. See you later."

Swann watched them leave, then carried a mug of coffee into the lieutenant's office. Slovecky had his head in both hands, staring down at the report of that morning's murder.

"Here's your coffee, Loo."

"Just put it on the table."

"Want me to make copies of that, Loo?" Swann asked.

Slovecky looked up at Swann, his eyes red-rimmed,

and then said, "Yeah, Swann, make copies and bring it right back."

"Right."

Swann took the reports and went into the other room. He used the Xerox machine there to make copies of the report for each detective, then made one for himself. Before taking all of the copies into the lieutenant, he tucked his away in his desk, with the copies of the others he had made for himself. When no one was around, he sometimes took them all out and went over them, hoping that something would occur to him, something no one else had seen. It hadn't happened yet, but he'd keep at it.

He closed the drawer and locked it, then picked up the other reports and took them back into the whip's office.

Chapter Fourteen

Corby came through. Keough had been at his desk an hour when the phone rang.

"Keough, Six-Seven Squad."

"Joe, it's Pat Corby."

Keough automatically scanned the room with his eyes. Huff was across the room, sitting on Vadala's desk. He, Vadala, and Goldstein were bullshitting over coffee and doughnuts.

"What have you got, Pat?"

"Names," she said. "You ready?"

"Go."

He wrote them down as she read them off, last names only. Mollica, Samuelson, Lee, Ashe, Diver, and the second whip, a sergeant named Dolan.

"The clerical's a cop, a detective named Swann,"

Corby said. "The whip is a lieutenant named Slov-ecky."

"Wait a minute," Keough said, recognizing only one name. "This guy Swann, is that Leonard Swann?"

"I got Len," she said. "I guess that's short for Leonard, right?"

"Right."

"You know him?"

"We went through the Academy together," Keough said. "Jesus, in thirteen years on the job, I haven't even run into him. I haven't thought about him for years."

"Well, he's on the task force," she said. "Looks like you got your in, Joe."

"Looks like it, Pat," he said. "Thanks a lot."

"Don't mention it," she said. "Uh, Joe, you want me to forget you called?"

That was why he liked her: She was sharp.

Chief of Detectives Robert LaGrange stared into the mouthpiece of his phone while holding the instrument to his ear. The damned thing felt like it was stuck to his ear. His mouth ached from saying, "Yes, sir," to Police Commissioner Raymond Steiger a couple of hundred times. He looked up at the ceiling of his office on the thirteenth floor of One Police Plaza and imag-ined himself looking at the broad ass of the PC on the fourteenth floor.

"I know you don't like hearing this, Bob," Steiger said, "but the mayor's on my ass, and that puts me on yours. Do you understand?"

"Yes, sir," LaGrange said for the 199th time.

"You assured me that Lieutenant Slovecky could handle this task force, Bob," Steiger said. "Don't make me look like an asshole. Uh, you know what that would mean, don't you, Bob?"

"Yes, sir." Two hundred.

"Get back to me on this."

"I will, sir."

Now, LaGrange picked the phone up again and buzzed his outer office.

"Yes, sir?" his clerk said. Ah, to hear someone call him that for a change.

"Where's Inspector Pollard?"

"In his office, sir."

"Well, tell him to get his ass in here forthwith."

"Yes, sir!"

LaGrange hung up and shifted in his leather chair. He had started to sweat during the conversation with the PC, and now his ass was itching. He stood up and walked around his desk, just to air it out. LaGrange was fifty-five, and had been C of D for two years. He liked the job, and he didn't want to lose it. This fucking Lover bullshit had to stop.

There was a knock on his door and he said, "Come in, damn it."

The door opened and his exec, Insp. Paul Pollard, strode in. Pollard was forty-seven and dressed as if he was on his way to stand in the window of Macy's or Bloomingdale's. LaGrange knew that the younger man would make a helluva better-dressed C of D than he did—but that wouldn't be for a while.

"You wanted me, sir?"

"I want you, Paul, yes," LaGrange said, sitting back down again.

Pollard started to sit and LaGrange said, "No, don't sit."

"Sir?" Pollard asked, his knees still bent in the act of sitting.

"I want you to get your ass over to Twelfth Street, Paul."

"Twelfth Street, sir?" Pollard asked, straightening. "The task force office?"

"Right," LaGrange said. "The mayor has his teeth in the PC's ass and the PC is biting my ass. Who does that leave for me to bite, Paul?"

Pollard swallowed and said, "Me, sir?"

"You," LaGrange said with a nod. "You assured me that this man, this Lieutenant Slovecky, could handle the Lover investigation, Paul."

"Well, yes, sir—"

"I appointed him on your recommendation."

"I know, sir—"

"Because you said he could handle the job."

"Yes, sir—"

"Well, he's not."

"Sir, I—"

"Get over there and tell him to get his ass in gear or I'm gonna replace him—and I'll replace you at the same time, Paul. Then you and Slovecky can go work in Greenpoint. How would you like that, Paul?"

"No, sir," Pollard said, "I wouldn't."

He hated when the C of D used his given name so often during a conversation. It always meant the man was royally pissed.

"Then do your job, Paul," LaGrange said. "Motivate Slovecky. Just like I'm biting your ass, Paul, go take a piece out of his."

"Yes, sir," Pollard said, "I will."

"I want to know what progress he's made on this case," LaGrange said. "I want something encouraging to tell the PC, so he can pass it on to the mayor." LaGrange leaned forward and said, "Don't make me look like an asshole, Paul."

"No, sir," Pollard said. "I won't."

"Get to it, then."

"Yes, sir."

When the phone on Len Swann's desk rang the first time, it was downstairs announcing that the C of D's exec had just entered the building.

Swann hung up and swiveled around in his chair.

"Sarge, Inspector Pollard's on his way up," he called out loudly.

Dolan, who had returned an hour ago without Mollica and Samuelson, looked at Swann and said, "Okay, thanks, Swannie."

Dolan got up, went to the whip's office, and gave a perfunctory knock on his open door.

"Pollard's on his way up, Loo."

Slovecky looked up and said, "Fuck me. Is the coffee on?"

Dolan looked over at the pot and saw that it was almost full.

"It's on."

"Get me the bottle."

Dolan opened the bottom drawer of a file cabinet just outside and to the right of the whip's door and removed a bottle of Jack Daniel's. He had just handed it to Slovecky when Pollard entered the outer room.

Swann started to rise, but Pollard waved him off and breezed past him.

"Sergeant," Pollard said at Slovecky's door.

"Inspector," Dolan said. "Coffee?"

"Yes," Pollard said, "and then I'd like to talk to the lieutenant alone."

"Yes, sir."

Dolan waved at Swann, who came over with two mugs of black coffee. He set them down on the whip's desk and then he and Dolan went out, closing the door behind them.

"Sweeten it, Paul?" Slovecky asked.

Pollard nodded.

Slovecky leaned over and poured a liberal dollop of bourbon into the inspector's mug, then added some to his own.

"To what do I owe this pleasure, Paul?" Slovecky asked then.

Pollard stared across the desk at Slovecky, a man he had nothing but contempt for. He'd no choice but to recommend—strongly recommend—Slovecky as the whip for the Lover Task Force because Slovecky was a blackmailing son of a bitch who knew where the bodies were buried.

He also knew that Insp. Paul Pollard, married twenty-five years to the same woman, had had something going on the side for the past five years. The department knew that cops cheated on their wives, but neither the wife nor her minister father would have appreciated it. It was information that Slovecky had "come by" over the years, the kind of thing he routinely tucked away for a rainy day—like the day he decided he wanted to command the Lover Task Force.

Robert J. Randisi

"The chief is boiling, Lieutenant," Pollard said.

"Is he now?"

"It's coming down from the mayor to the PC to the chief, and to me."

"And he sent you to come down on me?" Slovecky asked. "You know better than that, Paul."

Pollard sat forward so fast, he spilled coffee and Jack Daniel's on the razor-sharp crease of his pants. He was so upset that he didn't even notice it.

"I'm not coming down on you, Slovecky," Pollard said. "Lord knows, though, I wish I could."

"You should have thought of that when you first got interested in dark meat, Inspector," Slovecky said. "You should have made the move before you got into the chief's office, Paul. Either divorce your wife and marry your black junkie or cut her loose."

"I can't get divorced," Pollard said. "I'm Catholic . . . and Mary Alice would never go for it."

"And you can't give up the dark meat, can you?" Slovecky asked.

Pollard sat back. It was true, he couldn't give Rachel up. He was as hooked on her as she was on her drugs. If it ever got out that he was committing adultery, that he was supplying her with drugs, his life would be over. He knew that and yet he still couldn't. . . .

"We all have our own private hell, Paul," Slovecky said.

"And you," Pollard said with a sneer, "you're my own fuckin' Devil?"

"Not me, Paul," Slovecky said. "I didn't get you into this mess; *you* did. You're your own Satan."

Pollard sat back. Slovecky was right after all.

"Deliver your message, Paul."

Pollard closed his eyes and took a greedy sip of his bourbon-laced coffee. He then delivered his message with his eyes still closed.

"The chief wants to have a progress report," he said. "He wants something to give to the PC, something that shows you're making progress, or he's going to replace you." Pollard opened his eyes and added, "And me."

"And send us where?" Slovecky asked.

Pollard shuddered and said, "He mentioned something about Greenpoint."

"Ah well," Slovecky said, "at least we'd be together, Paul."

Pollard shuddered again.

Meanwhile, Slovecky's devious mind was racing. He knew he had to give Pollard something to give to the chief, even if it was bullshit.

"All right," he said.

"You have something?" Pollard asked hopefully.

"I have something, Paul," Slovecky said. "Last night, when the Lover hit? He left a note."

"What?"

"A note, Paul, that leads us to believe that the Lover lives in Brooklyn."

"My God!" Pollard said, shock plain on his face. "Do the papers have this?"

"No."

"Have you put it in writing?"

"The report is being typed up even as we speak," Slovecky lied. Swann was a helluva typist. He'd be able to get it done fast, so it was practically typed up.

"I'll take it with me," Pollard said.

"I'll send it over, Paul," Slovecky said with a smile. "I still have to work on the . . . subtle nuances of it."

Pollard sat forward slowly and set his coffee cup down on the edge of Slovecky's desk.

"Is this straight stuff, Slovecky?"

"I'll put it in writing, Paul," Slovecky said, spreading his hands in a benevolent gesture. "How much straighter can I make it?"

"Where's the note?"

"I'll send a copy with the report, by courier, in a sealed packet, for the chief's eyes only."

Pollard frowned and stood up. It was then that he noticed the spill on his pants.

"Shit," he muttered. He looked at Slovecky and said, "I'll go back and tell the chief."

"You do that, Paul," Slovecky said. "And Paul?"

"What?"

"Get your private life together, my friend," Slovecky said.

"Fuck you," Pollard said, and practically fled from the office.

Instead of getting angry, Slovecky chuckled. There went a man who had it all, a helluva future ahead of him, one that Lt. Dan Slovecky would kill for, and he was risking it all for sex with a nigger junkie.

Go figure, Slovecky thought, shaking his head.

Swann watched as Inspector Pollard left the whip's office and got out of there so fast he and Dolan had no time to stand at attention.

"What the fuck—" Dolan said, looking at Swann, who simply shrugged.

The phone on Swann's desk rang a second time, and when he answered it this time, it was Det. Joe Keough.

Slovecky sat behind his desk for several minutes after Pollard left. It was starting. The politicians were trying to take this case away from him. The fuckin' note was going to come in handy now. Of course, the whip agreed with his second whip, Dolan, about the contents of the note. The Lover was, indeed, trying to disavow any knowledge of the two Brooklyn murders, but that didn't matter to Slovecky. His explanation made as much sense as anyone's, and he was the boss. All he had to do was send a report to the C of D's office about the note, indicating that the killer lived in Brooklyn, and they'd leave him alone for a while— hopefully long enough for him to catch this sick fuck.

But of course, catching the killer was secondary in Dan Slovecky's mind, as it had been from the start. Advancing his career was first and foremost, and using lies and blackmail to do so was not an unusual way to accomplish that.

It happened all the time, didn't it?

Chapter Fifteen

Kopykat read the report of the Lover's newest victim in the late edition of the *Post*. She was in her twenties, a secretary in a Wall Street firm who, when she left for work the morning before, never suspected that she would not be returning home that evening—or any evening after that.

He put the newspaper down and walked to the window of the run-down house he shared with his mother. He looked out at the street. From where he was, he could clearly see the young mothers in their shorts and sleeveless tops—some of them halter tops—walking their kids to or from summer school. Some of them even looked younger than they were because he couldn't see their faces, only their firm, tanned bodies.

110

Up close, though, he knew they would be older—too old for him.

His mother was out now, probably sitting in some bar trying to line up her "date" for the evening. In fact, he even could have guessed which two or three bars she'd be hitting. He knew that she wouldn't find someone until it was late. It took her longer these days because years of drinking and rutting had taken their toll on her face and her body. Guys had to be pretty drunk and near the end of the day to consider scoring her. She didn't mind, though. He knew she liked sitting in the bars, drinking and sizing guys up, and it didn't matter to her *why* they came home with her at the end of the day, as long as they did.

It was too bad, he thought, that the Lover didn't like older women.

The Lover left his office, telling his teaching assistant he'd be back shortly.

"You have a six o'clock appointment, Professor," she told him.

"Yes, yes," he said impatiently, "I'll be back in time. I'm just going to get a newspaper—and a bottle of Evian."

"I could get it for . . ." she started, but he was out the door and gone.

Down on the street, he crossed over to the news-stand and picked up a copy of the *Post*'s late edition. He knew that his nocturnal doings wouldn't have made the morning papers, but there it was on the cover of the paper now.

LOVER STRIKES AGAIN.

Couldn't they be more imaginative than that? He demanded imagination from his students, above everything else. You could have all the talent in the world, but it would be totally useless without imagination.

Funny, he thought as he went inside and took a bottle of Evian out of the refrigerator, that his note wasn't on the front page, as well. He had envisioned it that way, the note reproduced right on the cover. Maybe the *News* or *Newsday* would have it tomorrow.

He paid for the paper and water and went back across the street. He waited until he was on the other side to study the paper more closely.

The story began on the front page and was continued on page three, but even as he read on, he could find nothing about the note. Here he had taken the trouble of writing it, to clear himself of the Brooklyn murders, and they hadn't even bothered to put it in the newspapers?

Angrily, he crumpled the newspaper in his hands, tossed it away, then whirled and threw the bottle of Evian. It struck the wall of the building, bounced off, and rolled into the gutter. He ignored it and stormed back into the building.

A homeless man hurried over from the other side of the street, barely avoiding being hit by a passing car, and grabbed up the unopened bottle of Evian. He tucked his treasure inside his dirty coat and then picked up the "clean" newspaper. Clutching his treasures, he scurried off down the street to find someplace private to enjoy them.

Chapter Sixteen

The next morning, Keough was drinking coffee in the Daily Caffe, in the McGraw Hill Building on Sixth Avenue, not far from Rockefeller Center. He had called Len Swann, who also remembered him from the Academy, that morning to suggest a meeting.

"I've got some information I think the task force should know about."

"Like what, Joe?"

"I don't want to go over that on the phone. We should meet somewhere."

"Can you put it in writing?"

"I don't think so."

"What are you being so mysterious about?"

Keough hesitated, then said, "Len, I think there are two different killers."

"Joe," Swann said, "don't say another word. Let's meet."

That was when they talked about a location.

"We shouldn't be seen together," Swann said.

There was something in Swann's voice that told Keough that he had found the right man.

They agreed on the Daily Caffe, which was far from the task force office.

Keough had gone to bed early last night—that is, early for him. Usually, when he worked a four-to-twelve, it took him some time to unwind after work, and he'd hit the sack about 3:00 A.M. Since he hadn't slept much the night before, though, he'd turned in as soon as he got home.

That morning, he had caught Cindy Valentine leaving for summer school. She had a friend in the building who was in the same class, and that girl's mother usually took them to school. It made it easier for Nancy to get herself ready for work and then get to work on time.

The other mother waited patiently while Cindy excitedly told Keough about her play and how good she'd been in it.

"Of course," Cindy added, looking at her friend, "Lisa was real good, too."

"I'm sure you were both great, honey," Keough said, smiling up from his crouched position at Lisa's mother. She gave him a wan smile in return.

"And I understand why you couldn't come, Joe," Cindy said. "Your work is important."

"Thanks, honey."

He stood up and watched Cindy, Lisa, and Lisa's mother head for the front door.

"If Joe was in charge, I bet he'd find that nasty Lover," Cindy told her friend Lisa proudly.

"We don't talk about that, Cindy. . . ."

Not that Keough could blame Lisa's mother for not wanting the kids to talk about some sick serial killer who was stalking the streets of New York, but it just showed how much newspaper and TV coverage the case was getting when even children on their way to school were discussing it. He felt even more foolish for not having followed it closely himself and for not knowing about the color of the roses.

Also, the confidence with which Cindy had spoken tugged at his heart and made him feel guilty for not having done something up to now. It wasn't so much that he could help catch the Lover, but he felt sure there was a killer in Brooklyn who might get off scot-free, with the murders being attributed to the Lover.

He had decided that he just couldn't see letting that happen.

Len Swann told the whip that he was taking a "personal" to take care of some pressing business.

"I've already sorted the morning reports," he said as he entered the whips' office, "and here are your copies."

"Fine," Slovecky said without looking up.

"I'll be back in a couple of hours, Lieutenant."

Slovecky looked up and said, "Just don't jam me up by being away half the day, Swann."

"No, sir," Swann said, "I won't."

Swann went to his desk and picked up his leather briefcase, which had been a gift from his wife. He barely used it, so it still had that scent of new leather

115

even though it was a couple of years old. Today, it had some very important papers inside—papers that could cost him his job if he got caught taking them out of the office.

Trying to appear casual and not clutch the briefcase to him as if it was filled with gold, he left the office and caught a cab for his meeting with Det. Joe Keough.

He remembered Keough from the Academy. Although they had gone through training together, Keough was several years older than Swann and most of the other cadets. They had gotten along well while not becoming particularly close, and after their initial assignments, they had lost touch over the years. In fact, he had not thought about Joe Keough in a long time, until he saw his name on the reports from the Six-Seven Precinct on the first Brooklyn murder. He was surprised to hear the man's voice on the phone and even more surprised to hear what he had to say.

He was anxious to find out how a cop he hadn't seen since the Academy—and had not talked to in all those years—had come to the same conclusion he had.

The Daily Caffe was a tiny shop in the basement of the McGraw-Hill Building. The only seating was a counter with four or five stools against the wall. On the counter were copies of that day's newspapers. Keough was studying the stories on the Lover's latest victim when Len Swann entered. The man was holding a leather briefcase underneath his arm as if it held a bomb.

"Bad body language," he said to Swann as the man approached.

Swann frowned, then looked down at himself and abruptly pulled the briefcase away from his body.

"Coffee?" Keough asked.

"Yeah, sure," Swann said, "black."

Keough went to the counter and ordered two black coffees.

"What kind?" the girl asked.

"What?"

"What kind of coffee?" she said. "We have several different types."

"Just coffee," Keough said as patiently as he could, "regular black coffee, in containers, not cups." Just in case Swann preferred to walk and talk.

The girl looked at him as if he had no imagination or adventure in his soul and gave him two containers of coffee.

He went back to the newspaper counter and sat next to Swann.

"How've you been, Len?" he asked.

"I've been better, Joe," Swann said.

"What have you been doing?"

"Clerical."

"As I remember," Keough said, "you had clerical skills already when we went through the Academy."

"My curse," Swann said. "That's all they been letting me do since I got on the job, clerical, roll call, payroll—I tell you, Joe, I wanted to quit more times than I can remember. I mean, I can do that kind of work outside for a lot more money."

"I bet you could."

"The thing is, I don't want to do that kind of work," Swann said, "I want to be a cop."

"Hey," Keough said, "you made detective, didn't you?"

"They gave me a gold shield," Swann said, "but they won't let me be a detective—that's why this is so important to me."

"This?" Keough said, looking at the briefcase.

"Joe," Swann said, leaning closer, "tell me why you think there are two killers?"

So Keough told him about finding the first girl and about all of the discrepancies he'd found in the case.

"Unfortunately," he said, "the brass in my precinct are worried about their stats, and were only too happy to pass the case on to your people."

"And the other Brooklyn killing?"

"Same thing," Keough said. "It's just easier for the precinct to pass it along to the task force."

"But tell me what specifically makes you believe there are two killers?"

"There are too many inconsistencies," Keough explained, "but two stand out to me."

"What two?" Swann asked.

"First, the Brooklyn victims are girls, not women," Keough said. "Neither of the Brooklyn girls was over eighteen, and none of the Manhattan women who have been killed have been under twenty. Second, in one of the Brooklyn cases the rose was striped."

Swann said nothing, and Keough went on.

"And the other was red."

He waited for Swann to say something and when he didn't, he said, "Well, Swannie? What color were the roses on the Manhattan victims? Were they red? Or something else? Any striped?"

"No," Swann said. "I see all the reports. There were no striped roses."

"What were they?"

"Red," Swann said, "they were all red."

Keough could see that it wasn't easy for Swann to talk about the case to someone outside the task force. He was going to have to pull it out of him.

"Okay, so why a striped one in Brooklyn?" Keough asked. "On just one girl, why striped?"

"I don't know . . ." Swann said thoughtfully.

"Did early accounts actually mention that the roses were found in their vaginas?"

"Yes."

"That, too."

"What's going on, Swannie?" Keough said, falling back on the old nickname. "Why are we meeting here? Jesus, we're underground, you know?"

"Joe," Swann said, touching the other man's arm tentatively, "I agree with you. I don't think the Lover did the Brooklyn killings."

Keough sat back and breathed a sigh of relief.

"You mean the task force is working them as separate cases?" he asked. "That's a relief, Swannie—"

"No, that's just it," Swann said, shaking his head. "The whip won't entertain the possibility that the cases aren't related."

Keough frowned.

"Who's the whip, again? Uh, Lieutenant Dravecky?"

"Slovecky," Swann said.

"What's his story?"

"Made lieutenant quickly and got stuck," Swann said "He hates everyone above him in rank, and below

119

him. He wants this case to make him a captain.''

"And he can't see the differences between the Brooklyn and Manhattan murders?''

"He won't see the differences," Swann said. "That is, he won't let anyone else see them. See, the bigger the Lover's rep when he catches him, the better he's going to look. At least that's how I read him.''

Keough frowned and said, "He's padding the Lover's record? I don't know why this should surprise me. Typical brass way of thinking. He cares more about making captain than about catching a sick killer—and while he's at it, he'll let another killer go completely free.''

"Basically," Swann said, "that's it.''

"So tell me why do you think there are two killers?''

"The main reason," Swann said, "is the note.''

Keough frowned.

"What note?''

Swann looked around to make sure they were alone, then said, "This note." He slid a piece of paper from his briefcase and handed it to Keough.

Keough saw that it was a Xerox of a note, written in a scrawling handwriting.

"Jesus," Keough said, "where'd this come from?''

"They found it on Julie Hansen," Swann said, "the latest victim.''

"Well, Jesus Christ," Keough said, shaking his head in disbelief, "the Lover himself is saying he didn't kill the Brooklyn girls!''

"That's what our second whip, Artie Dolan, said.''

"And what did Slovecky say?''

120

"He said that maybe the killer just didn't want us looking for him in Brooklyn."

"That's crazy," Keough said.

"Slovecky is devious, Joe," Swann said, taking the note and putting it back in the briefcase.

"What else have you got in there, Len?"

Swann looked nervous.

"Joe, I've been Xeroxing all of the reports on the Lover victims," he said, "and when those Brooklyn cases came in, I made copies of those, too."

"Why?"

"Why?" Swann repeated. "Because I want out, that's why. I want to get out of the office and into the street. I was figuring that maybe this case would be my ticket out. I don't think that I ever really expected that it would, though."

Keough stared at Swann, who seemed fairly desperate about this. How, Keough, wondered, did this make Swann any different from Slovecky? They both wanted this case to advance their careers. No, that wasn't fair. At least Swann wasn't lying and twisting the facts to suit him.

"Okay," Keough said. "Okay, so who do we go to with this?"

"What do you mean?" Swann asked.

"Len, we have to do something about this, or a killer is going to go free."

"You mean . . . go over Slovecky's head?"

"What else?" Keough said. "We can't go to him. He'll cover it up, right?"

"Well . . ."

"And he'll probably transfer you to the boonies."

Swann hesitated, then said, "That's true. . . ."

Robert J. Randisi

"We've got to bring this to someone's attention."

"But . . . who?"

Keough stared at Swann, then said, "The C of D."

"The chief?"

Keough nodded.

"We send him a written report, signed by both of us, with our conclusions," Keough said. "We're covered, and we let him take it from there."

"Jesus," Swann said, "we'd be sticking our necks way out there, Joe. Christ, if Slovecky found out about this, he'd kill me!"

"I know," Keough said, "but I don't think either one of us has that much to lose, Len. I'm not where I want to be, and neither are you. Look, if you want, I'll send the report with just my signature on it."

"No!" Swann said. "No, that wouldn't be fair . . . to you."

"Okay," Keough said, "so we write it up and send it to the chief's office."

Swann stroked his jaw with one hand and kept the other one on the briefcase, which was lying flat on the counter, next to his coffee.

"I'll write it," he said finally.

"All right," Keough said, since he hated writing and Swann had a knack for it. "Maybe," he added, "it'll be the last report you ever write."

Swann gave him a funny look, and for a moment Keough didn't realize that the last thing he'd said could have been taken two ways.

Chapter Seventeen

Marcia Swann had never seen her husband, Len, so worked up before. Oh, she had seen him angry, especially when he talked about being consigned for life to the "Palace Guard." But this was different. Len was not angry; he was not disappointed; he was not upset. He was . . . agitated, and she didn't like it one bit.

Although Swann had explained to his wife that Joe Keough was someone he had gone through the Academy with, and even though Marcia and Len Swann were married back then, she didn't remember Keough. Still, she agreed to having him as a guest for dinner and was polite to him before, during, and after. She also noticed that Keough and her husband were constantly exchanging glances she could only think of as

123

furtive. She wanted to ask what was going on but decided against it. She had always trusted her husband, and she trusted him now to tell her what was going on . . . eventually.

For now, she would just get the kids off to sleep—Billy, eight, and Jennifer, thirteen—and then get out of the way herself and let the two detectives talk.

Sometimes, though, she wished she didn't trust Len so much. Sometimes she just wanted to ask questions. . . .

It was after hours and Lt. Dan Slovecky was the only one still left in the task force office. There was one light left on, and that was the desk lamp on Det. Len Swann's desk. Slovecky laughed derisively to himself. Detective! The man was nothing more than a glorified clerical.

He had to give Swann one thing, though. The man was a damned good clerical—and he knew how to make this goddamned Xerox machine work.

Slovecky had been trying to Xerox the same piece of paper for the past five minutes, and he couldn't even get the damned machine to go on. Suddenly, he noticed that the doors in front of the machine were ajar. Shit, he hadn't even known that there were doors there.

He crouched down to try to close them and then opened them in order to see how they secured. He found himself looking at the inner workings of the machine, which included a big drumlike thing. He frowned then, because he saw a flash of white on the drum. He tried to reach in to get it but couldn't. There was a handle in his face and it turned out to be connected to the drum. He grasped it, pulled up, then pushed down and slid the drum out, where he could get at it. Sure enough, there was a piece of paper on it, a copy that someone had made and left in there. Whoever it was had probably not even realized it. He slid the paper off the drum and pushed the thing back in, where it locked into place. Next he closed the doors and locked them into place. All of that done, he was able to make his copy, which he did, and then he shut the machine off.

As he reached for the lamp on Swann's desk, he realized he was still holding the piece of paper he'd taken from the belly of the machine. He glanced at it, and then his eyes widened. He smoothed it out and took a good look at it under the light.

"Fuck," he said.

Somebody was making copies of the note from the Lover. All the copies should have been made earlier in the day, and they were accounted for. And he knew that the machine had been used since then. That meant that, just before closing up shop, somebody had made an extra copy of the note—and this one had gotten stuck in the machine.

Swann, he thought. That clerical fuck was the only one who really knew how to work the machine. Now why the fuck was he making a copy of the note . . . and what else had he been making copies of all along?

He went to Swann's desk and began going through his drawers. If he was hoping to find a duplicate file there, he was disappointed—until he really dug down to the bottom of the drawer. There was a piece of paper lying flat on the bottom, underneath the hanging files. He pulled it out and saw that it was another page of the report.

One page in the belly of the Xerox machine could be anything, but another page in Swann's drawer clinched it. The man was making copies, but why?

Swann watched Keough read for a short time, until it made Keough nervous. At that point, he asked the man for another beer, and Swann went to the kitchen to get it.

"Why don't you check on your wife and kids, too?" Keough asked.

"I'm making you nervous, right?"

"You got it."

"Listen," Swann said, "you've still got a lot of paperwork to go through. I'm gonna go and take a shower."

"Now that's a good idea." Keough hadn't wanted to tell Swann, but the man's constant perspiring in the small room had created an odor that was both pungent and unpleasant.

"I'll be back in a little while."

"Fine."

"You want that beer before I go?"

"Just bring it with you when you come back."

"Okay."

"And leave the door open, will . . ." Keough started to say, but he was too late. Swann had left the room and closed the door behind him. From his seat behind Swann's desk, Keough was able to reach over and crack the door open enough to let some air in—and some of Swann's odor out. That done, he turned back to the papers.

He had to hand it to Swann. The man had amassed every fact about the so-called Lover murders, and that included the Brooklyn cases.

By the time Swann returned, Keough was excited by what he'd read.

"Jesus, Len," he said as the man entered the room, "there are more discrepancies than I thought."

"You saw the thing about the thorns, huh?"

"Damn right I did."

As it turned out, the roses in the Manhattan cases had clean stems, while the two roses inserted into the vaginas of the Brooklyn girls had thorns on the stems.

"So even though the second rose was red, like the others, it was still different."

Swann nodded and stood behind Keough. The man smelled much better now that he was fresh from a shower. Keough, however, had begun to sweat . . . and smell.

"Jesus," Keough said, "imagine this sick fuck stuffing the roses, thorns and all, into these girls?"

"Did you see the thing about the rapes?"

"What about them?"

"Look." Swann leaned over him and started leafing through the pages. "Where is it, I know it's here . . . yeah, here. Read this."

Keough leaned forward and read what was on the sheet with growing annoyance, until he exploded. He sat back and glared at Swann in disbelief.

"You mean Slovecky is sitting on this, too?"

"Slovecky says a rose is a rose."

"But"—Keough leaned forward and pointed—"it says right here the Brooklyn girls weren't raped? Wait a minute—I asked Carcaterra if they were sexually molested and he said yes.''

"What would you call inserting the stem of a rose, thorns and all, into a girl's vagina?''

"Wait a minute," Keough said again. He looked around, starting to feel cramped in the small office. "Can we go into the living room?''

"Sure," Swann said. "Everyone else is in bed. Come on.''

They left the claustrophobic office and went into the living room, where Keough sat on the sofa and set the paperwork down on the coffee table.

"Let me get you that other beer," Swann said.

"Good. I could use it.''

Swann went into the kitchen and came back with two more beers. He'd changed his clothes earlier, and was now wearing a pair of jeans and a sweatshirt that said BROOKLYN BREWERY on it.

"Let's go over the differences between the Manhattan and Brooklyn cases," Keough said, after taking a swig of beer.

"Okay," Swann said. He ticked them off on his fingers. "We have a different color rose, we have the thorns still on the stems, and we have the fact that the killer did not rape the girls.''

"And they're sure of that part?''

"There was no semen.''

"What about condoms? Could he have used them?''

Swann shook his head.

"There would be trace evidence of the rubber, or the lubricant, and there was none.''

"Okay," Keough added, "there's also the age difference. The Brooklyn girls were in high school, while the Manhattan girls are college age.''

"Right."

"Four," Keough said, "four discrepancies, Swannie. That's too much to ignore."

"Apparently," Swan said, "not for Slovecky."

"What about the other detectives in the squad? What about the second whip, Dolan?"

"Come on, Joe," Swann said. "It's Slovecky's squad; he calls the shots. They don't want to rock the boat. After all, it's a temporary assignment for everyone."

"Jesus," Keough said, exasperated. "Then we have to go to the chief with this stuff, like we talked about."

"I don't know."

"We have to go to someone, Swannie, because your CO and mine don't want to hear about it."

Swan thought it over for a few moments, working on the bottle of beer, and then looked at Keough.

"Okay, let's do it."

129

Chapter Eighteen

Rather than go back to his empty apartment, Dan Slovecky decided to stop at a bar on the way home. Since the divorce, he had been living in the same basement apartment in the East Village, and the bar he chose was one that was near home, rather than any of the cop bars he knew of in the city. Slovecky didn't drink in cop bars, and he didn't hang out with cops. He was, after all, a lieutenant, a boss. It wouldn't do for him to rub elbows with the regular cops and detectives. He'd lose their respect, that way.

Slovecky, because of his size, was used to commanding respect, but he deluded himself by thinking it was because of his rank. Rather, he instilled fear in most men due to his size and his temper.

He lived in the Village because it was fairly inexpensive for him. He was, in fact, subletting a cheap apartment, which made it cheaper still for him. Under normal circumstances, he would never have chosen this neighborhood to live in. It was filled with homosexuals, and like most brutal men, he had a distrust and disgust of "fags." He found them a threat to his manhood, something he would never have admitted to anyone—least of all to himself.

A psychiatrist might have said that he subconsciously chose to live there, looking to feed a rage that was far from starved.

Like everything else in his life, though, Slovecky felt that he was stuck there. For a while, he felt that way about his job, felt he'd be stuck at lieutenant for good. That was when he decided to start using some of the information he'd been storing up for years. Dirt stuck to Slovecky's fingers, and sometimes it was other people's dirt, like Inspector Pollard's affair with a black junkie. He was able to take that little piece of information and use it to wrangle himself the job as whip on the Lover Task Force. From there, he expected to ultimately ride the task force job to deputy inspector.

It was 8:00 P.M. when he stopped in a bar called the Peculiar Pub, on Bleecker, west of La Guardia. It was a good walk from his apartment, an NYU hangout he knew didn't cater to gays, and he wanted to do some thinking without having some fag checking him out. Like most macho homophobes, he thought all gays were looking to hit on him.

He seated himself at the bar and nodded to the bartender, who might or might not have recognized him from other times he'd been there but who nodded back just the same.

"Draft," he said, and then cradled the mug the bartender put in front of him.

He scowled as he thought again about Len Swann making copies of reports. The task force was his ticket to better things, position, a nicer place to live, and he wasn't going to let some clerk mess it up for him. He remembered now how Swann wanted to argue about the Brooklyn murders not being Lover killings. What if Swann started asking more questions? What was wrong with the guy, anyway? Jesus, there were roses, weren't there? Naming a second killer would really start a panic, wouldn't it? Didn't it make sense to lump all the killings together and blame them on the Lover? That way, when the case was closed, people would feel safe, and Slovecky would look even better for a promotion.

All of that could be in danger now because of Swann. Slovecky had to find out why Swann was making copies of all the reports and whom he might have shown them to. After that, he was going to have to make sure that Swann didn't have a chance to show them to anyone else.

Over another beer, he decided the best thing to do was go out to Brooklyn and brace Swann at his house. He was going to have to take a cab, though, or the subway. He didn't own a car—his ex-wife had walked away with it—and he couldn't afford to use a task force unit.

He had a couple of more beers—with added shots of whiskey for fortification—and then left the Peculiar and walked unsteadily to the nearest subway stop.

It was 9:00 P.M.

"Okay," Len Swann said, "here it is."

He handed the report to Keough to read and sat back in his chair, rubbing his eyes. They were back in his little office again, and he'd just finished typing a two-page memolike report to the chief of detectives about the murders in Manhattan and Brooklyn.

Keough read it carefully, and when he was done, he had to admit that Swann really was good at this paperwork stuff. He'd never have been able to put it down on paper so simply and concisely.

"This is it," Keough said. "This is perfect; it says everything."

"You know," Swann said, "Slovecky's not going to like this when it comes out."

"Neither is the chief," Keough said, "or the commissioner. I think Slovecky's whip days are going to be over."

A sour look came over Swann's face.

"Len, are you afraid of Slovecky?"

"Well, no . . . yeah, I guess I am, but besides that . . . he's a cop."

"He's a boss," Keough said. "There's a difference, you know."

"Still, we're going over his head."

"Have you talked to him about this?"

Swann hesitated, then said, "I tried when the cases came in, but he was adamant. He insists that the rose is the overriding factor that links the cases."

"And he ignores everything," Keough said. "I said it before, Swannie, and I'll say it again. He's willing

133

to let a killer go free to make himself look good. I think that's wrong."

"I know, I know," Swann said. "I agree with you."

"Well, we can't let him get away with it," Keough said, brandishing the report.

"How about I talk to Sergeant Dolan again?"

"Your second whip?"

Swann nodded.

"Maybe I can get him to go along with us on this."

"And then what?"

"And then . . . I don't know," Swann said helplessly. "Maybe he can talk some sense into Slovecky."

"Is he intimidated by Slovecky?"

"Well . . . yeah, I think. I mean, he expressed his own opinion about the note. . . ."

"But nothing came of it, right? Slovecky shot him down?"

Swann lowered his head and said, "Yeah."

"I think we should send this." Keough put the report down on the desk in front of Swann. "I'm going to leave it with you, though. You do what you think you've got to do. You talk to Dolan, or send the report, or do it in whatever order you feel good with—but send it, okay?"

Swann nodded.

"Okay."

"And let me know when you do."

Swann nodded.

Keough looked at his watch. It was almost ten o'clock.

"It's late, Swannie. I'm going to head home."

"Okay." Swann stood up. "I'll walk you to the door."

At the front door, Keough turned and shook hands with Swann.

"We're doing the right thing, you know."

"I know," Swann said uncertainly, "I know."

As Keough walked to his car and Swann watched him, neither of them was aware of the man standing across the street in the shadows, watching them. Keough got in his car, started it up, and drove away. Swann closed the door and turned off the outside light.

The man in the shadows started across the street.

Marcia Swann woke up, rolled over, and looked at the red glowing numerals on the bedside clock radio. It was 2:15 A.M. and her husband hadn't come to bed yet. She doubted very much that Joe Keough was still downstairs with him, but she rose and paused to put on a robe just the same. Sufficiently covered, she went downstairs to find her husband.

When she got downstairs, the lights were still on in the living room, but her husband wasn't there, not even in the recliner he often fell asleep in. She decided to check the kitchen next. Sometimes when Len Swann couldn't sleep, he sat in the kitchen with a cup of tea. Usually, she'd find the cup still on the table, half-filled with cold tea. She never understood what the point was for her husband to make tea, then not drink it.

The kitchen was dark, and there was no teacup on the table when she turned on the light. She saw several empty beer bottles in the garbage, though. Maybe Keough had left and Swann had fallen asleep at his desk. He didn't do it often, but he had done it once or twice.

She went to the door of the small office and saw the light from beneath it. She knocked once, and when there was no answer, she opened it and entered.

"Len?" she called. "Honey, are you asleep?"

He was seated in his chair, his back to her. His head was cocked to one side, and she felt sure he was asleep. She moved alongside him, at the same time putting her hand on the back of the chair and turning it toward her.

"Honey," she started to say, "time to wake up and go to sl—"

She stopped short and caught her breath when she saw that her husband was not asleep. He looked asleep, with his eyes closed and his head lolling to one side the way it did when he complained of a stiff neck from falling asleep that way in his recliner. He could have been asleep, if it wasn't for the handle of the little sword he used as a letter opener. It was protruding from his chest, and blood had dripped down the front of his shirt and pooled up in his lap.

As a cop's wife, she was always prepared for the worst, for a policeman appearing at her door to tell her that her husband was injured, or worse, dead. She was not, however, prepared to find her husband dead herself, in their own home, and she did what any other woman would do, cop's wife or not: She screamed.

Chapter Nineteen

When Keough arrived at the Swann home at 5:15 A.M., there were a number of vehicles parked out front, including the medical examiner's wagon. It was just starting to get light out, and the heat was creeping in.

"Stand back, bud," a uniformed cop said to him, holding his arm in front of him to block his way.

"I'm on the job." Keough showed the man his shield.

The cop studied him and said, "I don't recognize you from the squad."

"I'm not with your precinct," he said. "I'm with the Six-Seven Squad. I was called in."

"By who?"

"The wife. The dead man was a friend of mine."

The cop, fresh-faced and young-looking, wasn't sure what to do.

"If you ain't with the squad, I don't know if I can—"

Keough, still in shock from the call he'd received from Marcia Swann, brushed past the cop and said, "Take it up with the duty captain, pal," and walked to the house. The young cop did not try to stop him.

Keough got to the door, which was open, and had to show his shield to another cop. This time, he hung it from the pocket of his jacket.

"You ain't with the squad," this cop said. He was older than the other, and his demeanor was more relaxed.

"No," Keough said, "but I was called in."

"Go ahead, then."

"Thanks. Do you know where they have the wife?"

"I think she's upstairs with the kids. She scared the shit out of them when she screamed."

Keough flinched, imagining that he could hear Marcia Swann's scream when she found her husband.

"Who's here from your squad?"

"Clapton and Hancock," the cop said. "Clapton's catchin' the case."

Keough didn't know Hancock, but he knew Clapton slightly from working a night watch with him a few times.

He entered the house and looked around. The door to Swann's little office was open and Forensics was working inside. The ME was standing outside, and Keough walked over to him. As he got closer, he could see Swann's head and knew that the man was still in his chair.

Dr. Mahbee saw Keough approaching and looked surprised.

"Did you get transferred?"

"No," Keough answered, "the wife called me."

Mahbee indicated the body and asked, "Friend of yours?"

"Yes."

"Want to take a look?"

Keough nodded and entered. He walked around so he could see Swann's body. The hilt of the little sword was sticking out of his chest, approximately where his heart would be. For just a moment, he imagined a pain in his chest—sympathy pain.

"I don't know how sharp that thing was," Mahbee said behind him, "but it would have taken a lot of force to do that with a weapon that small."

Keough didn't know how sharp it had been, either. He'd seen it on the desk but hadn't paid it much mind.

"Ho, what've we got here?" a voice said.

Keough looked up and saw Det. Keith Clapton standing in the doorway. He was in his late forties, average height, slim to the point of emaciation. He wore wire-framed glasses and sported a pretty ragged beard and mustache.

"Hey, you're Keough," the man said. "The wife told me she called you."

Mahbee backed out of the room so Clapton could enter and shake hands with Keough.

"Too many people in the room," the Forensics man said.

"That's okay," Keough said, "I was just stepping outside."

Clapton exited the room with Keough right behind

139

him, wishing he'd had a chance to look at Swann's desk and see if the memo they'd drafted the night before was there.

"Okay," Clapton said, opening a small spiral notebook, "the wife says you were the last one to see him."

"No."

"No?"

"The killer was the last one to see him."

Clapton surpressed a grin.

"Okay, you're the last one we know of."

"Right."

"When did you leave here last night?"

"Around ten."

"How long were you with him?"

"Hours . . . probably, oh, five or six hours."

"Why were you here?"

"We're—we were friends. Went through the Academy together."

"You make a habit of coming here?"

Keough studied the man for a moment before answering.

"You already asked his wife that."

"Yeah, I did," Clapton said, "and now I'm askin' you."

"We ran into each other recently and renewed acquaintances. Last night was the first time I'd ever been here. He didn't live here when we were in the Academy."

"You still workin' the Six-Seven Squad?"

"That's right."

"And he was working the Lover Task Force."

"Right."

"Any connection?"

"Between what?"

"Do me a favor, Keough," Clapton said, "don't make me pry everything out of you?"

"The task force was just one of the things we talked about."

"Like what?"

"Like he was upset that they were only using him as a clerical."

"Was that unusual?"

"No, he was a good clerical."

"Then why was he upset?"

"Because he said he wanted to be a real detective."

"Like you and me, huh?" Clapton asked.

"Yeah, like you and me."

Clapton jerked his thumb toward the little office and said, "You got any ideas about this?"

"Not right now." Keough shook his head. "I'm still a little bit in shock. Does she want to see me?"

"Yeah," Clapton said, "she does. Why don't you stay here and I'll get her. She's upstairs with the kids and my partner."

"How are they?"

"She scared them when she screamed."

"Have they been told?"

"Yeah, they have. It was rough."

"Does she have someone to stay with them?"

"Her mother's up there, too. I'll bring her down. Why don't you wait in the living room."

"Okay. Who's got the duty?"

"Captain Dulfer."

"I don't know him."

"He's the exec over at the Seven-One. They call

him Candy, 'cause he's always sucking on something—cough drops, a lollipop—hey, like Kojak. I never thought of that before.''

"He's not here yet?''

"No,'' Clapton said. "I'm thinkin' about callin' him again.''

"What about a sergeant?''

"Here and gone.'' Clapton laid his finger alongside his nose and said, "He had to go and get some breath mints.''

That meant the sergeant on duty was a boozer and might or might not be back.

"Detective?'' Mahbee said.

"Yeah?'' Clapton replied.

"Can I move him?''

"Not until the captain shows up, Maybe,'' Clapton said, "you know that.''

"Yes, I know that,'' Mahbee said, "and don't call me Maybe.''

"Sure.''

Clapton went upstairs to get Marcia Swann, and Mahbee gave Keough a look.

"This department is going to the dogs,'' he said. "The sergeant was drunk; the duty captain's not here—''

"Clapton's a good man,'' Keough said.

"Well,'' the medical examiner said, "I guess we'll have to settle for one out of three, huh?''

"When was he killed, Doc?''

"Near as I can figure,'' Mahbee said, "between ten and midnight.''

"I left here at ten.''

"That puts me right on the money, then, doesn't it?"

"I guess it does."

Keough took one last look at the office. From where he stood, he could only see part of the desk, and he didn't see anything that looked like a memo.

"Looking for something?" Mahbee asked.

"No," Keough lied, "just looking."

Keough turned and went into the living room. The last bottle of beer he'd had was still there on the coffee table, half-full.

He turned as he heard someone approaching and saw Marcia Swann enter with Detective Clapton. He wasn't sure how to react. Should he embrace her? Give her a sympathetic shoulder? She made the decision for him by keeping her distance, not crying, but hugging herself as if she was cold. Maybe it was her own icy calm that was chilling her.

"Marcia, I'm . . . so sorry." It sounded lame to him.

"Don't be sorry, Joe," she said. "Just find who killed him."

"Marcia," Keough said, "Detective Clapton will do everything he can—"

"No," she said, interrupting him, "I don't want Clapton; I want you."

Keough looked at Clapton, who shrugged.

"Keith, could I talk to Marcia alone?"

"Sure," Clapton said, giving a wave. "I'll be in the other room."

Clapton left and Keough looked at Marcia.

"Marcia, are you all right?"

Another lame question.

"No, I'm not all right." She looked at him angrily.

"I'm so fucking mad, Joe. How could someone do this? In our own house?"

"That's what Clapton will find out—"

"I told you," she snapped, "I want you!"

"I don't understand, Marcia. Why do you insist that I work on the case?"

"Because you were his friend."

Some friend, he thought. They hadn't seen each other since the Academy until this week.

"Because I know my husband, Joe," she went on. "He was excited about something, and nervous, and it had something to do with you."

"Marcia—"

"You and he were working on something together, Joe," she said accusingly. "Did it get him killed?"

"No," Keough said right away, "of course not."

"Are you sure?"

He opened his mouth to answer, then closed it abruptly. Was he sure? But how could the murders have had anything to do with it? It had to be a coincidence.

"Joe?"

"Marcia, I don't think—"

"There was no forced entry, Joe," she said quickly. "I'm a cop's wife. No forced entry means nobody broke in. This wasn't done during the course of a burglary."

He didn't know how to respond. He still couldn't see how the murders could have anything to do with Swann's murder. Where would he even start? There weren't any suspects.

"He was killed by someone who knew him, Joe."

"Marcia—"

"Somebody he let in the house after you left."

"I was the last one to see him, Marcia," Keough said. "Why not suspect me?"

"Maybe I do, Joe."

That stung him.

"Then why ask me to investigate?"

Suddenly, she lost her icy calm and her eyes darted about before they finally settled on him again.

"All right," she said miserably, "I thought about you because you were the last to see him, but I don't really think you did it, Joe."

"Thank you, Marcia." His tone was stiff.

"But I think you can find out who did."

"I won't be assigned to the case, Marcia."

"You will if I insist on it, Joe. If I make a big-enough fuss."

If she made a fuss, then he was going to have to explain to someone what he was working on with Swann, and he wasn't quite ready to do that—not until he had some time to think things over.

"I'm working on something else."

"Something you were working on with Len."

He hesitated before answering.

"Something Len was helping me with, yes, Marcia, but I don't think—"

"There's a connection, Joe."

"There can't be," he said, but his denial was too forceful, even for him.

"I want you to work on this, Joe . . . please?"

They stared at each other for a few moments, and then he said, "Don't make a fuss yet, Marcia. Let me see what I can do."

"I'll go along with you, Joe," she said, "but don't disappoint me, you hear?"

"I'll try not to, Marcia," he said. "Now tell me, do you know any reason why someone would want to kill Len?"

Marcia returned upstairs to be with her children. Keough went to the little office, where Clapton was still waiting for the duty captain.

"Keith, I think I'm going to get going." He tried to get a surreptitious look at the desk. "You want me to come by your precinct later today and make a statement?"

"Sure," Clapton said, "I'd appreciate it."

He started away, then stopped and turned around again. His eyes raked the desk one more time, but he didn't see the memo.

"You going to get in trouble for letting me go before the duty captain gets here?"

"I'll handle it," Clapton said with a smirk. "It's my case, not his."

Keough looked over at the body again, and Clapton shook his head.

"This is bad, Joe. Every cop in the city is going to be up in arms."

"I know."

Clapton looked at Keough.

"Is there anything else I should know before you go, Joe?"

Keough looked at Clapton and thoughts ran through his mind quickly. What could he tell him? That he and Swann were preparing to go over the head of the CO of the Lover Task Force? Would that make that very same CO—Lieutenant Slovecky—a suspect? The way Clapton was looking at him, the man figured there was more to Keough's presence than what he was telling, but the other detective was not pressing him—not yet, anyway.

No, Keough still had to get away to put some thought into his next move.

"Nothing right now, Keith," he said. "If I think of something, I'll give you a call."

"Okay," Clapton said, "then shove off before the captain gets here, or you'll never get out of here."

"Appreciate it, Keith."

Clapton waved Keough's gratitude away and stepped back into the little office. Keough wished he had time to look around the office alone. He wondered what Clapton would do when he found the memo he and Swann were going to send to the C of D.

He also wondered what it would mean if Clapton didn't find the memo at all.

Chapter Twenty

Keough was on the day tour that day, so he went home, showered and dressed, and went directly to work. On the way, he went over Swann's death in his mind. Coincidence or connection? How could there be a connection? he wondered. Could the Lover have found out the names of the task force detectives? Was he going after them? If so, he was acting like no serial killer Keough had ever heard of. He'd never heard of a killer turning around and going after the cops.

Was Swann cheating on his wife? Had he been killed by a jealous lover? Or a lover's husband or boyfriend?

Marcia had given him no potential reason for the murder.

"Len wasn't like the rest of you, Joe," she'd said,

which he assumed was supposed to sting. "He didn't stop off on the way home; he didn't cheat; he was a good family man. No, I don't know why anyone would have wanted to kill him. I think you'd know more about that than I do."

Marcia Swann was convinced that her husband had been killed as a direct result of his working on something with Keough—only as far as Keough was concerned, they had barely even gotten started.

Could it be that Swann had told his two-killer theory to someone who wanted it covered up? The only person Swann had even mentioned in connection with a cover-up was the lieutenant, Slovecky.

Now with Swann dead, Keough thought, he was the only one with the two-killer theory.

Did he have to watch his back now?

"You look like shit," Pete Huff said as Keough entered the squad room.

"Thanks."

Det. Jim Diver came over to the desk and said, "We heard about Len Swann, Joe."

Keough looked at Huff.

"You went through the Academy with him, didn't you?" Huff asked.

"That's right."

Huff shrugged and said, "I remembered."

That surprised Keough. Maybe Huff wasn't such a complete asshole after all.

"You heard, right?" Diver asked, as if suddenly afraid he'd been the one to deliver the bad news.

"I heard, Jimmy."

"Were you friends?" Diver asked.

"We knew each other, Jimmy," Keough said. "We knew each other."

"Well . . . I'm sorry."

"Thanks," Keough said. "Are we catching?"

"Third in line," Huff said happily.

That satisfied Keough, too. He didn't know how he was going to juggle his own cases—of which there were plenty—and also spend time on the Lover and his copycat, as well as Len Swann's murder.

Keough felt bad about Swann. You were a cop, you felt bad when another cop was killed. He would have felt bad even if he still hadn't seen him since the Academy. Renewing acquaintances with him—for whatever reason—just made it worse, and having met his family was the capper. Still, he didn't want to drop the other thing because of it, and yet if it came out what he was doing—messing in a case that wasn't his—he'd be called on the carpet. Now he had two cases that weren't his—the Lover case and Swann—and he needed the time to work on both.

He stood up, walked to the coffeepot, poured himself a cup, and carried it back to his desk. He took a deep breath and decided what his next move had to be.

Swann was to have sent their memo that morning. Now it was going to be up to him. He'd read the memo; now he was going to have to try and duplicate it from memory and send it to the C of D. After he'd gotten that done, he'd think about Len Swann's murder.

He pulled a sheet of letterhead from his desk, rolled it into his typewriter, and started hunting and pecking.

"Whataya writing, a book?" Huff asked after a while.

"Just a memo."

"I'm gonna go get something to eat," Huff said. "Want something?"

"No thanks."

"Suit yourself."

Huff got up and left, then came back, and Keough was still hard at work on the memo. He didn't know how Swann had managed to do stuff like this so fast.

It was almost three by the time he finished his third and final draft and pulled it out of the typewriter.

The original was to have been from both him and Swann, but with Swann dead, Keough's name went at the bottom all by itself. He stared at his name for a few moments, then took a deep breath and signed the thing. It wasn't word for word what Swann had written, but it was close enough.

"Pete," he said, "I've got to go out for a while. Are we next up?"

"Naw," Huff said, "only one case came in so far. We're second. Where you headed? Want me to come?"

"I've got to mail this," he said, holding the envelope in his right hand, "and then I've got to go make a statement to the squad about Len Swann's murder."

"Why you?"

"I was with him last night," Keough said. "Apparently, I was the last one to see him alive."

"Jeez, I didn't know that. They called you?"

Keough nodded.

"Early this morning."

"Jeez," Huff said again, "no wonder you looked

like shit—aw, jeez, I'm sorry I said that this morning—''

"Forget it, Pete, just forget it. I should be back pretty soon."

"Don't worry about it," Huff said. "You don't make it back by end of tour, I'll sign you out. Don't even come back here."

"Thanks, partner," Keough said. "I owe you one."

Keough left, wondering if he and Huff had made a breakthrough in their partnership.

He went down to the front desk to drop the envelope in the mail. The precinct had a special basket there for mail that was going out to other commands. He knew that the mail was picked up twice a day, and he wanted to make the second pickup. He trusted the department mail better than the post office—although just barely.

"Hey, Keough."

He turned and saw the cop behind the desk who had called him. His name was Sal Adamano, and he had gone through the Academy with Keough and Swann.

"Hey, Sal."

"I heard about Swannie," Adamano said, leaning across the desk.

Adamano was working as the station house officer, who was basically to assist the sergeant or the lieutenant on the desk. Today, the desk officer was Sgt. Phil Greco. At the moment, Greco was listening to a woman who was complaining about someone doing something to someone named Rosa Mundi.

"Damned shame," Adamano went on.

"I know."

"Guy works as a clerical, for Chrissake, and somebody breaks into his house and kills him. How are his wife and kids?''

"His wife's strong, Sal," Keough said. "The kids'll lean on her."

"I'm gonna be going to the service," Adamano said. "See you there?"

Keough hadn't even thought about a service. It probably wouldn't be for a while, though, since Swann was the victim of a homicide.

"Yeah, I'll be there."

"Lady," Phil Greco was saying, "I can't have someone stake out your garden, for Chrissake."

"Don't curse at me, young man," the old woman said. "I watch *Law and Order*, and I used to watch *Hill Street Blues* and *Police Story*. I know all about stakeouts. Baretta used to do them all the time. Sometimes he'd take that bird along. . . ."

Keough didn't want to hear any more. He waved at Adamano and then left to go make a statement to Det. Keith Clapton.

He hadn't expected Clapton to have anything new yet, and he wasn't disappointed.

"I did some interviews in the neighborhood while some of the uniforms canvassed. Nobody saw nothing, and ain't that a surprise."

"Keith, I don't know if you heard, but Marcia Swann wants me to work on this."

"Are you going to?"

"How can I? It's not my case."

"Did you tell her that?"

"I did."

"Well, she was upset. She's a cop's wife; she'll understand."

Clapton was assuming that Keough had no intentions of working the case. Keough decided to allow the man to continue thinking that. After all, he wasn't sure what he was going to do himself.

He made his statement to Clapton, answered some more questions warily, and then decided to take a shot at something.

"Keith, since Len was on the Lover Task Force, do you think his murder is connected with that?"

"I don't know, Joe," Clapton said. "At this point, I don't have many theories. I'm gonna talk to the other detectives on the task force, though."

"Did he have any files or anything in his office?" Keough asked, trying to make it sound like nothing but natural curiosity.

"I went through the place, Joe, including his file cabinets and desk, and I didn't find anything. Did you think he was taking files home?"

"Not really," Keough said carefully, "but he was always talking, you know, about doing real detective work. It wouldn't have surprised me if he had."

"Well, we didn't find anything."

Keough nodded and rose to leave. Apparently, whoever had killed Swann had taken his Lover file. Keough didn't like the implications of that.

He was just about to leave when the phone on Clapton's desk rang.

"Clapton, squad," the man said. "No, he's still here. Wait a minute." He held the phone out to Keough and said, "It's for you."

"For me?"

Clapton nodded and Keough took the proffered phone.

"Keough."

"Joe, it's Pete."

"What's up, Pete? We catch a case?"

"Oh, no, Joe, that's not what I'm calling about," Huff said. "Uh, I think you better get back here."

"I thought you were going to sign me out," Keough said, momentarily annoyed.

"Something came up, Joe."

"What?"

"I think you better—"

"Can't you just tell me?"

Huff fell silent, then Keough heard an intake of breath before his partner spoke again.

"It just came in a few minutes ago on the Teletype, Joe," Huff said. "You've been transferred."

Transferred! After months of trying, what a time for it to come through.

"Joe, did you hear me?"

"I heard, Pete," Keough said, "I just am not sure how to react."

"Well, you should be glad, I guess."

"I guess. I'm on my way back."

"Okay."

"Thanks for calling."

"Sure."

"Oh, by the way, where was I transferred to?"

Another moment of silence and then Huff said, "Joe, you got transferred to the Lover Task Force."

Chapter Twenty-one

Driving back to the station house, Keough's mind was reeling. First he was thinking about Swann's death and what it meant that his Lover file had been taken, and then he thought about his transfer to the Lover Task Force. How did that come about? Were they moving this fast to replace Swann?

By the time he reached the station house, the next tour of detectives had already come on. Lieutenant Carson was still there, though, and Keough decided he'd rather discuss his transfer with his squad CO than with the precinct CO.

"Sorry to see you go, Joe," Carson said as Keough entered his office.

"Can you tell me what this is about, Loo?"

Carson shrugged helplessly.

"All I know is what came across the Teletype. You're to take a two-day swing and report to the Lover Task Force Monday morning."

"But how did this happen? Was I requested?"

"You'll have to ask your new CO that."

Keough left Carson's office. Obviously, there was little the man could tell him. His new CO was going to be Lt. Dan Slovecky, and at the moment Keough wasn't so sure he wanted to talk to the man. If Swann's murder was connected with the Lover Task Force, then that made Slovecky a damned good suspect. Keough didn't like thinking about cops killing cops, but it had happened before and it would happen again. Also, if Slovecky was guilty, what was his motive for having Keough transferred? It was clear he was going to have to watch his back very carefully.

It was good news that he had two days before reporting to Slovecky. He was going to try to put those days to good use. For one thing, he was going to investigate Slovecky and see what kind of man he was. Swann had already said Slovecky was concerned with making himself look good when he finally caught the Lover. What Keough had to determine was just how badly Slovecky wanted to look good. Bad enough to kill Swann when he thought the detective was going over his head with his own investigation? If word got out Slovecky was padding the Lover's dance card to make himself look better, it would—or should—have exactly the opposite effect.

Keough paused at his desk and wondered if he should take the time now to clean it out. Suddenly, he became aware of someone standing next to him.

"Heard the news, Joe," Det. Les Roberts said.

Roberts was a handsome white-haired man in his fifties who had been a detective for more than fifteen years, and on the job for over twenty-five.

"Yeah," Keough said, "I'm out of here."

"You don't sound happy about it."

"It's a surprise, is all."

"Well, if you want to trade places, just let me know. I've been trying to get out of this place since they first dumped me here."

"I'll let you know, Les."

"Good luck, huh?" Roberts said, sticking out his hand.

"Yeah, you, too." Keough shook Roberts's hand, and then the other man walked out. After a couple more detectives shook his hand and wished him luck, he decided to clean the desk out now and get it over with so he wouldn't have to come back.

He went in search of a box.

When Joe Keough entered his apartment building, he was carrying a cardboard box with the contents of his desk in it. Keough had always been ready to leave the Six-Seven Squad at a moment's notice, and to that end, he had not kept a lot of personal belongings in his desk. Now, however, as he carried the box to the elevator, he thought how surprised he was that, now he'd finally gotten the transfer, he had mixed feelings about it.

"Hold the elevator, please?" he heard a voice call as the doors started to close. He stopped them by using the DOOR OPEN button, and Nancy Valentine got into the elevator with him.

"Oh, hi, Joe."

"Hello, Nancy."

Her face was flushed from running for the elevator, and she looked very pretty. She was wearing her nurse's uniform under her coat, but he noticed she had removed the white hose that usually went with it. She had once told him that her theory about why men were turned on by nurses was not that it was because of the uniform, but the stockings.

"You're not moving out, I hope," she said kiddingly, eyeing the box in his arms.

"Um . . ." he said, because he hadn't thought about that. Would his transfer to the task force make it necessary for him to move?

"Joe?"

"I was transferred today."

"Really? That's . . . well, that's wonderful," she said, although she didn't sound like she thought so.

Actually, she did think it was wonderful for him, because she knew how much he'd wanted a transfer, but she did not like the thought of losing him as a neighbor, and as a friend, or as what he could possibly have become. . . .

"Back to Manhattan?" she asked.

"As a matter of fact, yes."

The elevator stopped at their floor and the doors opened.

"You'll be moving, won't you?" she asked as they stepped out and walked down the hall together.

"I really don't know yet, Nancy," he said. "It only happened a little while ago, and I've got mixed feelings about it."

"Oh? But . . . I thought this was what you really wanted."

159

"It was—that is, it is, but . . ."

They stopped, he in front of his door and she by hers, and faced each other across the hall. There were about twenty apartments per floor, but no one else was in the hall at the time.

"But what?"

"It's . . . complicated."

"Complicated is my specialty," she said. "You want to come over and talk about it?"

He hesitated and thought about it a moment. He didn't feel he could talk to anyone in the department—especially after what happened with Swann. Maybe he needed to talk about it to someone outside the department, even if it was just to hear himself say it all out loud.

"Cindy won't be home until late," she added. "She's having dinner at a friend's house. That's why I'm late getting back. I'll make us a small dinner."

"I do need to talk to someone, Nancy, but—"

"I know," she said, holding up her hands, "a lot of it is official. Maybe you can just talk about the unofficial stuff?"

"All right," he said finally. "I appreciate it, Nance, I really do."

"Dinner at seven? And then we can talk?"

"Seven's fine." It gave him time to shower and change.

"Good." She seemed delighted as she opened her door. She stepped inside, turned to close the door, and said to him, "See you then."

Keough held the box beneath one arm while he worked his key in the lock. Inside, he set the box down on the floor by the door and went directly to the kitchen. He took a bottle of John Courage from the refrigerator and drank it standing right there, mulling things over in his mind.

By the time he got to the bottom of the bottle, he was convinced that trying to work all of it out in his head would only drive him crazy. Talking it out with someone would be the best thing for him, but preferably someone who was not in the department. He needed someone who would listen, make intelligent comments, and not try to tell him what his duty was.

Nancy Valentine had already proven herself, time and again, a good listener.

Chapter Twenty-two

Over a hastily put together but delicious dinner of chili over white rice, corn bread, and a salad, Keough explained his dilemma to Nancy Valentine, who listened intently. She seemed to realize that he had more of a need to speak aloud to someone than to have that someone make comments.

"So your big problem, about the serial killer, has been solved by you being transferred to the task force?" she asked when he was done.

"No," he said, "and I'm not sure that's my biggest problem."

"Okay, wait a minute," she said, holding her hands up. "If that's not the big problem, what is?"

"I'm not sure," he said, "maybe the murder of Len Swann."

"Because he was your friend?"

"That, and because he was a cop, and because his wife seems to think I'm to blame for his death."

"All you said was that she wanted you to work on the case," Nancy interjected. "Why does that mean she blames you?"

"She's convinced that he's dead because of whatever it was he and I were working on."

"The serial killer?"

He nodded, then added, "Although she doesn't know that's what we were meeting about."

"And what do you think?"

Here was the tricky part, admitting to someone outside the department that he thought a cop might have killed Len Swann. That was sort of like airing your dirty laundry on Fifth Avenue, and the department would have frowned on it if they knew.

"Joe?"

He poured himself another glass of wine and then held the bottle out, silently asking if she wanted more. She didn't. That suited him. He had designs on finishing the rest of the bottle himself, anyway.

"Nancy . . . I think another cop may have killed Len."

"Why do you think that?"

"Well, for one thing, he let the killer into the house. It was someone he knew."

"And?"

"And a memo that he and I had worked on that night and were intending to send to the chief of detectives was missing."

"Who would have taken it?"

"A cop."

163

She eyed him and asked, "Just a cop?"

"No," he said, "I have a specific cop in mind."

"And you don't want to tell me his name."

"No."

"But if this memo had been sent, it would have hurt him?"

"Yes."

"And there are no other suspects?"

"All he was working on was the task force."

"What about outside the job? Maybe a girlfriend?"

"His wife says no."

"Isn't the wife the last to know when her husband is fooling around?"

"Sometimes the wife—or the husband—is the first to know. A lot of spouses—mostly wives—can tell, and they don't mind when their husbands stray."

She frowned.

"Why?"

"Because then the husband isn't bothering them."

"For sex, you mean."

"Right. In many cases, the wife just wants the husband to provide while she takes care of the children and the house, and they don't mind when their man gets sex from someone else."

"Oh my," she said in an odd tone.

"What is it?"

"Do you believe that?"

"It's not what I believe, Nancy; it's what I've seen," he replied.

"I don't believe my husband ever cheated on me, Joe."

He stared at her for a moment and then said, "He would have been a fool to."

Joe Keough was always aware of how attractive Nancy Valentine was, and he wasn't sure why nothing had ever happened between them. He had never had a lot of luck with women. For one thing, he found it hard to talk to them. The only woman he hadn't had that problem with was Nancy. If he tried to get closer to Nancy, though, to have a "real" relationship—well, then there was Cindy. As much as he liked Cindy, he didn't know how he'd do on an everyday basis with her.

Maybe it was Cindy that scared him the most from having a relationship with Nancy.

"Joe? You went away," Nancy called across the table.

"I'm sorry, Nancy," he said, picking up his wine-glass. "I'm tired, and I'm confused."

"Is talking it out helping any?"

"Not yet," he said, but then hastily added, "but it's not hurting any . . . and dinner was wonderful."

"Let me clear the table and I'll bring out some coffee," she said, standing up.

"I'll help—"

"You'll do no such thing. I don't want you zoning out again and dropping my plates and glasses on the floor. Stay there and . . . think."

She went into the kitchen, and Keough did just what she suggested: He thought.

From the beginning, he thought there were two different serial killers at work, and he still did. Now, however, he also had to deal with Len Swann's murder. He doubted that one of the serial killers was the culprit, so that meant he was looking at three murderers.

Was the third a cop? Swann's boss, Lieutenant Slovecky? Did he kill Swann to try to preserve the number of murders he'd attributed to the Lover? To answer those questions, he was going to have to find out what kind of man Slovecky was—and he had two days to do it before he had to report to the man at the Lover Task Force.

"Coffee's on," Nancy said, coming back into the room with a tray in her hands.

Keough wanted to leave, to go back to his own place to plan his moves for the next day, but he didn't have the heart to do so now. He stayed for some coffee and some more talk, and when that was done, he stood up to leave.

"Joe?"

"Yeah?"

She smiled.

"Did talking to me help?"

"It helped a lot, Nancy."

"I guess since it's police work, I really don't have to know how, huh?"

"I think it's better you don't."

They walked to the door together.

"What about moving?"

"What?"

"Are you going to be moving to Manhattan?"

"I don't think so."

"Why not?"

He opened the door and turned to face her.

"If things work out the way I think they're going to, I think this will be a temporary assignment."

"Well," she said, touching his arm tentatively, "I hope things work out the way you want them to."

He started to leave, hesitated, then took a step to her and kissed her. He meant it to be a short kiss, a gentle thank-you kiss, and he was surprised when she put her arms around his neck and melted into him. The kiss went on for some time, her mouth soft and supple beneath his, and she was breathless when it ended, her eyes shining.

"Good night, Joe."

He stepped into the hallway and she closed the door in his face, but not before he saw her satisfied smile.

He went back to his apartment to work up his moves for the next day, but the kiss kept intruding. He'd kissed Nancy in the past, but never like that. He was afraid of the consequences of a kiss like that.

He thought about Nancy and Cindy, but he eventually pushed them aside to think about Len Swann, Marcia Swann, and their children, as well as Dan Slovecky and two serial killers who liked to use roses to defile their victims.

He fell asleep in a chair and dreamed that he was walking barefoot on a bed of roses—with thorns.

Chapter Twenty-three

Keough spent the next two days talking to as many people as he could who either worked with, under, or over Dan Slovecky.

The people he worked with didn't like him. The partners he'd had didn't stay partners with him very long, and the other men he'd worked with were glad they'd never been partners.

"Dan was out for himself." Ivan Rogoff had been partners with Slovecky for four months in a radio car when both of them had been on the job for five years. Rogoff now worked as a desk sergeant in a Staten Island precinct that was generally known as a "country club."

"You sure he's not gonna hear about this?"

"I'm sure."

"Why'd you say you were askin', again?"

"I've got to work for him," Keough said, "and I heard he was a tough nut. I'm just trying to find out some stuff about him."

"Well, that was Danny boy's specialty."

"What was?"

"Finding out stuff about people."

"How do you mean?"

Rogoff leaned across the desk to get closer to Keough. He was so big around the middle that the move didn't get him all that closer.

"I mean he watched people, other cops, usually anybody who had a higher rank than him. He watched them real careful, and he noticed things."

"Noticed things?"

"Yeah, you know, like who was seein' who, who was shacking up with who—he caught a lieutenant doin' a female civilian in the captain's office one time. The lieutenant swore him to secrecy and Danny boy kept the secret—until he needed somebody to sign him a transfer. You get what I mean?"

"He blackmailed people?"

"Only when he needed something, and never for something big. I mean, he never had enough on anybody high enough to get himself promoted, but he was able to get little things for himself—better shifts, vacation days, and transfers. Get it?"

"I got it."

"You're sure he ain't gonna hear about this?"

"Not a word."

Keough found that when people heard he was asking questions about Slovecky, they acted hesitant but were actually eager to talk. Apparently, Dan Slovecky had made very few friends during his years on the job.

"He was a pig," Detective Second Grade Andrea Service said. She was another old partner of Slovecky's, seven months' worth, when they were both working Narcotics during the late seventies. He had been a detective, while Service had simply been a plainclothes cop.

She was a handsome woman in her early forties with white hair cut very short. She had a face that looked better in profile, because from there all you could see were the strong nose and jaw. When you looked at her head-on, she had a weak chin and close-set eyes, but she was still attractive.

"He tried to get me to sleep with him the first night we worked together. Told me he had friends who could help move me along in the department."

"And he didn't?"

She snorted.

"If he did, they didn't do me any good. No, what Danny Slovecky had was a way of getting things on people—little things, things that would get him certain favors. Hey, maybe he even got laid because of these things, but he never got into my pants."

"You said he had a way of getting things on people?"

She stared at him for a moment, then said, "Oh, I see. You want to know if he got anything on me?"

"Sorry, but—"

"That's okay. No, the only thing he got on me is that I was young, and I thought my pants were pure gold. I worked damn hard to get this far—and this is as far as I've gotten, because I wouldn't put out.''

Det. Andrea Service was assigned to the Missing Persons Squad, and she did most of her work taking reports over the phone.

"Maybe if I'd slept with him, I'd be a sergeant by now, huh?'' she asked. "Not!''

Keough wondered if Service had actually gotten no further because of her refusal to trade sex for promotions. He was no choirboy, but he would hate to think that was how women had to get ahead on this job.

After Keough had interviewed enough of Slovecky's peers and ex-partners to determine that he was far from a well-liked man, he decided to find someone whom Slovecky had worked for. He wanted to get a perspective from the other side.

He ended up visiting a retired captain named Truxton Lewis. The man lived in a small wood-frame house in Queens, and when Keough arrived, he was working in his garage. His wife answered the door and directed Keough around to the garage.

As Keough approached the two-car garage, he could see that it was set up as a woodworking shop. The man inside was in his sixties, with white hair and large hands. He was tall and lanky, and at the moment was bending over an electric saw that was affixed to a homemade table. Around his feet, the fresh sawdust was being stirred by the small fan that was sitting on a shelf. Outside the garage was a Chevy wagon that no longer fit in the garage.

Keough waited for the sound of the saw to die down and then called out, "Captain Lewis?''

Lewis looked up and stared at Keough from behind a pair of plastic goggles.

"Who wants to know?"

"My name is Keough, Captain. I'm on the job."

Lewis pulled off his glasses and a heavy pair of work gloves that he was wearing, then set them both down on the table. Obviously a careful man, he switched off the electric saw before speaking again.

"Let's see it?"

Keough knew that the man was talking about his shield. He took out his wallet and let the man see his badge and his ID.

"You're not with IAD, are you?"

Keough frowned.

"No. Why would you think I was from Internal Affairs, Captain?"

"Those sons of bitches come out here every once in a while to hassle me."

"Why?"

"You don't know?"

"No, sir."

"Don't call me sir," Truxton Lewis said, "and don't call me Captain."

"Yes, sir—I mean, no sir—I mean—"

"Call me Tru," Lewis said. "That's what everybody calls me. Tru. Got it?"

"Yes . . . Tru."

"Where'd you get my name from?"

"A file."

"What file?"

"Lt. Dan Slovecky's personnel file." Keough had a friend in personnel.

The look on Lewis's face changed abruptly, as if a dark cloud had suddenly settled on him.

"If that son of a bitch sent you here, you can turn around and get the fuck away from me and my house."

"Slovecky didn't send me."

"You a friend of his?"

"From what I've been able to find out, uh, Tru, Dan Slovecky had very few friends on the job."

"Try no friends."

At that moment, Mrs. Lewis appeared carrying two cans of Budweiser beer.

"One for you and one for your guest, Truxton," she warned him. "Don't go drinking both of them."

"I won't."

"Here," Lewis said, handing Keough a beer. The other, he pressed to his sweaty forehead.

"Thanks."

"Well, if you're not friends with that bastard, you might as well come over here and sit."

Keough followed Lewis to two folding chairs that were set up to the left of the garage.

When they sat, Lewis was staring off in the direction his wife had gone.

"She's the only person in my whole life I've let call me by my given name."

"Truxton?"

Lewis looked at Keough.

"Bet you wonder where a horrible handle like that came from, huh?"

"It had crossed my mind."

"Well, I ain't gonna tell you." Lewis drank some

beer and then looked directly at Keough. "What's this about Slovecky?"

"I've been transferred to his squad, Tru, and I'm trying to find out what kind of a man he is."

"His own squad? What squad would that be?"

"It's a task force, the Lover Task Force."

Lewis snorted.

"No wonder that maniac hasn't been caught. Slovecky is in charge of that squad?"

"Yes, si—uh, that's right."

Lewis thought that over for a moment, shaking his head, and then directed his attention to Keough again.

"Son, do I look like a fool?"

"Uh, no, of course not."

"Then don't treat me like one. I have never heard of a cop being assigned to a squad and then trying to dig up dirt on his new CO—except for Slovecky himself. Are you like him, son?"

"No, I'm not."

"Then tell me what the hell is goin' on here, or this conversation is over."

Keough thought it over for a few moments and then figured, What the hell. After all, Lewis wasn't on the job anymore. So he told the retired captain more than he'd intended, but not the whole story. He told him about feeling that there were two killers, and about Slovecky covering that fact up to make one man—his killer—look better.

"So he makes himself look better when he catches him," Lewis finished.

"That's what I think."

"Well, you've got no problem, son."

"Why not?"

"Slovecky isn't gonna catch him. He's not smart enough."

"He's got detectives working for him, Tru; they're good men."

"You know 'em?"

"I knew one."

"Knew?"

Keough found himself telling Lewis the rest, about finding out that Len Swann felt the same way he did, about the memo, and then about Swann being killed.

When he was finished, Keough found Lewis staring at him intently.

"Tru?"

"You think Slovecky killed him, don't you?"

"The thought had crossed my mind, yeah."

"Sure, that's why you're out here talking to me. You've talked to others, haven't you? Others who have worked with him?"

"Yes, I have."

Lewis smiled.

"You're a good detective, son," he said. "I can tell a good detective when I see one."

"Thank you."

"That's not idle ass kissing. I retired from my own squad, you know. My men were good. They were like you, thorough and not afraid to rattle a few doors. Tell me something?"

"If I can."

"Why are you doing this?"

Keough hesitated before answering.

"It started because of a young girl being killed, and I didn't think anybody was looking for the right killer. Now I'm in it for a lot of other reasons."

"To find out who killed your friend?"

"That's one of them."

"It's a bad thing," Lewis said, shaking his head, "a cop killing a cop."

Keough didn't say anything.

"You want to know if I think Slovecky is capable of it?"

"I'd like to know what you think, yes."

"Son, I haven't seen that man in ten years, but if he continued to develop the way he was going, and he thought that killing your friend—a cop—would get him what he wanted, then I wouldn't put it past him."

Keough digested that and then said, "Thank you, Tru." He put the empty beer can on the ground and stood up.

"I'll give you a piece of advice, too." Lewis stood up and walked as far as the open garage with Keough.

"What's that?"

Truxton Lewis stepped into the garage and picked up his plastic goggles.

"I was you," he said, "I'd check into how Slovecky managed to get himself assigned whip of that task force."

It sounded like good advice.

Chapter Twenty-four

It occurred to Keough later that if Slovecky had had bigger visions throughout his years on the job, he might have been able to get himself moved further along instead of trading what he knew for small favors. Apparently, he'd been a small thinker all his life.

There were things in Slovecky's file that Keough didn't have to talk to people about. When he was on the street, Slovecky had been the recipient of more than his share of brutality beefs. When he became a detective, there were fewer, but they were still there. Even as a sergeant, he'd gotten himself into trouble for being quick-tempered, and quick with his fists, or his baton.

What was clear was that Slovecky had always been a brutal man, as well as a thoroughly disliked one. Did that mean he was capable of murder? That probably depended on how badly he wanted to catch the Lover with more murders to his credit than he actually had.

Keough decided that the man to talk to now was Sgt. Arthur Dolan, the second whip on the task force. He could offer some insight on the kind of man Dan Slovecky was now—that is, if he was willing to talk about—or against—his superior.

Also, Keough wanted to find out—as Truxton Lewis had suggested—how a man like Dan Slovecky managed to wrangle himself the assignment as CO of the Lover Task Force.

Keough called the task force office, hoping to catch Dolan still in. He was lucky. Whoever answered the phone caught Dolan as he was walking out.

"Yeah, Dolan."

"Sergeant, this is Joe Keough. I'm supposed to report to the task force tomorrow?"

"Keough, right. What's the matter, calling in sick already?"

"No, that's not it. Sarge, I'd like to meet with you tonight."

"Meet with me? For what?"

"I'd rather talk to you about it in person."

"What's the gag, Keough? You looking to transfer out before you even transfer in? I can't help you—"

"It's not that."

Dolan heaved an impatient sigh. Keough imagined the man shifting from one foot to the other and looking at his watch.

"Do you have anything to do tonight?"

"Not really—not other than going home, and I'm not all that sure I want to do that."

Keough had heard a lot of married cops echo that sentiment.

"How about letting me buy you dinner?"

There was a pause.

"Is this important, Keough?"

"It's about Len Swann's murder."

"Swannie," Dolan said, sounding sad. "Jesus, that makes me mad. You got something? Are you working on that? What's your interest?"

"Swannie and I were friends, Sarge," Keough explained. "We went through the Academy together, and we were working together on something when he was killed. In fact, I was the last person to see him alive that night."

Another moment's hesitation and then Dolan said, "Then you should be talking to the investigating officer."

"I have, twice. Now I want to talk to you."

"About what?"

"Again, I don't want to talk about it on the phone."

"Ah shit, you're lucky me and my old lady aren't getting along these days, Keough. Where do you want to meet?"

"You pick it," Keough said, "but don't make it a cop hangout."

"I fucking hate cop hangouts," Dolan said. "You know a burger joint called Those Were the Days?"

"On Thirty-third and Eighth?" Keough was drawing on his former knowledge of Manhattan.

"That's the one. I stop in there sometimes on the way home from work, for a beer and a burger. I'll be there in . . ."—Keough saw in his mind's eye the man looking at his watch again—". . . about fifteen minutes, and I should be there for a couple of hours. If you show up, we can talk."

"I'll show up, Sarge," Keough said. "Thanks."

It took Keough forty minutes to drive from Queens, over the Fifty-ninth Street Bridge to Manhattan, and then downtown to West Thirty-third and Eighth. The bar was across the street from Madison Square Garden. It was after 6:30 when he arrived, and some parking spots had opened up nearby. The work day was done and this busy section of Manhattan—on the edge of the Garment District—was winding down to a halt. Maybe that was why Dolan liked it.

He entered the place and realized that he didn't know what Arthur Dolan looked like. He suspected, however, from the way the man talked that he'd probably take his burger and beer right at the bar. At the moment, there was a man in one seat, working on a hamburger, and a woman a bit farther down who seemed to be working on the man.

"... good looking man shouldn't be eatin' alone," she was saying as Keough entered. She looked to be in her forties, a professional bar bimbo looking for an early pickup.

"For the last time, lady," Dolan said, "I'm not interested."

"Whataya, gay or somethin'? Come on, I'll show you how it feels to be with a woman."

The man turned and said something to the woman that Keough didn't hear, then showed her his palm.

"Jesus," she said, sliding off her seat fast. She headed for the door, and as she passed Keough, she

180

was muttering something about "... if they're not gay, they're cops."

Keough went over and sat down on a stool next to the man.

"Sergeant Dolan?"

"You Keough?" Dolan asked.

"That's right."

"Drop the Sergeant stuff, okay? I eat here a lot and nobody knows I'm a cop."

"Have it your way."

"You want something to eat?"

Keough realized how hungry he was and nodded.

"What you're having looks good."

"Hal, bring my friend a bacon burger and a Watney's."

Keough had not ever had Watney's before, but he was willing to try it.

Dolan was in his late thirties, a red-faced Irishman with the road-map face of a drinker, brown hair, green eyes, and a mouth that turned up at the ends. He had the face of a man who should be smiling, but Keough doubted he smiled much. Maybe at one time he had, but not much anymore.

"Okay, so you're here," Dolan said. "What's this all about?"

"I want to talk to you about Lieutenant Slovecky."

Dolan frowned.

"You said on the phone you wanted to talk about Len Swann's murder?"

"I do, I do, but I'd like to start with Slovecky."

"Why should I talk to you about my boss—our boss, since starting tomorrow you're part of the squad. Are you a clerical?"

181

"No, why?"

"That's what Slovecky said he wanted, a clerical to replace Swann."

"Well, I'm not a clerical. Did Slovecky ask for me specifically, Sarge?"

Dolan studied Keough, as if he wasn't sure he wanted to answer the question.

"As a matter of fact, he did."

"Now why would he do that?"

"I don't know; maybe you'd like to tell me. Tell me something, anyway."

"Okay," Keough said, "but I'd rather do some asking before I do any telling."

Dolan rubbed his hand over his face and thought about that, then looked down at his half-eaten burger.

"You've got until I finish this to get to the point," he said finally. "After that . . ."

"That's fair."

Before he could start, though, the bartender came back with his food and beer.

"That's quick service."

"That's one of the reasons I eat here," Dolan said. "Now I'd appreciate *some* quick service from you. Give."

Keough's mouth was watering now that the burger had arrived, but he decided to give Dolan something before he took the time to chew.

"Do you think there are any discrepancies among the Lover cases you fellas are working on?"

Dolan gave Keough a slow look, during which the detective took a bite of his hamburger. It was bad, but he was hungry.

"What do you mean 'discrepancies'?"

"Specifically between the Manhattan and Brooklyn cases?"

"What's your interest?"

"I caught the first Brooklyn killing."

Dolan sat up straighter.

"Now I remember your name."

"There were differences I noticed right on the spot, Sarge, but before I could do anything the case was referred to the task force—wrongly, I think."

Dolan had stuffed the last of his burger into his mouth, and he was chewing slowly.

"Then came the second Brooklyn case, and again there were differences, but that one was referred to the squad, as well—again, wrongly."

"You thought."

"And I still do."

"And what did Swann have to do with anything?"

"Swannie agreed with me," Keough said. "We talked about it that last night, before he was killed."

"And?"

"He had a duplicate file, and it wasn't found at the scene."

"A duplicate file?" Dolan said. "If Slovecky knew that, he would have skinned him alive."

"Maybe he did know."

"What?"

"Maybe Slovecky knew about the file."

"What are you saying? That Slovecky killed Swann to get the file? That's crazy."

"That's what I'm here to find out from you, Sarge," Keough said. "Is it crazy?"

"Of course it is."

"Did Swann ever talk to Slovecky about the differences in the cases?"

Dolan frowned.

"Once, I think."

"After the note?"

Dolan looked surprised.

"You know about the note?"

Keough nodded.

"Swann told me."

"Jesus, if Slovecky knew that . . ."

"What happened when Swann questioned Slovecky."

"The loo put him in his place and explained away Swann's remarks."

"Did he explain them away to your satisfaction?"

Dolan hesitated, then said, "His explanations made sense."

"You accepted them?"

"He's the boss, Keough."

"Didn't you look into them yourself?"

"Why should I?"

"You're second whip."

Dolan laughed derisively.

"That doesn't mean a thing to Slovecky. He runs the squad alone."

"So if he wants to suppress evidence, nobody questions him?"

"Why would they? He's the boss."

Dolan took some money out of his pocket and tossed it on the bar.

"If you're going to work in the task force, you better get used to that."

"So you don't think that Swann's death had anything to do with the Lover case?"

"I wouldn't know," Dolan said impatiently. "I'm not investigating Swann's case."

"And what about me?" Keough asked. "I was the last person to see Swann alive, and all of a sudden Slovecky asks for me to be reassigned to the task force?"

"Maybe he just thought you were the best man for the job."

"He doesn't even know me, Sarge."

"Yeah, well . . . like I told you, he runs the squad."

"With an iron hand?"

"That's right." He picked up his glass and drained the last of his beer.

Keough thought he could see now why Slovecky had picked Dolan as second whip. Slovecky seemed to have an ulterior motive for everything he did.

"I see."

"No," Dolan said, slamming the empty glass down on the bar, "you don't see. You don't get anywhere on this job, Keough, by bucking the system. What do you care if the Lover gets convicted for two more murders?"

"I care because then the real killer of those two girls goes free."

Dolan stared at Keough for a few moments, then looked away uncomfortably. He got off the stool, picked up his coat from the stool next to him, and started putting it on.

"I'm going to do you a favor, Keough."

"What's that?"

"I'm going to pretend this meeting never happened."

Keough turned on his stool and watched Dolan leave, then turned back and took a thoughtful sip of his Watney's. It was much better than the burger. In the end, he finished the beer, left half the burger, and headed home feeling that not much had been accomplished by talking to Dolan—except possibly to have the man watching him from the moment he walked into the task force office.

When he got home, he took a John Courage out of the refrigerator and sat in the living room with it. It was better than the Watney's, but not by much. At least he'd discovered a new beer tonight.

He'd also discovered—or rediscovered—what he had known all along: The attitude of most cops was still "don't rock the boat." Swann had been the only one willing to do a little of it, and now he was gone and Keough was alone again.

Keough still had one thing he wanted to find out, and maybe he could do it early in the morning before reporting to the task force. He wanted to know how Dan Slovecky had managed to get himself assigned as the CO of the task force. From what he'd discovered over the past two days, it was fairly obvious that Slovecky had something on somebody. All he had to find out was who the recommendation had come from and then maybe he'd be able to get something on Slovecky.

Chapter Twenty-five

It was raining Monday morning when Keough left at 7:45, a miserable gray drizzle. He turned up the collar of his raincoat, but while he waited for the bus, the water seemed to seep down the back of his neck, anyway. Before getting on the train, he bought a container of coffee and drank it on the way.

He'd only ridden the subway to Manhattan a few times since moving to Brooklyn, and never at this hour. Now he looked around at the bored faces of the people who made this trip at this time of day, every day. He didn't think he would like to do this every day. It would be interesting to see where he ended up after this task force assignment was over. Would he end up back in the Six-Seven? That would probably depend on Slovecky and whether or not the lieutenant was in a position to control that.

Even if Slovecky wasn't Swann's killer, it was clear to Keough that he had mishandled the whole Lover investigation. If he could just prove that and get the Brooklyn cases investigated separately, he'd be happy. As for Swann's murder—well, if the task force wasn't involved, there was really very little he could do about it.

When he had returned home last night, there had been one message on his phone, from Marcia Swann. He really didn't want to talk to her, but he hadn't the heart to ignore her, either. So he returned her call.

"Joe," she said when she answered, "what's going on?"

"What do you mean, Marcia?"

"What have you found out? What have you done so far?"

"Marcia—"

"Don't tell me you can't work on this, Joe," she said, cutting him off. "Maybe you don't know this, but Len was the easygoing partner in this marriage. I'm a bitch when I want something, and I want this, Joe."

An idea occurred to Keough at that moment.

"I wasn't going to tell you that, Marcia. What I was going to tell you is that I managed to get myself assigned to the task force to fill Len's spot."

"Why did you do that?" she asked, sounding puzzled.

"You told me that there was nothing happening in

Len and your personal life that would account for his murder, right?''

''That's right.''

''Well, that leaves his job, doesn't it?''

''I suppose it does. How did you manage that, Joe?''

''Trade secret, Marcia. Look, I'll keep in touch with you, okay?''

''Sure.''

''One more thing.''

''What's that?''

''Don't mention this to Detective Clapton. He wouldn't like me meddling in his case.''

''All right, Joe. I won't say a word.''

''That's good, Marcia.''

''Joe? Thanks.''

''Marcia? Len was my friend, and I want to know who killed him, too.''

''Not as much as I do.''

''No,'' Keough said after a moment. ''No, not anywhere near as much as you do.''

When Keough entered the task force office, he spotted Dolan across the room. The sergeant saw him, came over, and pretended not to know him.

''Help you?''

''Yeah, my name's Keough.''

''The new guy.''

''Yeah, the new guy.''

''The lieutenant wanted to see you as soon as you got in.''

''Big surprise,'' Keough said, loudly enough for Dolan to hear him.

The sergeant gave him a warning look and said, "Let me introduce you to the others, and then I'll take you in to see him."

He walked Keough around the room, introducing him one by one to the other members of the task force, none of whom he had ever met before.

"Now I'll take you in to see the boss."

"Great." He was finally going to get to meet Slovecky face-to-face. The first thing he was going to ask the man was why he'd picked him.

Dolan knocked on Slovecky's closed door and opened it without waiting for an invitation.

"Boss? Detective Keough is here."

"Good," Keough heard a deep voice say, "bring him in."

Keough slid past Dolan and entered the room, with the sergeant behind him. The man behind the desk didn't stand, but Keough could see the powerful build on him even while he was seated.

"Lieutenant Slovecky?"

"That's right." The man still made no move to stand or shake hands. "Have a seat, Keough."

Keough sat right across from the man and studied him. He had a bullet head, hair very close cut, almost no neck, and powerful forearms and shoulders. He would hate to run into Dan Slovecky in a bar or an alley. He knew from Slovecky's file that he was thirty-four years old.

Dolan took the seat on Keough's right and Slovecky stared at him.

"You can go, Dolan."

"Uh, I thought I'd stay during the orientation, Loo."

"You thought wrong," Slovecky said coldly. "Close the door on your way out."

Dolan looked stunned, but he finally stood up, walked slowly to the door, and closed it on his way out.

"I've seen your file, Keough," he said. "You're a fuckup."

No dancing around, right to the point. Keough decided to stay calm.

"No more or less than anybody else."

"No, no, don't be modest," Slovecky said, "a lot more. That stunt you pulled in the men's room of the courthouse, that was a beauty."

"The asshole had it coming."

"Maybe," Slovecky said, "but not from you."

"That sounds funny, coming from you, Lieutenant."

Slovecky frowned.

"What do you mean?"

"This beef I had was nothing compared with some of the ones you had in the past," Keough explained. "That one in Eight-Five? When you broke the hand of a city councilman's son? That was a bit of a beaut, don't you think?"

"You son of a bitch!" Slovecky said. "You saw my file, didn't you?"

"I like to know who I'm working for, Lieutenant," Keough said, deciding on the spur of the moment how to play it. "You never know when you might find out something . . . useful."

Slovecky stared at Keough, thinking that the new detective in the squad sounded a lot like somebody he knew.

"You're a smart-ass, is that it?" he asked. "Who showed you my file?"

"Let me ask you a question, Lieutenant. Why did you pick me for this assignment? I'm not a clerical."

"You are now."

"Yeah, but why?"

Slovecky sat back in his seat and Keough could now see that the man had some extra pounds around his middle. Still, being locked in a room with the man would certainly not be Keough's idea of a good time.

"Should we put our cards on the table, Keough?"

"We could try."

"I didn't ask for you to be assigned here. Your name has been in for some time for a transfer, and somebody decided to have you dropped in here. That's okay—I need a man to fill Detective Swann's spot. But you've spent the last two days asking questions about me." Obviously, Keough had talked to at least one person who was a friend of Slovecky's, or maybe Dolan had already told him about their conversation. "I don't like that."

Keough shrugged.

"Like I said, Lieutenant, I like to know who I'm working for."

"What did you and Swann have going?"

"What?" The question surprised Keough.

"I want to know what you and Swann were working on. Did he give you copies of any files? Because, you know, if you have copies of any of my files, I'll have your ass."

The stupid son of a bitch, Keough thought. The man had just admitted that he knew that Keough and Swann were working on the Lover case independently of the task force. How would he know that unless he'd seen them together? Maybe outside of Swann's house? Like the night of the murder?

Suddenly, Keough wanted to leap across the desk at his superior, but he quelled the urge. If he was going to prove anything, he had to make sure it would stick. Attacking his boss on his first day wouldn't enhance his credibility when the time came.

Slovecky stared back at Keough.

"Well?"

"I don't have any files, Lieutenant."

"No? What *do* you have?"

Keough shrugged.

"Some thoughts."

"About what?"

"The same thoughts you should be having," Keough said, "about two killers."

"There are not two killers, Keough. I went through that with Swann, I'm not going through it with you. If you have thoughts about that, forget them. I run this squad; nobody here thinks but me."

"Swann did."

"Swann's gone."

"But not forgotten."

"What's that supposed to mean?"

"Just what I said."

Slovecky sighed heavily and shook his head sadly.

"Keough . . . you and I ain't gonna get along, are we? I can tell."

"Fine, then transfer me."

"Not on your life. I want you right here where I can see you. I'm gonna be watching every move you make."

Keough grinned at the man and said, "That makes two of us . . . sir."

Slovecky sat back, his hands in his lap, out of sight.

"Get out," Slovecky said. "Dolan will show you where Swann's desk was. Get our files in order."

"You computerized?"

"Of course we are."

"I don't know how to use a computer."

Slovecky's face darkened.

"Fake it."

Keough stood up and walked out of the office, closing the door behind him.

"First meeting's a bitch," Detective Samuelson said to Keough, "but the boss is okay."

"Uh-huh." He looked over at Dolan, who was standing nearby. "Slovecky said you'd show me Swann's desk."

"Sure, it's over here."

Keough followed Dolan to a corner of the room with a computer and some file baskets. The baskets were full of reports that had come in that morning from precincts all over the city, and beyond.

"How'd it go, uh, with him?" Dolan asked, out of earshot of the others.

"I think we understand each other, the lieutenant and I." He decided not to accuse Dolan of giving him up—not yet, anyway.

"Is there going to be trouble?"

"Oh," Keough said, almost laughing, "oh yeah, if I can help it."

Dolan got a pained look and walked away.

Keough sat at Swann's desk and wondered if Slovecky was telling the truth. Could it possibly have been a coincidence that brought him here, right where he would have chosen to be, given the chance? Now he'd not only be able to work on the serial killer cases but on Swann's murder, as well.

September

Chapter Twenty-six

Over the course of his first week with the task force, Keough was left alone in the office often, and he couldn't believe his luck. All he had to do was figure out the damned Xerox machine.

Initially, Keough made no attempt to file the reports that came into the office. After all, Slovecky really hadn't had him assigned to do that. He figured if the lieutenant was lying to him and had actually arranged for his transfer, then he just wanted him where he could watch him, which suited Keough, because it afforded him the very same opportunity. On the other hand, if the transfer was truly a coincidence, it was one he could take advantage of. By the second day, however, he figured trying to keep the files in order might eventually benefit him. He did his best, but he was no Len Swann.

On the Monday beginning his second week—Labor Day—he called his old partner Pete Huff. He'd thought he'd have his answer from the C of D's office by now.

"How do you like your new assignment?" Huff asked.

"It's fine, Pete."

"Boy, what I wouldn't give to change places with you."

Keough doubted that Huff would feel that way if he knew all the facts.

"Callin' 'cause you miss us?"

"I'm calling because I mailed something out before I left, and the answer is going to come back there, if it's not there already. Is there anything for me?"

"I'll check. . . . No, nothing, Joe."

"When it comes, would you give me a call?"

"Sure. Want me to send it to you?"

"No, Pete, I want you to call me. I'll come and pick it up myself."

"Okay, okay, you got it. Hey, can you put in a good word for me up there?"

"I'll try."

Keough hung up, thinking that, to his mind, he was more "down" there than he was "up."

While most of the others were out of the office, including Slovecky, Keough was alone with Arthur Dolan. Dolan had avoided contact with him for most of the first week, and Keough decided to press the issue today.

"Hey, Sarge?"

Dolan looked up from his desk.

"What is it?"

"Can you show me how to work the Xerox machine?"

Dolan frowned.

"I'm not really sure how to do it. Swann used to make all the copies."

"Does the lieutenant know how to work it?"

"I think so."

"Hey, tell me something. Do you know how Slovecky got this assignment?"

"Not really."

"Well, is he friends with the chief?"

"Hell no."

"Then someone must have recommended him for the position. Who has the chief's ear?"

"Pollard."

"Who?"

"Inspector Paul Pollard, the chief's right hand. If he was going to take a suggestion from anyone, that's who it would have been. Pollard and Slovecky know each other."

"What's Pollard's story?"

"He's a yes-man, good at what he does."

"Any skeletons?"

"There must be."

"Why do you say that?"

"Because he's too good to be true—married, churchgoing, the whole nine yards. You just know somebody like that's got something in their closet."

Dolan stood up then and said, "I'm going out for a while."

"When will you be back?"

"I don't know," the sergeant said. "I'll call in."

"Okay."

Keough figured Dolan was leaving rather than stay with him alone and answer more questions.

An hour later, he was still alone in the office when the phone rang again. He considered not answering it, but the morning was slipping by and he figured he should probably wait for Slovecky to come back and go out again before he started Xeroxing.

He answered.

"Keough, task force."

"Detective Keough, is it?"

"That's right."

"This is Lieutenant Skerrit, over in Brooklyn at the Six-Three Squad?"

Keough suddenly went cold from head to foot.

"Yes, sir?"

The latest Brooklyn victim had been found at the base of the stairs leading down to the subway station at the corner where Nostrand Avenue and Flatbush Avenue intersected. It was an area that was generally called "the Junction." It was a commercial area filled with small stores and restaurants. Also in that area was Brooklyn College.

The victim was not college age, however, but high school age. She was found lying at the base of the subway steps and, according to a preliminary ME's report at the scene, had been dead several hours. The body had been found by a token-booth clerk who was reporting to work.

The phone call from the Six-Three Squad commander was a courtesy notification that they had a case involving a dead girl and a rose—"Yeah, it's in her cunt"—and that they'd be forwarding a copy of the report forthwith.

Keough hung up the phone and covered his face with his hand. The Brooklyn killer had struck again, on the heels of the Lover, and he had no doubt that Slovecky would simply lump it in with the rest of the cases.

There was a television in the squad, a portable color set, and Keough turned it on. The lieutenant from the Six-Three said that the body had been found too late to make the newspapers but that some television reporters had made it to the scene.

Sure enough, as Keough changed channels, he came upon a special report by one of the stations. While he was watching it, Dolan and Samuelson came walking back in together. Obviously, they'd hooked up some-place outside.

"What's that?" Dolan asked.

"Another murder in Brooklyn," Keough said.

Dolan and Samuelson joined him by the set.

"Say anything about a rose?" Samuelson asked.

"Not yet," Keough said, "but I just got off the phone with the Six-Three commander. He said there was a rose involved."

"Shit!" Dolan said.

"A high school-age girl," Keough said, turning and looking at Dolan.

"Just like the other ones in Brooklyn," Dolan said defensively. "So our man likes Brooklyn girls high school age."

"That's funny, don't you think?" Samuelson asked.

"What's so funny about it?" Dolan demanded, looking at the man.

Samuelson backed off a few steps.

"Hey, I was just making a comment."

"You got some reason to believe that the Brooklyn girls aren't being killed by the same man?" Dolan demanded.

"Now that you mention it—"

"Save it," Dolan said. "If you got something to say, say it to the boss."

"Forget it," Samuelson said. "If he wants to lump all these murders together, it ain't no skin off of my nose."

"Is this a live feed?" Dolan asked Keough.

"Yeah."

"Come on, Eddie," Dolan said, "let's take a ride out to Brooklyn."

"Whatever you say, boss."

Dolan gave Samuelson a sour look, tossed an even more sour one to Keough, and the two men left.

So even Samuelson had noticed the discrepancies, huh? Keough thought. How many of the other detectives on the squad had noticed it and ignored it in the face of Slovecky's position?

Chapter Twenty-seven

Kopykat sat in front of the TV and watched as the pretty people talked about his handiwork—first the handsome man with the raincoat and microphone, then the pretty lady in the studio.

While he was watching, his mother came out of her room, scratching herself. She had come home with another man last night, thank God, and had left him alone. The man was still sleeping in the bedroom. Kopykat could hear him snoring.

"Whataya watchin'?" his mother demanded. "I wanna see Jane Whitney."

"Jane's not on, Ma."

"Whataya mean she ain't on? It's after twelve."

His mother went over to the TV to take a look.

"What's that?"

"A special report."

"About what? Oh, is that about another murder?"

"Well, yeah, Ma—"

He stopped when she slapped him in the back of the head.

"Change that, damn it. I don't want you watchin' that stuff. Gimme that." She took the remote control from him and started switching channels. "Maybe Ricki's on, or what's'er name, that Rolanda? God, everybody's gettin' a talk show, these days. Even that blonde from *Entertainment Tonight*, uh, Leeza . . ."

Kopykat tuned his mother out as she kept talking. What would she think if she knew that those pretty newspeople were talking about something he'd done?

Wouldn't she just shit.

The Lover couldn't believe his eyes, but there it was on the television in the faculty lounge. Live from the scene in Brooklyn, they were talking about what "appeared to be" another murder by the Lover. But he hadn't even left his apartment last night.

He watched and listened with growing horror as they described the girl as "apparently" of high school age. The fiend! How could he bear to touch girls that young? And people were blaming it on him!

He became aware that someone was speaking to him, but he couldn't be bothered now with things like faculty meetings. He waved the person away and staggered out into the hall, feeling sickened but knowing that he had to regain control. He had to do something so people would know this was not his handiwork.

He rushed down the hall to his office. He had tried a note; now he was going to have to do something more direct.

Chapter Twenty-eight

Keough was still watching the television when the phone rang.

"Detective Keough, task force."

"I sent a note."

"What?"

"I said, 'I sent a note.' " A man's voice, impatient, educated. "Didn't anyone read it?"

Keough felt a chill. Had a whole series of events taken place just to get him here, at this moment, alone, when the phone rang? To talk to him?

"What note would that be, sir?"

"I think you know what note, Officer."

"Detective."

"Who is in charge there?"

"At the moment, that would be me," Keough said, "as I'm the only one around."

"Did you see my note?"

"Uh, are we talking about the note about—"

"Please don't waste my time," the voice said. "You fellows are up there for one reason, and that is to catch me. That is your job. What other note would I be calling about?"

"If you'll excuse me, sir, you could be anybody calling up here. Somebody looking for attention."

"Well, of course Im looking for attention, you idiot. Why else would I be . . . doing what I'm doing?"

No admission there.

"Besides," the man went on, "there has been nothing in the newspapers about the note, so how else would I know about it unless I wrote it?"

The man had a point there. Keough decided that he actually was talking to the Lover.

"Did you see the note?"

"I did."

"Then why wasn't it published?"

"My superior decided not to release it."

"If you had, I wouldn't be receiving the blame for what happened last night, would I? Have you heard?"

"Yes, sir, I've heard."

"And have you seen the television?"

"I have it on now."

"It's preposterous. I would never touch a girl of that age, never!"

"I believe you."

"What? Excellent! Then you are now operating

with the knowledge that I have not killed anyone in Brooklyn?''

Keough's mind raced as he tried to figure out how to play this. The man seemed genuinely concerned that his ''reputation'' was being muddied. Keough decided to play to the man's ego.

''Well, actually, no.''

''What do you mean 'no'?''

''Our people have decided to believe that you were using that note simply to throw us off the track.''

''In what way?''

''The belief here is that you live in Brooklyn and do not want us looking for you.''

The man expelled a disgusted breath.

''That's preposterous! I would not live in Brooklyn. It is filled with cretins!''

''Well, maybe—''

''You must make them believe otherwise.''

''I can't do that.''

''And why not?''

''They wouldn't believe me,'' Keough said, making it all up as he went along. ''You called while I was here alone. When the others come back and I tell them you called, they won't believe me.''

''Why not?''

''I am not considered very reliable.''

''And are you?''

Keough hesitated and then said, ''I'm something of an oddity in the police department.''

''In what way?''

''I care a little too much.''

''And most policemen do not?''

''Most policemen these days,'' Keough said, ''want

to put their time in and retire with a nice pension.''

The Lover sighed and said, ''It is not so different in my profession.''

Keough remained silent.

''You did not ask me what my profession was.''

Keough laughed.

''I don't think you'd be foolish enough to answer me correctly, so what would be the point?''

''Let me ask you something.''

''Go ahead.''

''What would you suggest I do now?''

''Well, you could call back and talk to my superior.''

''Would you recommend that?''

At that point Keough got an idea.

''No.''

''And what would you suggest I do?''

''Call a newspaperman.''

''Really.'' The man sounded surprised. ''Wouldn't your department rather keep this matter out of the press?''

''Definitely.''

A chuckle filtered through the phone.

''What is your name, Detective?''

''Keough, Detective Joe Keough.''

''Mr. Keough, let me ask you something.'' The man's tone was that of a teacher addressing a student. In fact, that had been the attitude Keough detected from the beginning of the conversation.

''Go ahead?''

''Do you believe I killed those girls in Brooklyn?''

''I do not,'' Keough replied, ''but I am a minority of one.''

"I see, and you are in a position where the majority rules."

"That's correct."

"So you are saying that unless I announce in the newspaper that I did not kill those girls, I will continue to be thought responsible?"

"That's correct." Keough was aware that his own speech pattern had become more and more proper during the phone call.

"I see."

The man fell silent, but Keough could still hear him breathing. He decided to wait and let the man make the next move.

"I should think about this," the killer finally said, "but tell me, Mr. Keough, what newspaperman would you suggest I call?"

After hanging up on the man who claimed to be the Lover, Keough sat back and waited for his heart to slow down. He'd never spoken to a serial killer on the phone. The voice had been so calm, so cool, and he knew that his voice had sounded the same way. Were the killer's palms, then, sweating the way his were at the moment?

Although the man had never admitted to anything, Keough was absolutely certain that he had spoken to the killer. He also believed the man when he said that he had not killed the girls in Brooklyn and that he did not live in Brooklyn. Lastly, he knew that Slovecky was not going to believe that he had spoken to the killer on the phone. Neither would Dolan. He didn't know about the other detectives in the task force, but he decided not to tell any of them. In fact, he wasn't going to tell anyone else who was on the job.

There was only one person he was going to talk about it to.

He dialed the phone and when it was answered, he asked for his party.

"Mike O'Donnell, please."

When O'Donnell came on, Keough said, "We've got to have dinner."

"Why?"

"Have I got a story for you."

Chapter Twenty-nine

When Mike O'Donnell walked into Brendan's, Keough was already seated at a back booth. He'd gone straight to Brendan's from the task force office, after a brief discussion with Slovecky.

"You managed to stay out of my way the first week, Keough," Slovecky had said at the end of the shift. "That's good."

"It's not going to do your filing any good to keep me on clerical, Lieutenant," Keough had said. "You'd be better off putting me on the streets."

"So you can muddle the picture with hogwash about a second killer? No, I think you'll stay inside, where you can do the least damage."

"Suit yourself," Keough said, and left, secretly pleased that Slovecky was going to keep him inside, where he could stay in contact with the Lover—if the killer ever called him again.

When O'Donnell appeared, Keough waved him to the booth. O'Donnell stopped at the bar for an Irish coffee and carried it to where Keough was sitting, nursing a beer.

"What's this story you've got for me?" he asked. "Have you broken the serial killer case?"

"Not yet."

"Then why the urgent summons to dinner—and when is dinner, by the way?" He picked up a menu from the table and turned to look for a waitress.

"Let's eat after we talk, Mike."

"Okay," O'Donnell said, "then talk."

"You should be getting a phone call this week—a very important phone call."

"Oh yeah? From whom?"

Keough hesitated, then said, "The Lover."

O'Donnell stared at him.

"The Lover?"

"That's right."

"The serial killer Lover? With the roses? That one?"

"That's the one."

O'Donnell stared at Keough for a few moments, then said, "Joe, if this is a joke—"

"No joke, Mike. It's on the level."

At that moment, a waitress came.

"Would you like to order dinner?"

"Not yet," Keough said.

"Honey," O'Donnell said, putting his hand on her arm to stop her from leaving, "would you bring me an Irish whiskey—make it a double?"

"Sure, Mr. O'Donnell."

As she went off to get it, the newspaperman turned back to Keough and asked, "How did you manage this? And why is he calling me? What the hell is going on, Joe?"

"If you'll quiet down for a minute, I'll explain it all to you," Keough said.

"Okay," O'Donnell said, "I'm quiet. Give."

Keough told O'Donnell again about his belief that there were two separate killers. He told him about working with Swann, about Swann's death, and about being transferred to the task force so that Slovecky could keep an eye on him and keep him quiet. He did not tell O'Donnell that he suspected Slovecky of killing Swann. That would be putting too much temptation in the way of the newspaperman. Keough only paused when the waitress came back with O'Donnell's drink.

"The killer in Brooklyn is using different roses, and he's using them with the thorns still on the stems," he went on.

"Also, he's hitting high school girls, while the Lover is killing women."

"And the task force doesn't know this?" O'Donnell asked.

"The commander of the task force is covering it up," Keough said. "He wants the Lover's reputation to be that much bigger when he catches him."

"And he'll let another killer go to do it?"

"Yes."

"Do you have proof?"

"I will have, when you want to go press with this."

"Which is not yet . . . right?"

"You can't go to press with anything I've told you, but you will be able to after you talk to the Lover."

"Jesus," O'Donnell said excitedly, "he really is going to call me?"

"He is."

"Why?"

"It's very important to him that people don't think he's having sex with high school girls."

"And killing them."

"After I told him I thought he should call a newspaperman, he said, and I quote, 'I am not a pervert; I would not have sex with high school girls.' Apparently, he's not worried about people thinking he killed them, just that he had sex with them."

"This is a sick bastard."

"Yes, but an educated one. He sounds like he could be a teacher."

"And he's gonna call me," O'Donnell added proudly.

"Well, after I told him to call you, he asked me what paper you wrote for."

"He didn't recognize my name?" O'Donnell asked sadly.

"No," Keough said, "apparently he doesn't read the *Post*. He, uh, asked if I didn't know somebody at the *Times*."

"And you told him to get fucked, right?"

"Something like that."

"Jesus, I can't believe this. Do you know what kind of story this will be? This is Pulitzer stuff."

"Not to mention the book you could get out of it."

"Hell yes."

"Well, when is he gonna call?"

"If he calls, it will be this week."

"If he calls?" O'Donnell asked. "I thought it was all set?"

"He has your name and number, Mike, but whether or not he calls is up to him."

"Jesus, what if he doesn't call?"

"He'll call."

"How can you be so sure?"

"He wants everyone to know that he's not killing in Brooklyn. He'll call."

"What if he calls some jerk at the *Times*?"

"I talked you up."

"What if he doesn't take your word for it?"

"It's funny."

"What is?"

"I really thought we hit it off, you know? He seemed to know what I was up against, and he sympathized. He said he'd often come up against the same sort of thing in his business."

"And what business was that?"

"I didn't ask."

"Why the hell not?"

Keough studied O'Donnell for a few moments before speaking.

"Mike, I think you're going to have to handle this guy a certain way so he doesn't hang up on you."

"I've done interviews before, Joe."

"Not like this," Keough said, "and that's my point. This is not an interview I've set up. You can't start asking him a lot of questions. If you do, you'll lose him."

"What am I supposed to do, then?"

"Just listen to him," Keough said. "He wants to tell his side of this Brooklyn thing."

"There's something I don't think you've thought of," the newspaperman said.

"What's that?"

"I'm going to have to call the task force before I run with this. I'll need to have a statement from the commander—what's his name?"

"Lt. Dan Slovecky."

O'Donnell wrote the name in his notebook.

"He's going to deny everything," Keough said.

"That's okay," O'Donnell said. "I just have to hear his side and cover it—but that's not what I was talking about. I meant you."

"What about me?"

"You're gonna get into a lot of trouble over this. You're gonna get jammed up; that's what's gonna happen."

"I'll worry about that."

"Do you want me to check in with you when he calls?"

"No, just print it, Mike."

"You want this guy bad, don't you?"

"The Lover?" Keough shook his head. "I care about him the least in all of this. Oh sure, I want him caught before he kills again, but he's really the least of my worries. I want Swann's killer, and I want the department to recognize that there's someone else at work in Brooklyn. That's the guy I want to catch. He's a sicko."

"And this guy isn't?"

Keough sat back in his chair.

"Let me see if I can explain this."

"Wait, wait," O'Donnell said, taking out his notebook again. "You mind if I take this down for the book?"

Keough thought a moment, then said, "Why the hell not. If I lose my job after all this, I can do talk shows."

O'Donnell found a clean page and said, "Okay, shoot. You were gonna tell me why the guy in Brooklyn is a sicko and the guy in Manhattan's not."

"Don't get me wrong, Mike. The Lover is a killer; he's just not a sicko. I mean, they're both crazy, but the Lover isn't . . . mad. Am I making sense?"

"No," O'Donnell said, "but I'm taking it all down, anyway. Keep going."

"It's just that the Lover sounded so educated on the phone, and so hurt that people would think he was raping high school girls. Hell, he even removed the thorns from the roses he—Jesus . . ."

"What?"

Keough put his hand to his forehead and shook his head.

"I was just going to say he removed the thorns from the roses he inserted in his victims' vaginas. Christ, Mike, do I even know what I'm talking about? What kind of man does that, and I'm making excuses for him?"

"Hey, hey." O'Donnell reached across the table with real concern in his voice. "Don't start comin' down on yourself, Joe. If you're right about this, you're doing a lot of good by taking two killers off the streets."

"Maybe."

"No maybes. Besides, I know what you're tryin' to say."

"You do? Then tell me."

"This Brooklyn guy is trying to copy the Lover, but he's picking younger girls, and he's shoving roses up their, uh, twats without removing the thorns. Jeez! What you're saying is that this guy's brutal and mad, while the Lover is . . . well, in need of psychological help."

Keough made a face.

"I'm not saying that at all. The last thing I think about either one of them is that they're killing girls because they used to wet their beds, or because their daddies drank. I don't believe in that shit."

"So what *are* you saying?"

"Maybe I'm just saying that the second guy is mine. I found him; he's my responsibility—not the Lover, but his copycat."

O'Donnell closed his notebook, but not before Keough noticed that it was full of indecipherable scribblings that were obviously the newspaperman's own personal shorthand.

"Joe, I think you better go home—uh, after you buy me dinner, that is."

"Don't worry," Keough said, "I didn't forget." He picked up a menu. "Where's that waitress?"

After dinner, they left Brendan's together, pausing only to wave at the owner before leaving. The same unusual cold drizzle that had been falling all day was still there. They both turned up the collars of their raincoats.

"Crummy day," O'Donnell said.

"Yeah."

"I've got to go back to the office and finish up some work. You goin' home?"

"I guess."

O'Donnell looked over at Keough.

"You having a problem with this, Joe?"

Keough returned the look.

"With what, Mike?"

"Going outside channels like this?"

"Maybe I am," Keough said after a moment, "but if I don't, then the second killer gets away with what he's done, and whoever killed Swann gets away with what he's done—"

"Joe, do you think you know who killed Swann?"

Keough hesitated, then said, "No, Mike, I don't . . . not yet."

O'Donnell was not convinced.

"Uh, Joe, is there some stuff here that you aren't telling me about?"

"Some maybe," Keough said, patting the newspaperman on the shoulder and then shoving his hands in his pocket, "but it will all come out in the end."

He hoped.

Chapter Thirty

It took three days for the story to appear, and when it did, it was splashed all over the front page.

The dead girl in Brooklyn was indeed added to the Lover's dance card by Lieutenant Slovecky, who warned Keough with a steely glance about saying anything. Keough decided not to say anything to anyone and just to wait and see what happened between the Lover and Mike O'Donnell.

Keough had been buying the *Post* every day since his dinner with O'Donnell. On the day the story broke, he approached the newspaper stand and was able to see the headline from far off.

"All right!" he said under his breath. He bought a newspaper and read it on the subway on the way into the city.

O'Donnell embellished and extrapolated around a simple statement by the Lover that he had not raped or killed any girls in Brooklyn and that he resented the implication he would molest girls of high school age. Keough was sure that this was a sincere statement on the part of the killer, but anyone reading it in the newspaper would have to laugh. Here was a man who had killed several women in a particularly brutal manner, and he was sounding insulted by the implication that he would touch high school girls. O'Donnell also printed the contents of the Lover's original note, which must have been dictated to him over the phone by the killer. There was also a very short "no comment" from Slovecky. Keough thought it odd that the lieutenant hadn't said anything after the phone call from O'Donnell, which must have come in the previous evening, before they'd all left for the day.

One man who wasn't laughing, however, was Lt. Dan Slovecky. Keough was walking in the door of the task force office when Slovecky was calling everyone into his office for a meeting. When he entered the office behind everyone else, Keough noticed that Slovecky was seated behind his desk.

"My guess is you've all seen this morning's *New York Post*." Slovecky was holding the paper up over his head and then he slammed it down on his desk with such force that the pages separated and scattered all over the office. "This son of a bitch called the *Post!* Can you believe it?"

"Maybe it wasn't him," Dolan suggested.

Red-faced, Slovecky shouted, "It was him all right. He knew about the note. We never released any information about the goddamned note."

Through much of Slovecky's tirade, he kept his eyes on Keough, but how could he even think that Keough had anything to do with this? Slovecky could never suspect that Keough had actually spoken to the Lover and had him call O'Donnell at the *Post*.

The phone rang at that point and Slovecky picked it up. He listened for a moment and then said, "No comment . . . I said no fucking comment!" He slammed the phone down.

"The goddamned *Daily News*. They're a little behind. So far, I've had calls today from the *Times*, and from NBC and CBS News."

"What, no ABC?" Keough asked.

They all turned and looked at him.

"You think this is funny, Keough?"

"Yeah, as a matter of fact, I do, Lieutenant."

Slovecky glared at Keough for a few moments, then shouted, "Everybody out . . . except Keough."

The other detectives moved toward the door, Dolan trailing behind them. Keough stayed where he was, standing at the back of the room, leaning against the wall.

"Close the fucking door!" Slovecky shouted.

Dolan, last out, closed the door gently.

"You know," Slovecky said, glaring at Keough, "if I didn't know better, I'd think you had something to do with this."

"I did."

"What?" Slovecky looked surprised.

"The Lover called me and asked me what newspaper he should talk to. I like the *Post*. They have the best sports section."

Slovecky stared at Keough for a few moment, then shook his head and snorted.

"Yeah, right. The killer calls here to talk to you."

Keough spread his arms helplessly and said, "Hey, I was the only one here. I'm the clerical, remember?"

"You like this, don't you?" Slovecky asked. "You like that the killer called the newspaper and disavowed any knowledge of the Brooklyn killings. It supports your theory, don't it?"

"*Disavow,*" Keough said thoughtfully. "That's a big word for you, isn't it?"

Slovecky's face reddened even more—if that was possible. Keough decided then and there to push even harder.

"Maybe I just want to see where your limits are, Lieutenant. Maybe I just want to see at what point you'll pick up a letter opener."

"A letter opener? What the hell are you talking about?"

"I'll tell you what I'm thinking, Lieutenant, and then you can tell me how you feel about it, all right?" Keough moved away from the wall to Slovecky's desk, where he rested his hands. "I think it's time for you to step down as commander of this task force."

"And why is that, Keough?"

"The obvious reason, Lieutenant," Keough said. "You have royally fucked up this investigation by insisting that the Brooklyn murders are part of it."

"Bullshit! The roses—"

"The roses don't even match, Slovecky!" Keough cut him off loudly. "Swann noticed that, too. What happened that night, Slovecky? Were you outside the house, waiting for me to leave?"

"You're crazy."

"You went in to talk to him, to see what was going on. Somehow, you found out he was making copies of files, right? Maybe he left a sheet in the Xerox machine?"

Slovecky stared at Keough without saying a word.

"That was it, wasn't it? You found an errant copy, and you went to his house. You waited until I left, went inside, killed him, and took back the duplicate file—and you removed the memo he'd written."

"You're crazy, Keough," Slovecky said, "and you're bucking for a suspension."

"Come on, Dan," Keough said. "Get it off your chest. Maybe you didn't mean to kill him. Was there a struggle? Come on."

"Shut up."

"Maybe when you saw the memo and realized that he and I were going over your head, you just flipped, huh?"

"Stop. You're getting in deeper."

"And what about me? Why simply transfer me here? Why not kill me, too?"

"I'm warning you . . ."

"That memo went through, you know. Yeah, you thought you stopped it by taking it from his desk, but I rewrote it. Maybe I didn't do as good a job as he had, but the gist of it was there. I rewrote it and sent it to the chief's office."

Keough expected that to ruffle Slovecky's feathers even more, but all of a sudden the lieutenant looked calm.

"The chief will never see it," Slovecky said with a slow smile. "You wasted your time trying to go over my head, Keough. You wasted your time taking me on. You're not in my league."

"Your league?" Keough laughed. "Your fucking league? Why would I want to be in the same league with a man who would kill a fellow cop?"

"I told you—"

"You're a cop killer, Slovecky," Keough said tightly, "and I'm going to prove it!"

Keough was surprised by Slovecky's reaction, because the man seemed to have gone so calm, but suddenly the lieutenant came over the desk at him, his hands closing around Keough's neck.

"Call me a cop killer, you son of a bitch!" Slovecky shouted. He lifted Keough off the floor with incredible strength and ran with him until he slammed the detective's back into the wall.

The office door slammed open and the other detectives charged into the room. When they saw what was going on, they rushed to separate the two men, but they had difficulty prying Slovecky's hands from Keough's neck.

The edges of Keough's vision were getting fuzzy as Slovecky continued to squeeze. He had done everything he could to get away, including kneeing Slovecky in the groin, but the man seemed so incensed, so enraged, he apparently was impervious to pain.

Keough knew that if the others couldn't get Slovecky off of him, the man was going to kill him.

The phone rang then, just as three of the detectives finally managed to pull Slovecky off of Keough. Keough fell to the floor, dazed, and Slovecky was shouting and spitting and trying to get away from the men holding him.

Dolan answered the phone, then held his hand over the receiver and shouted, "Quiet!"

Everyone in the room turned to looked at him, because they had never heard the normally soft-spoken man ever yell like that.

Dolan looked at Slovecky and said, "It's the chief."

Slowly, Slovecky's eyes came back into focus, the rage flowing out of them.

"Let me go!" he said, pulling away from the other men.

He went around the desk and took the phone from Dolan.

"Get out, and take him with you," he said, pointing to Keough. "And don't let him leave. I'm not through with him yet."

"Come on," Dolan said to the others, "pick him up."

They helped Keough off the floor, walked him out of the office, and closed the door behind them. In the other room, they lowered Keough into a chair.

"What the hell happened in there?" Dolan demanded.

"He's crazy," Keough said, rubbing his neck. His voice was coming out raspy. "He killed Len Swann, and he just tried to kill me."

"What?" Samuelson said.

"Keough . . ." Dolan said warningly.

"I'm telling you, Sarge, he killed Swann!"

"That's crazy," Det. Tim Mollica said. "Why would Slovecky kill Swann?"

The door to the office opened before Keough could offer an answer. Slovecky stood in the doorway, staring at all of them.

"Keough, I want your gun and shield. You're on suspension."

"Lieutenant—" Dolan started.

"Shut up! Keough, your gun and shield . . . now." Slovecky extended his hand for Keough's hardware.

"You can't do this, Slovecky," Keough said, even as he was taking his gun out of his holster and his shield from his pocket.

"I can and you know it. Don't worry, you'll get to tell your side of it at your disciplinary hearing."

Keough handed his gun and badge to the lieutenant, who was suddenly once again in control. Keough wondered what the call from the chief had been about.

"Sergeant, see Detective Keough out. If he doesn't leave, arrest him."

"Oh, don't worry," Keough said, standing up, "I'm leaving, but you haven't heard the last of me, Slovecky. You and I know what you did."

"Well, good luck proving your charges, Keough." Slovecky turned and looked at Dolan. "Search his desk first, and search him before he leaves. I don't want a scrap of paper to leave here with him, Xerox or original. You got it?"

Slovecky turned and went back into his office, closing the door behind him.

"Let's go, Keough," Dolan said.

"Going to walk me out, huh?"

"I don't even know what I'm looking for," the sergeant said, shaking his head.

"A Xerox copy of the file on the case, Dolan," Keough said. "Swann had one at his house."

"He did?"

"I saw it the night he died." Keough lowered his

230

voice and added, "I told you that the other night."

Dolan looked around to see if anyone had heard that.

"It wasn't there after Swann was killed, Dolan. The killer took it with him."

Dolan slammed a drawer.

"Nothing here. This your coat?"

Keough had tossed his raincoat on the desk when he got there.

"Yes."

Dolan picked up the coat, felt it, checked the pockets, and then tossed it to Keough.

"Time to go, Keough."

"You keep following that man's orders, Dolan, and you're going to go right down with him."

"Let's go."

Once they were outside the office, Dolan's attitude changed.

"You had to do it, didn't you?" he demanded. "Not even here two weeks and you had to push him? You know, if you screw up this investigation, you're gonna screw everybody. I don't want to be a sergeant forever, Keough!"

"The article in the paper pushed him," Keough said. "I just helped a little."

"By accusing him of murder? That is what you did, isn't it? We could hear what was being said from outside."

"He killed Swann, Dolan, I know it."

They went down the stairs and out onto the street.

"You attacked a superior officer, Keough."

"He attacked me!" Keough said. "He tried to kill me, Dolan."

"Well, that's gonna be your word against his, isn't it?"

"And who's going to believe me, right?"

"I would suggest that between now and then you get some facts—some hard facts, Keough—to back up your allegations."

"Well," Keough said, "now that I'm suspended, I'll have the time to work on it, won't I?"

"Without a badge, Keough," Dolan said. "Don't forget you're working without a badge."

Chapter Thirty-one

When Slovecky went back into his office, he dropped Keough's gun and shield on his desk and sat down. Suspending Keough was not going to stop the man, but it would discredit him to a degree, at least until Slovecky could figure out what to do.

The call from the chief was another concern.

"Slovecky, this is Chief LaGrange. Get your ass over here, and you better be ready to explain yourself."

That had been the whole call. Obviously, the chief had seen the newspaper headline and read the article, and now he wanted to know what was going on.

Slovecky sat back in his chair and tried to slow down his breathing. Losing it with Keough like that was not a good thing.

The first thing he had to do, even before going downtown to see the chief, was call Pollard and see if Keough had indeed sent a copy of Swann's memo to the C of D's office.

He knew that if he dialed the chief's office, he wouldn't get the chief himself, so there was no danger in calling the number back.

"Chief of Detectives," a woman's voice answered.

"Inspector Pollard, please."

"One moment."

He waited about that long until Pollard came on the line.

"Inspector Pollard."

"It's Slovecky."

"Jesus," Pollard said, lowering his voice, "the chief is beside himself!"

"I know, I just talked to him. I'll come over there and calm him down."

"You're going to have to show some progress, Slovecky," Pollard said. "You're not going to be able to get around him the way you do me."

Slovecky knew that was true. The chief was as clean as Pollard was supposed to be.

"Did you get a memo from a Detective Keough about the Lover case?"

"A memo? Wait a minute . . . yes, I did. It came across my desk several days ago. I'm still trying to decide if it's a crackpot, or if I should show it to the chief."

"Whatever you do, don't show it to the chief."

"Why not?"

"The man who sent it is in my squad. He just at-

234

tacked me, and I suspended him. He's unstable, Pollard. His record indicates that.''

"Why was he in your squad?''

"I needed a replacement for Swann, the man who was killed.''

"What's happening with that case?''

"I don't know,'' Slovecky said irritably. "I'm not working on that case, am I?''

"No, I just thought—''

"Don't think, Pollard, just listen. I'm on my way over there. Meet me downstairs with that memo. Understand?''

"Meet you . . . in the open?''

"Why not? We're both cops, aren't we? Just meet me right out front so I can get that memo from you. After that, I'll go up and see Chief LaGrange.''

"I don't know if this is such a good idea—''

"Just do it, Pollard,'' Slovecky said, and hung up.

Putting his jacket on to leave, he thought that maybe his losing control and attacking Keough might work out for the best. He hoped that discrediting Keough would be enough to keep anyone from listening to him.

Stepping out of his office, he caught Sergeant Dolan's attention.

"I've got to go and talk to the chief. I'll be back later.''

"Do you want someone to drive you, Lieutenant?''

"No, I'll drive myself.''

"Uh, Loo, about Keough—''

"Forget Keough. He doesn't fit into our chemistry.''

"Uh, yes, all right. . . .''

Robert J. Randisi

"I should be back within two hours. Don't do anything until I get back."

"But Loo—"

"Dolan," Slovecky said, cutting him off, "you're a good second whip because you do what you're told. Keep it up, all right?"

Dolan hesitated, then said, "Yes, sir."

"Good. Just hold down the fort."

He patted Dolan on the shoulder. It should have been a gesture of camaraderie, but to Dolan it felt more like a master patting a dog: Stay.

Dolan watched Slovecky go out the door and found himself hoping that the man would never be back. Maybe the chief would be impatient enough to replace him. Maybe he'd even promote *him* to lieutenant and put him in charge. Dolan had been telling the truth when he told Keough he didn't want to be a sergeant for his whole life. He'd seen this assignment to the task force as his chance, and now it looked like it might blow up in his—in everybody's—face.

Because of Joe Keough.

Insp. Paul Pollard hung up the phone, his hand lingering there. His stomach felt hollow, as it always did after speaking to Dan Slovecky. The man held his future in his hands, and there was nothing Pollard could do about it.

He found the memo on his desk and read it again. If what the memo said was true, then Slovecky was grossly negligent in the way he was conducting the serial killer investigation. If Chief LaGrange saw this, he would replace Slovecky in a second. If he did that, however, Slovecky might take it upon himself to pull Pollard down with him. On the other hand, if Pollard hid this memo—handed it over to Slovecky, as the man had demanded—and it turned out to be true, *and* LaGrange found out about it, Pollard would be finished, anyway.

He was in a no-win situation.

He decided to do as Slovecky asked and turn the memo over to him, but just to cover himself he'd stop by the Xerox room on his way out of the building.

Keough left the task force office and the building and stopped on the street. What should his next move be? He looked up at the window of the task force and shook his head. He'd played it wrong, and now he was going to be discredited—again. Not only would Slovecky charge him with assaulting a superior but he'd point to Keough's personnel file as an indication of his instability.

Who was going to listen to him now?

On the plus side, he had managed to duplicate most of the paperwork in the Lover cases, and he had that file at home. That's where he'd be doing most of his work from now on, which should please Nancy and Cindy Valentine at least.

He decided to head straight for home, and during the subway ride he realized that if the Lover happened to call the task force office again, he wouldn't be there to get the call. What would happen, he wondered, if the killer ended up on the phone with Slovecky?

He shuddered at the prospect.

* * *

When Lieutenant Slovecky reached One Police Plaza, a nervous Insp. Paul Pollard was waiting for him right out in front.

"Got it?" he asked.

"Yes."

Pollard passed over a white number-ten envelope and Slovecky looked inside of it. The piece of paper there resembled the memo he had removed from Len Swann's desk the night he . . . the night of the . . . the night Swann died.

"All right," he said, putting the envelope in his inside breast pocket, "let's go."

"Let's go . . . where?"

"To the chief's office. You're gonna want to be there when I talk to him. And Paul?"

"Yes?"

"Go along with anything I say. Understand? If I lose this assignment . . . well, the prospects wouldn't be bright for any of us."

"For Chrissake, Dan—"

"Take it easy," Slovecky said, playing with the lapels of Pollard's jacket. "Just go along with everything I say and things will work out for the best." He smiled and added, "I guarantee it."

Chapter Thirty-two

As they entered the office of Chief of Detectives LaGrange, Slovecky hoped that Pollard would be able to keep it together.

"Lieutenant Slovecky, sir," Pollard said by way of introduction.

LaGrange was standing at the window with his hands clasped behind his back. Slovecky stood there staring at the man's broad back, waiting for him to speak.

"You know," LaGrange finally said, "I blame myself for this."

"For what, sir?" Slovecky asked.

LaGrange stared out the window a moment longer, then turned to look at Slovecky over his shoulder. His eyes were a startling blue beneath snow white eyebrows. Slovecky found himself oddly mesmerized by the effect, as most people did.

"I never should have put you in charge of that task force sight unseen," the chief said. "When Inspector Pollard recommended you for the job, I should have brought you in here and checked you out myself."

"With all due respect, Chief . . ." Slovecky began, but he allowed it to trail off when LaGrange put his hand out like a traffic cop.

"I'm not saying you're not qualified, Lieutenant. All I'm saying is that I wouldn't have to be wondering now if I had made it a point to meet you then." LaGrange turned around to face Slovecky and added, "But I am wondering, Lieutenant. What do you have to say to me about the story in the *New York Post* today?"

"Sir, I can't say for sure if the man who called the *Post* really was the Lover—"

"Let's assume that he was, shall we? After all, he did mention the note, did he not?"

"Yes, sir."

"And we didn't leak the information about the note to anyone, did we?"

"No, sir."

"At least I didn't."

"It wasn't leaked from my squad, sir."

"Well," LaGrange said, looking past Slovecky at Pollard, "that would leave Inspector Pollard, then, wouldn't it? Do you think the inspector leaked the information, Lieutenant?"

"No, sir, I don't."

LaGrange stared at both men long enough for Pollard to begin shifting from foot to foot.

"Sit down, gentlemen," LaGrange said, and seated himself behind his huge desk. Slovecky and Pollard sat across from him, side by side.

"I'm a little surprised, Lieutenant."

"At what . . . sir?"

"I was told that you weren't . . . that you were a little . . . crude? Don't be insulted, but from your file I had assumed you to be . . . unpolished."

"I am, sir," Slovecky said. "I don't make any excuses for that. I'm not like everyone else."

"Well, so far you've conducted yourself admirably," LaGrange said. "I'd advise you to continue to do so for the rest of this conversation . . . no matter what happens."

Slovecky was puzzled but said, "Yes, sir."

"Good," LaGrange said, then suddenly shouted, "Now what the fuck is going on?"

"Sir?"

"Why haven't you caught this maniac yet, Lieutenant?" The well mannered man had been replaced by an angry, red-faced man who oddly reminded Slovecky of himself. Maybe there was hope for him to rise even higher than he had first thought.

"We're working very hard on it, Chief—"

"The commissioner wants results, Lieutenant," LaGrange said. "Do you know what that means?"

"Yes, sir, that you want results, too."

"That's very good, Lieutenant, right on the button. I want results, and if I don't get them, do you know what will happen?"

"I can guess, sir—"

"Never mind, I'll save you the trouble. I will replace you and every member of your squad. Now, tell me what's being done.''

"Well, sir, we're still working with VICAP, with department psychologists; we're still investigating the background of all the girls to see what acquaintances they had in common; we're continuing to have the note analyzed—''

"In other words," LaGrange said, cutting him off, "you're still going through the motions."

"We're doing everything we can, sir," Slovecky said. "If you don't mind my saying so, if you replace the entire squad, you'll be trashing months of work. Anybody you assign to the case would have to start from scratch. I don't think—''

"I'll worry about that, Lieutenant," LaGrange said. "You just worry about catching this sick fuck. Have you talked to the reporter yet—I mean, beyond this scintillating quote from you in the paper?''

"Not yet, sir," Slovecky said, "I was planning on doing that myself today, though."

"Well, then, get the fuck out of here and do it. I want a progress report. If this killer is going to keep in touch with this guy, we should be able to use that. Get phone taps. Get the works, Lieutenant. Understand?''

"Yes, sir," Slovecky said, "that was my plan."

"Then go . . . go!"

"Yes, sir," Slovecky said, standing up.

Pollard stood as well, but LaGrange said, "Stay a minute, Paul."

"Yes, sir," Pollard said as Slovecky went out the door.

"What do you think, Paul?''

"About Slovecky, sir?"

"Of course, about Slovecky."

"Well . . . he's doing all he can—"

"He's jerking my chain," LaGrange said.

"Sir?"

"He's pulling an Eddie Haskell on me. 'Yes, sir, no, sir.' "

"Eddie Haskell?"

"Didn't you ever watch *Leave It to Beaver?*"

"Was that a television show, sir? I never did watch much—"

"Never mind, Paul, never mind. Your lieutenant was right about one thing."

"My lieutenant?" Pollard repeated, but LaGrange ignored the remark.

"To replace the entire squad right now would put us even further behind this maniac. Slovecky better come through, Paul, for his sake, your sake, and my sake."

"Yes, sir," Pollard said sadly, "I'm sure he will."

As Keough entered his apartment, he was thinking about Marcia Swann. What would she do when she heard about his suspension? And what would it matter at this point? If she made a fuss now, how much more trouble could he be in? Once Slovecky wrote him up, the department would come down on him—unless he showed some progress before that, unless he gave them a reason to come down on Slovecky and not him.

He went directly to his phone and played back his messages.

"Joe, it's Mike. Call me."

There was one more, and when he played it back, he felt a chill.

"Detective Keough, this is . . . a friend. We spoke earlier in the week. I hope you saw the *Post* today. I just wanted to thank you for the referral." *Click, buzzzzz* . . .

That son of a bitch. He didn't want to thank him; he wanted to let him know that he knew where he lived.

The only call he could return was to Mike O'Donnell, and he'd planned on calling him, anyway. When the *Post* operator picked up, he asked for the reporter and was connected immediately.

"Mike, it's Keough."

"Joe. Jeez, did you see the story?"

"I saw it."

"My phone's been ringing like Grand Central Terminal. I got a call from your Lieutenant Slovecky."

"He's not my lieutenant anymore."

"Huh?"

"I've been suspended, Mike."

"Whoa, tell me about that."

Keough could visualize the man hunched over his notebook, taking down information for the book.

Keough explained to O'Donnell what had happened and then waited for a comment.

"So he attacked you, but he's gonna write you up for jumping him."

"Right."

"And nobody witnessed it?"

"They all heard what was happening from outside, but when they rushed in, we were already struggling. The son of a bitch is strong. He almost killed me."

"Whataya gonna do?"

"The only thing I can do is keep working on things, unofficially."

"You could get in a lot of trouble for that."

"I think I'm already in trouble, Mike. Now I've got to work to get myself out of trouble."

"Well, good luck. Let me know if I can help. I owe you big, buddy."

"Thanks, I'll remember that."

"Listen, I've got to tell you about the conversation I had with your friend."

"Did you give him my phone number?"

"What? Hell no, but he did ask."

"Well, he got it from somewhere."

"He called you at home?"

"Left a message on my machine. A thank-you message."

"That's all?"

"No. It was a 'thank you/I know where you live' message."

"Just because he's got your number doesn't mean he knows where you live."

"He got my number, Mike. How hard could it be to find my address?"

"Not very."

"Did he say he'd be calling you back?"

"He said he'd be watching the newspaper to make sure I kept my word. I started to ask if he'd be calling back, but he hung up. Jesus, I hope he calls again now that the story's out."

"Let me know if he does, okay?"

"And let me know if he calls you back."

"Deal, Mike."

Robert J. Randisi

"You got nobody to work with you on this now except me, Joe."

"Don't try to depress me any more than I already am, Mike."

Chapter Thirty-three

Keough awoke the next morning and sat up in bed. It wasn't his regular day off and he didn't have to be anyplace, and it was an odd feeling. He decided to get up and make himself a big breakfast, something he hardly ever did. He checked his refrigerator and discovered two eggs, four strips of bacon, and a green pepper. In his closet, on the floor, was one lone potato in a bag. He made all of this into an omelette, along with two pieces of white toast and a pot of coffee. All he needed now was a newspaper to read with it. He was headed for the door to check the hall and see if anyone had not picked up their newspaper yet when the phone rang.

"Hello?"

"Keough? Huff. Bad break, buddy."

Robert J. Randisi

"What are you talking about?"

"What am I talking about? Your suspension, that's what I'm talking about."

"How the—how the hell did you know about it?"

"Whataya mean? It's in the newspaper."

"What newspaper?"

"The *Post*."

Keough couldn't believe it.

"How the—"

"Yeah, it's right here in Mike O'Donnell's column."

Keough frowned, then realized that while O'Donnell covered major news stories for the *Post*, he also did an occasional column, whenever he had something to say.

"What's it say?"

"Don't you have a copy?"

"No, if I had a copy, I wouldn't be asking you what it said."

"It says that you were wrongfully suspended from the Lover Task Force when your opinions on the case radically opposed those of your commanding officer. What opinions is he talking about, Joe?"

"It doesn't matter. Look, Pete, I got some bacon cooking . . ."

"Makin' yourself a big breakfast, huh? That's good. Listen, I just called to say tough break, but good luck, huh? From the other guys, too."

Oddly touched, Keough said, "Uh, yeah, well, thank all of them for me, huh?"

"Sure thing, partner."

Keough hung up, shaking his head. Apparently, O'Donnell had taken it upon himself to question

248

Keough's suspension in the newspaper, and Keough wasn't sure at the moment what he thought of it.

He went to his front door and opened it. Checking the hall, he saw that everyone had taken their newspaper in. He looked across the hall at Nancy Valentine's door and wondered what shift she was working today.

He was wearing only a robe over his underwear, so he went back inside and pulled on a pair of sweatpants and a sweatshirt, then went to Nancy's door and knocked. When she answered, she looked surprised to see him.

"Joe! I was going to knock on your door in about a minute."

"Hi, Nancy."

She was wearing a blue pullover sweater with stars and moons on it and a pair of black stirrup pants. Her hair was down and her feet were bare.

"I saw the column in the paper."

"Uh, yeah, that's why I'm here, Nancy. I haven't seen it, and I thought—"

"Do I smell bacon from your apartment? Are you cooking?"

"Oh, yeah," he said, looking over his shoulder, "it's probably burning—"

"Well, go and save it, and leave your door open. I'll bring the paper over."

"Oh, hey, good, thanks. Uh, come over for coffee, too, why don't you?"

She smiled, apparently pleased at the invitation, and said, "Fine." He went back into his apartment and saved his breakfast, then put out another coffee cup. He had scraped his breakfast onto a plate and was pouring the coffee when Nancy appeared with the newspaper.

"Here it is."

She had taken the time to comb her hair, and she had obviously put on perfume. The kitchen suddenly smelled of vanilla.

She handed him the paper and said, "I thought we were friends, Joe."

"I—what? We are friends, Nancy."

Nancy had been in his apartment exactly three times—he forgot the last time, when she and Cindy had put him to bed—but she walked right to the refrigerator and took out the milk as if she had been doing it forever.

"Why didn't you tell me about this?" she asked, sitting opposite him, pouring milk into her coffee.

"It just happened yesterday."

"We were home last night. You didn't have to be here alone."

"Well . . . I had a lot of work to do."

"Work? But you've been suspended. Why should you be—oh, I think I see. You're going to continue working on this case, aren't you? The serial killer?"

"Nancy," Keough said, making a sudden decision to confide in her—once again!—"he called me."

"Who called you?"

"Him, the serial killer."

"Which one?"

He could have kissed her then. She asked, "Which one?" so naturally, demonstrating so completely that she believed in him.

"The original one, the Lover."

"He called you on the phone?"

"Twice," he said, nodding, "once at work and once here."

She put her hand to her mouth.

"My God, here?"

"I didn't get a chance to talk to him here, but he left a message."

"Oh my God."

He lowered his voice and asked, "Would you like to hear it?"

"Oh . . . no, I couldn't. I mean . . . no, thank you, but . . . no. . . . How did he get your number?"

"There are a lot of ways to do it."

He realized that he was eating his breakfast right in front of her.

"Can I get you something?"

"No, I had my breakfast. The coffee is fine—and it's good, by the way."

"Does that surprise you?"

"Truthfully . . . yes. Can you cook anything else?"

"No," he said, shaking his head, "what you see here is it. Eggs, bacon, toast, and coffee, that's it."

"Then you're lucky you have me as a neighbor."

He stared at her and said, "Yes, I am, aren't I?"

He could have sworn she blushed, but she turned her head at that moment.

"What about this man O'Donnell? The one who wrote the column."

"He's a friend of mine. I used to see him a lot when I worked in Manhattan."

"Did you know he was going to do this?"

"No, I didn't," Keough said. "If I had, I might have stopped him."

"Why? Why not let people know what's going on?"

"Well . . . it would be better for me if I didn't try to show up the department."

"Are you really worried about that?"

"Actually, more and more of late, no. I've been getting real frustrated—even more than usual."

"Then maybe this will be good for you. Maybe somebody will listen to you after this."

"Well, somebody will listen all right. I'll have a departmental hearing about my . . . altercation with Lieutenant Slovecky."

"That's something else you didn't tell me about."

"Well, I haven't seen you for a few days—or Cindy, for that matter. Oh, hey, did Cindy see this?"

"No, she didn't, and I don't know if I should show it to her. She loves you a lot, Joe. I don't know how she'd react to this."

"She'd react a lot worse if she heard it from someone else. Maybe I should tell her myself."

"I'll leave that up to you. What are you going to do today?"

"Work," he said. "And I've got to talk to O'Donnell about this column."

"What are you going to say?"

"That I appreciate his help but don't think he should give me any more without checking with me first."

"That's probably wise.

"Well, I'll just be going then. Thanks for the coffee, Joe."

"That's okay. Thanks for the paper."

"Sure." She started for the door.

"Nancy?"

"Yes?"

He walked to where she was standing by the door. "Having you to talk to means a lot to me."

She smiled, touched his face tenderly, and said, "It means a lot to me, too, Joe."

His cheek burned as she went out the door.

He went back into the kitchen, scraped off his plate, and put it and the coffee cups into the sink. He thought briefly of Nancy and smiled. It wasn't as if he didn't have other options in the sex—uh, romance—area. Why hadn't he thought of this before? She was right next door, and she was certainly pretty enough—more than pretty enough—and wasn't he already telling her things he didn't tell anyone else?

Why was it that the girl next door—or in this case, the woman—was always too close to see? Thinking back it was obvious that she was interested in him. When this was all over, if he was even in a position to have a normal relationship with a woman, it would be something for him and Nancy to talk about.

Chapter Thirty-four

Keough decided to stay in all day and see if the killer called back. While he was waiting, he intended to go over the histories of the victims to see if he couldn't link them up somehow. First, though, he called Mike O'Donnell.

"Joe!" O'Donnell said when he heard Keough's voice. "How'd you like the piece?"

"I don't know whether to kiss you or kick you, Mike."

"Uh . . . if I have a choice, I'll take the kick."

"I think that'd be my choice, too."

"What's the matter? I thought you'd be pleased that somebody came to your defense."

"I am, Mike, I just wish you'd talked to me about it first."

"Ah, hell, Joe, I knew you wouldn't go along with it beforehand."

"You did, huh?"

"You would have said something about alienating the department, or prejudicing your case. . . ."

"And you don't think that's so?"

"My friend, I think when you took up this particular banner, you knew what you were doing. Throw in the death of your friend, and your belief that he was killed by a cop—a lieutenant, no less—and I think you either cave in or put up a helluva fight and say good-bye to your career, win or lose."

"You've got it all figured out, do you?"

"Look, don't worry," O'Donnell said, "When my book comes out, you'll be a celebrity. I'm gonna play up your part in this big. Maybe there'll even be a movie. Maybe you'll get to play yourself. Maybe—"

"Lots of maybes, Mike."

O'Donnell paused, then said, "Look, Joe, I believe in you. I think you're doing the right thing here, and I want to support you. If you wanna kick me for that, I'll bend over for you."

"Ah," Keough said, "if you're going to put it like that, just forget it. You're taking all the fun out of it."

"So what are you going to do now?"

"I'm going to keep working, Mike."

"Did he call you again?"

"No, not yet, but I'm going to stick around and see if he does. I'm also going to go over some files."

"You rascal," O'Donnell said, "you duped the task force files."

"Yes, I did."

"That's great. I can use them for the book."

"You're jumping the gun here, Mike. The case isn't solved yet, you haven't even written the story, and you're thinking about the book already?"

"Hey, I've got an open contract and this is the book I'm gonna do. You're in, pal."

"Thanks, Mike."

"Keep me informed, huh?"

"You do the same."

Keough hung up, wondering if his career as a police officer was indeed over. If that was what happened, if he lost the job, it would be no one's fault but his own, and yet he didn't think he would regret it. He could still see that first girl, Mindy Carradine, lying at the base of the steps at Erasmus High School, the promise of her future gone, taken from her by some psycho who happened to idolize a sick serial killer and wanted to emulate him. If he could have convinced someone then that there were two killers, none of the rest of this would have happened. Hell, Len Swann might even still be alive.

But Swann wasn't alive, and two other girls had been killed in Brooklyn. Keough wouldn't be able to sleep or live with himself if he allowed the Brooklyn killer to go free.

Of course, he could just sit back and wait for the Lover to be caught. At that time, the copycat killer might stop—but then again, he might not.

Wouldn't that be a kick in the head? If Slovecky and the task force caught the Lover and put him away, and while he was in jail another girl was killed in Brooklyn? What would the brass say then? How would Slovecky explain that to the chief of detectives?

There was a time in every cop's life when the job

was the most important thing in the world.

For Det. Joe Keough, that time had passed.

It was time for justice to move to the forefront, and that meant finding Len Swann's killer and proving to everyone that there was not only one serial killer at large in New York but two.

Keough had all of the girls' histories spread over his desk. Under normal circumstances, a single individual had no chance in the world of catching a serial killer. In this case, however, most of the work had already been done by the task force detectives, and all of the VICAP and psychological-profile information was all in place.

Keough didn't put much faith in the psychological profile, though. On the one hand, he thought the Lover was too smart to be caught that way, and the second killer might just be too dumb. After all, he was trying to copy his hero's methods, and yet had bungled at every turn, from the color of the rose, to the thorns to the ages of the girls. If anyone could be bothered to look, the copycat was stamping his own killings as individual.

The dead women—the Manhattan victims—were all college-educated, but they had not all gone to the same school. There had to be another way, then, for them to have come in contact with the same man.

At that moment, the phone rang. He stared at it as it rang a second time. On the third ring, he knew that it was him.

He picked the phone up in the middle of the fourth ring.

"I hope I'm not disturbing you."

"Not at all," Keough said. "I'm just doing some work at home."

"On me?"

It was the same cultured, educated voice he had spoken to the first time. His heartbeat quickened as he tried to keep his voice level and calm.

"What else?"

"I read about you in the newspaper today." The killer chuckled. "I never used to read the *Post*. Its coverage of current events has always been banal, at best."

"I read the sports page."

"Ah, yes," the man said, "I have been given to understand that their coverage of sports is . . . adequate. I myself am not interested in sports."

"What are you interested in?"

"Justice."

Now it was Keough's turn to laugh.

"What is funny?"

"I was just sitting here thinking about the same thing."

"Were you?"

"Yes, I was."

"Amazing. Did you get my message?"

"I did."

"And of course you read the story."

"Yes."

"And now you are in no position to help me."

"Helping you was never my intention."

"Granted. You expected my statement to vindicate you somehow?"

"It was a possibility."

"And now you have been suspended . . . because of me?"

"You get only partial credit."

"Are you an educated man, Detective Keough? I can still call you Detective, can't I?"

"Yes, technically, and to answer your question, I'm nowhere near as educated as you. I was educated on the streets, and then at the Police Academy."

"Ah yes, the vaunted street smarts that people talk about. I've never felt that to be the equal of a formal education."

"Is that what you tell your students?"

There was a long silence, during which Keough started to think the man had hung up.

"We will get nowhere, Detective, if you continue to try to trick me."

There was enough in the man's voice to convince Keough that he had struck a nerve.

"Are we going anywhere?"

"Actually, no."

"Then why did you call me?"

"Truthfully?"

"I don't get much of that in my business. It would be a refreshing change."

The killer chuckled again.

"I called because I enjoyed our talk the other day. Indeed, I am enjoying this one even more. You know, I haven't had anyone to talk to about . . . what I've been doing."

"And you want to talk to me about it?"

"Well, why not?"

"And why would I want to talk to you about it?"

"Who knows? I might let something slip during our

conversation . . . something that would help you catch me."

"There's not much danger of that," Keough said, "you slipping up or me catching you."

"And why is that?"

"Well, first you're too smart to slip, and second, I've been suspended, so I don't have the facilities to properly—"

"Oh nonsense," the killer said, interrupting him. "I have been following the efforts of your task force to catch me, you know. Grossly ineffective."

"Well, you can't blame me for that. The day we talked was the beginning of my second week."

"Ah, so they have not had the benefit of your expertise to call upon. Too bad for them. I would wager quite a bit that you would catch me before they did."

"I'm flattered."

"Truly, I am only basing my opinion on our conversations, but they have had adequate time to make some headway, haven't they? What's been holding them up?"

"Their leadership."

"Ah, this superior officer you scuffled with?"

"Yes."

"A bad sort?"

"The worst."

"Will no one listen to what you have to say?"

"No."

"Then you and I are the only ones who know that I did not kill those Brooklyn girls?"

"I guess so."

"That is, unless the story in the *New York Post* does

some good.'' He said '*New York Post*' with the disdain of a *New York Times* reader.

''Somehow I doubt that.''

''Oh? Why?''

''Because nobody will want to believe that there are two killers loose in New York—especially when the police aren't admitting it.''

''I find that . . . disturbing.''

Keough decided to take a shot.

''So I guess everyone will just go on thinking that sometimes you just get a craving for high school girls.''

There was a pause and then the killer said, ''I resent that.''

''Resent what?''

''Your attempt to manipulate me. You know, Detective Keough, I had thought that you would be someone I could talk to from time to time, but now I am not so sure.''

''Listen, I—''

''I am not at all sure that I shall ever call you again.''

''Hey, come on—'' but he was talking to a dead line.

He hung up the phone and cursed. It had been going well, and he had had to push it. Now he might never hear from the guy again. Contact with the killer was the only thing he had going for him. If the man was so concerned about people thinking he was a pervert—instead of simply a killer—he might have been able to talk him into giving himself up. Maybe he could convince him that this was the only way to get people to believe him.

And what was that business about being interested in justice? Did he somehow equate killing all these girls with some misguided sense of justice?

How many cops, he wondered, actually had the opportunity to talk with a serial killer before he was caught, while he was still active? Had he been given this opportunity through an unbelievable series of events, only to blow it?

Nah, he thought. He'll call back. He had to call back. This was the only chance Keough had of solving this thing. If he could talk to the man long enough, he was sure he could convince him to turn himself in. True, the man was well educated, but he thought the killer might just be underestimating the power of street smarts.

Chapter Thirty-five

Later in the evening, Keough was cleaning up after a frozen dinner when there was a knock at the door. He was surprised at whom he found standing in the hall.

"Are you going to ask me in?" Truxton Lewis asked.

"Captain Lewis."

"I thought I told you to call me Tru."

"What are you doing here?"

"Standing in the hall," Lewis said, "and I don't like it."

"I'm sorry," Keough said, "come in."

He allowed Lewis to enter, then closed the door and turned to face the man. Lewis was wearing an un-zipped leather jacket with a checked-pattern shirt underneath and blue jeans. There were minute specs of sawdust on the pant legs, and he smelled like fresh-cut wood.

"It was just a surprise to see you," Keough said. "How did you find out where I live?"

"I made a phone call, son," Lewis said, removing his jacket. "Have you got a beer anywhere?"

"Sure," Keough said, still puzzled by the man's appearance. "Have a seat and I'll get you one."

Keough went into the kitchen, took a John Courage out of the refrigerator for the retired captain, then took a second out for himself.

"I saw the column in the paper today," Lewis said as Keough handed him the beer. "You know the department is not gonna like you taking your problems public."

"I know it, but it wasn't me who took them public. O'Donnell did that on his own."

"You and O'Donnell are friends?"

"That's right."

"I've read his books," Lewis said. "He's good. Is this serial killer business gonna be his next one?"

"He hopes."

"Well, it's got everything he needs to be a best-seller, doesn't it?"

"Except for the end."

"Well," Lewis said, "maybe I can help you with that."

"You? How? You're out of the loop, so to speak."

"I'm retired," Lewis said, "but I'm not dead. I've still got some friends in the department."

Which must have been how he got Keough's address from his file. First the Lover, now Lewis. Pretty soon everyone was going to have either his number or his address.

"Have a seat, Tru, and tell me how you think you can help me."

Lewis sat down on the sofa. Keough reversed the wooden chair, set in front of the desk, and straddled it, holding his beer bottle by the neck.

"I think I can get you an audience."

"With who?"

Lewis smiled and said, "With Chief LaGrange."

"You know the chief of detectives?"

Lewis nodded.

"We went through the Academy together."

"How long ago was that?"

"Many years," Lewis said. "True, we went our separate ways after that. I was never good at politics, so I made it to captain and stalled there. He went on to become chief of detectives—but I think I know him as well as you knew your friend from the Academy . . . Swann?"

Keough nodded. "Len Swann.

"So you can just call him and get me in to see him?"

"I think I can."

"Then what?"

"Then you make your case," Lewis said. "Convince him that Slovecky screwed up the investigation. Convince him that there are two serial killers, not one. And then prove to him that Slovecky killed Len Swann."

"That'll take a lot of convincing."

"I'll call Robert tomorrow," Lewis said. "He's probably planning on talking to you, anyway, but maybe I can get him into a different frame of mind.''

"Tru, do you know Inspector Paul Pollard?"

Lewis laughed.

"Oh, yes, Mr. Clean."

"Is he?"

"What?"

"Clean?"

"Nobody is as clean as he claims to be."

"I was told that it was likely that Slovecky was given this assignment on Pollard's recommendation."

Lewis thought a moment, then said, "It makes sense. I don't know why, but Robert always seemed to like having Pollard at his elbow. Maybe it was because Pollard is the perfect yes-man."

"But would he take Pollard's suggestion, then? If he's just a yes-man?"

"You get used to having someone around, someone to talk to, to rely on for menial tasks, and little by little you give them more and more to do—and more credit than they deserve."

"Okay," Keough said, "so suppose Pollard is not as clean as he's supposed to be. Slovecky's good at digging up dirt, right?"

"I see where you're going with this. You might be right. Slovecky might have blackmailed Pollard into giving him the nod with LaGrange."

"Tru, I sent a memo to Chief LaGrange about my theory of there being two serial killers. Would that memo have to go through Pollard?"

"It sure would."

"Shit! No wonder I haven't gotten an answer."

"LaGrange never saw it. Did you keep a copy?"

"No, I didn't."

"Too bad."

"But wait a minute."

"What?"

"It would probably still be in Swann's computer. All I'd have to do is get his wife to print me a copy."

"Good. When you go and see LaGrange, take it with you, and whatever other evidence you have."

"Tru," Keough said, turning and looking at the man, "I don't have all that much evidence."

"Well, you've got about two days to come up with some. That's probably how long it will take me to set this up. Two days to make sure that two—and maybe three—killers are brought to justice, and maybe you'll save your job at the same time."

Lewis walked over to the coffee table and put his empty John Courage bottle down on it.

"Time for me to head home."

"I appreciate you stopping by."

Keough walked the man to the door, where they shook hands.

"Tell me something, Tru?"

"What?"

"Why are you doing this?"

Lewis shrugged.

"I like you, I don't like Slovecky, and maybe I can save my old friend Robert LaGrange's butt in the bargain, too. I'll call you tomorrow, Joe, after I've talked with the chief."

"Thanks, Tru. Thanks a lot."

The older man waved away Keough's gratitude and walked down to the elevator.

Keough went inside and checked his watch. It was

after 8:00 P.M., but he didn't think it was too late to call Marcia Swann.

"Yes, I know how to work the computer, Joe," she said in reply to his request. "Is this going to help you find Len's killer?"

"It might, Marcia."

"I'll make a copy tonight. How do you want me to get it to you?"

"I'll come by and pick it up."

"When?"

"I'll call first."

"I'll have it ready."

He hung up, made a pot of coffee, and spent the rest of the evening going through the files on the victims. Finally, he was so tired, he had to stop. As soon as his head hit the pillow, he was asleep.

Chapter Thirty-six

The Lover was concerned.

He'd been thinking all day about his conversation with Detective Keough.

He was sitting in his living room, in his favorite chair, wearing a blue silk bathrobe. The curtains were open so that he could stare out at the view of the New York skyline while he drank his second martini of the evening. Tonight he did not have a young female student waiting for him in his bed, waiting to earn an *A* in philosophy. Tonight he wanted to be alone, to ponder his future.

He enjoyed teaching, he enjoyed the lecturing he did, both in his own university and on the road. He also enjoyed the killing. He realized that he could stop the killing and continue to do the other things he en-

joyed. However, there would always be that stigma of
the public thinking he was some pervert who preyed
on high school girls.

Granted, they did not know that it was *he*. They
thought it was this Lover character, as the press had
named him. Still, he knew that he would never stoop
to having sexual contact with a high school girl, and
he didn't like anyone thinking otherwise—not even if
it was under a nom de plume.

The dilemma had a very interesting solution, one he
did not know if he was quite ready to explore. He
found that he was also quite angry at this second killer.
The man was keeping these girls from moving on to
college, where they might have become students of
his, benefiting greatly from his knowledge. The man
should pay for that, but there was no way he would
unless he could convince people there actually was a
second killer.

He decided to have a third martini before he pon-
dered the problem further.

Kopykat had been upset.

There it was in black and white in the *Post*. His idol
was denying him. All Kopykat had ever wanted to do
was be like his idol, add to his idol's reputation. And
now to know the Lover was telling everyone on the
newspaper that he did not kill the girls in Brooklyn,
that *he* would not touch high school girls! He said that
obviously whoever was killing the girls in Brooklyn
was a pervert and he wasn't.

A pervert!

Kopykat became distraught. He had lain around the

house all day yesterday after reading the article, and his mother had yelled at him.

"Goddamn it, I keep tellin' you you're too big to just lay around here. God, you stink. Take a shower. Go out and do something. Don't you have to work today?"

"I called in sick."

"Again? Jesus, why don't they fire you. You call in sick alla time."

In the end, it was his mother who went out, and when she came back that night, she had a man with her.

Now this morning, he was more angry than upset, because it was clear to him that the Lover was jealous of him. Yeah, that was it. His murders were better than the Lover's, and his idol—his former idol—was jealous.

It was clear to him that he now had to make his own presence known.

Chapter Thirty-seven

When the phone rang the next morning, it woke and startled Keough.

"Hello?"

. "Detective Keough," the Lover said, "I think I have a solution to my problem."

"Really?" Keough asked, leaning back. "Why don't you tell me about it."

When Mike O'Donnell looked up from his desk and saw the man standing in the doorway of his office, he was at first surprised, then pleased.

"Well, well, what brings you into my neck of the woods, Detective?"

"I've got a story for you," Keough said, "and it's going to knock your socks off."

O'Donnell stood up, grabbed his coat, and asked, "Brendan's?"

Once they were settled into a booth at Brendan's with a beer each, Keough told his story.

"I had the most amazing phone call today."

"From him?"

Keough nodded, his eyes bright with excitement.

"Jesus, Mike, I was waiting for the guy to call so I could try to talk him into surrendering."

"And?"

"He told me he was surrendering."

"Christ! To whom?"

Keough grinned.

"Well, thanks to me, he's giving himself up to you and me."

O'Donnell sat back in his booth, stunned.

"The royalty checks on this book are gonna be phenomenal," was the first thing he said.

"If you think your book is going to be phenomenal, wait until his comes out."

"What?"

"The slick son of a bitch says he's going to write a book."

"Wait a minute," O'Donnell said, taking out his notebook, "give me this from the beginning."

Keough related his conversation with the Lover. . . .

"I wish to give myself up."

"Why?"

"I thought you would be thrilled," the killer said. "My reign of terror will come to an end, thanks to you."

"To me?"

"Well, I intend to give myself up to you."

"And then what?"

"Well, there will certainly be months, perhaps years of psychiatric evaluations before there is even a trial. During that time, I intend to write a book."

"You won't be able to benefit financially from the book." The words were out of his mouth before he could stop himself.

"That is quite all right. The point of the book will be to clear my name."

Keough hesitated for a moment, frowning, then realized what the man was talking about.

"Oh, of the Brooklyn murders."

"Well, of course. After all, I will be surrendering, so I will naturally be confessing to the Manhattan murders."

"That's decent of you."

"Exactly." The killer did not recognize the sarcasm in Keough's voice. "And the point of the book will be to tell once and for all, in my own words, how my reputation was tarnished by this madman who is killing young girls in Brooklyn. So all we need do is work out the arrangements of my surrender. Of course, I will need an attorney. . . ."

"Do you need a recommendation?"

"Oh, no. No, I think I can manage that on my own."

"Well, then, get your attorney and let him arrange the surrender."

"I see. Yes, that makes sense."

"Here's something else that might make sense."

"And what is that?"

"Make sure the newspapers know about this, so they're on hand when you surrender."

The killer hesitated a moment, then said, "That is a good idea. In fact . . . your friend Mr. O'Donnell, doesn't he write books such as the one we're discussing?"

"True crime, yes."

"Wonderful, then we can make sure that he is present when I surrender to you."

Keough had a thought.

"Television coverage might not be such a bad idea, either."

Why not get himself some publicity out of this? He'd be the man who brought in the Lover, plus he'd be involved in O'Donnell's book. The newspaperman was right: He could parlay this into some money, because he knew that after he brought in the Lover and as soon as there was another murder while this killer was in custody, the department was going to have egg on its face, and he was going to be blamed.

"Excellent idea. Would you be kind enough to take care of that for me?"

"It would be my pleasure."

"You know," the killer said, "this will do you almost as much good as it does me."

Keough smiled grimly and said, "I've already thought of that. . . ."

"Jesus," O'Donnell said. "You know, me boyo, you and I are likely to get filthy rich off of this."

"I can handle that."

"What about this Brooklyn killer?" O'Donnell asked. "Think you can get him to surrender, too?"

"I'd have to find him first."

"What do you think will happen when you bring in the Lover?"

"A media circus, I imagine."

"Well, your Lieutenant Slovecky won't be able to take credit for it, that's for sure. What do you think the chief of detectives will think?"

"You know," Keough said, "maybe I'll ask him beforehand."

"You mean tell him about the surrender?"

"Mmmm . . . not right away. I'm supposed to have a meeting with him. Maybe I'll make a deal."

"You know, you're getting crafty in your old age. You'll make him a 'what if I can deliver' deal."

"Right."

"When I was a kid, my sister and I would sometimes race to see who could get into their pajamas first at night. One night, I put the bottoms on, and then we said, 'Ready, set, go.' I thought I'd beat her, but she jumped out of her room right away. She had put both the top and the bottom of hers on, so we both cheated."

Keough stared at O'Donnell and asked, "Why are you telling me this?"

O'Donnell frowned.

"I don't know. It seemed appropriate when I thought of it."

Both men shook their heads.

"Okay, so when does this surrender take place?"

"He's got to get himself a lawyer, but he doesn't anticipate any problem with that."

"Huh, I guess not. Any lawyer would give his eyeteeth for the exposure this case is gonna give him."

"Once he's got his representation, he'll call me and I'll set it up. I say inside a week."

"That'll give you time to make your deal with the chief."

"Right."

"How are you gonna get in to see him?"

"Somehow," Keough said, "I don't think that's going to be a problem."

"Chief LaGrange?"

"Yes, Mary."

"There's a Captain Lewis on the line, sir—retired Captain Lewis?"

"Truxton Lewis? Put him on, Mary."

"Hello, Bob?"

"Tru, what the hell are you up to?"

"Not much these days, Bob. Building some furniture in my garage."

"Can you build a home-entertainment center? My wife's been bugging me for one."

"We'll talk about it."

"What can I do for you today, Tru?"

"Got a favor to ask, Bob."

"Finally going to use me to get IAD off your back?"

"Fuck IAD, Bob. No, this favor involves someone else."

"Who?"

"Do you know a detective named Keough?"

"Do I . . ."

After LaGrange agreed to see Det. Joe Keough on Truxton Lewis's say-so, he sent for Inspector Pollard.

"I've just agreed to meet with Detective Keough."

"Uh, Lieutenant Slovecky suspended the man, sir."

"Why?"

"Uh, apparently, they had an altercation."

"Well, I doubt that's the last altercation the lieutenant will have in his career, Paul. Detective Keough will be here tomorrow morning at nine. I want you to be here."

"Uh, yes, sir, all right."

"That's all, Paul."

In his own office, Pollard sat down and worriedly chewed his bottom lip. There was no doubt that when Keough came in to see the chief, he was going to bring up the subject of his memo. Pollard had given the memo to Slovecky, but he still had a Xerox copy in his desk. If he gave it to the chief now and insisted that it had been lost, maybe he'd be able to escape the man's wrath. On the other hand, if he did that, Slovecky might deliver on one of his many threats.

Pollard eventually decided to get the memo to the chief without actually giving it to him personally.

LaGrange was hanging up his phone, shaking his head, when his secretary, Mary Francis, walked in carrying a sheet of paper.

"What is it, Mary?"

"I found this under my desk, sir."

"What is it?"

"It's a memo, dated more than several days ago. Have you seen it before?"

She handed it to LaGrange, who started to read it

ALONE WITH THE DEAD

and stopped short when he came to the name Det. Joseph Keough.

"I'll take care of it, Mary."

"Yes, sir."

After his secretary left the office, LaGrange started at the top again and read the entire memo.

"Son of a bitch!"

He depressed the button on his intercom and said, "Mary, get Inspector Pollard in here."

Chapter Thirty-eight

Even though he'd already heard from the Lover, Keough didn't have much reason to leave his apartment the next day. The man still had to call him back when he found an attorney. Consequently, he was in that afternoon when Truxton Lewis called.

"You've got your meeting, lad."

"That's great, Tru. When?"

"Tomorrow morning at nine."

"Can't tell you how much I appreciate this."

"Just make the most of it."

Keough's heart was racing. There was still the possibility that the Lover would change his mind about turning himself in, but he didn't think so. Tomorrow he'd make his deal, and then it would depend on the killer being a man of his word.

He had just hung up when there was a knock on the door.

"You wouldn't believe the day I had," Nancy said, walking in past him with arms full of groceries.

"What's all this?" he asked.

"You've been inside so long, I just knew your refrigerator had to be empty."

He followed her into the kitchen, where she deposited the bags on the counter. He came up behind her and put his hands on her shoulders. What happened next could have happened for a lot of reasons. He'd been seeing Nancy in a different light lately, and he was in a good mood because his meeting was set. Whatever the reason, the next thing he knew, he was kissing her, unlike any good-night kiss they'd ever shared. Her tongue was in his mouth and it felt like wet velvet. He pulled her close to him, crushing her breasts against his chest, and she moaned deep in her throat as the kiss went on and on, until they moved away from each other, both breathless.

She leaned against the counter, bracing herself on it with her hands.

"God . . ." she said.

"I know. . . ."

She looked at him, her eyes shining.

"What do we do now?"

"I think . . . I think I'd like to continue this, Nancy, but not until after all of this . . . nonsense is done."

"Well, I'd like to continue it, too, Joe. Tell me, how long do you think we have to wait?"

"Not long," he said, "not long at all. . . . Okay, that's long enough. . . ."

He lifted her up onto the counter and captured her

surprised mouth with his. She got over her surprise, though, and helped him with her pants . . .

Later, he told her his news, after they'd made love a second time, this time in the bedroom.

"Is that good?" she asked when he was done. She was serious.

"It's wonderful news, Nancy. Once this guy gives up, I'll be able to prove there's a second killer."

"How?"

"Because he'll strike again, and when he does, the Lover will be in custody."

"What if he doesn't strike again? What if once the Lover is caught, the second man just stops? Wouldn't that be good enough?"

"No, not really."

"The killing would stop."

"But he'd get away with killing three women."

"You really believe in this stuff, don't you?"

"What stuff?"

"Justice."

"Yeah, I guess I do."

She smiled, put her hand on his belly, and said, "I guess that's one of the reasons I . . . like you so much."

"What are some of the others?"

"Mmm," she said, moving her hand lower. . . .

Later still, Nancy put a meat loaf together that put to shame any Keough had ever had before. Cindy came home from school and started looking oddly at both her mother and Keough. She did her homework on Keough's kitchen table while her mother cooked and he sat at his desk, trying to put together his presentation for Chief LaGrange. At one point, Keough turned in his chair and could see both of them in the kitchen. Nancy had stopped what she was doing to help Cindy with one of her homework problems. The whole scene was very domestic, and it surprised him that he liked the way it felt.

After dinner, Nancy and Cindy cleaned up while Keough continued his work.

"Are you two gonna get married?"

The question startled him and he looked at Cindy, who had come up next to him quietly.

"What?" Keough said.

"Cindy!" her mother called from behind them. Her tone was shocked.

"Well, are you?"

"Whatever gave you that idea?" Nancy asked. Keough decided to let the girl's mother handle this situation.

She turned and looked at her mother.

"You're acting funny, both of you."

"Funny, how?"

"All through dinner, you were giving each other goo-goo eyes."

"We were not!"

"You were, too." She eyed both of them suspiciously and then asked, "Did you two have sex today?"

"Cindy!" Nancy said, a guilty flush coming over her face. "That'll be enough of that, young lady."

"Well, I was just wondering," Cindy said, smiling a self-satisfied smile.

"Well, you can stop wondering. I think it's time for you to go across the hall."

"That's okay," she said, "it's time for my programs, anyway."

She grabbed her books off the table and started for the door, but she stopped short and detoured over to where Keough was sitting.

"Just in case I have a vote, Joey," she said, "I'd love for you to be my new daddy."

She kissed Keough's cheek as he stared at her in astonishment, then went out the door to the apartment across the hall.

"Joe," Nancy said, looking mortified, "I'm so sorry—"

"You know something?" he asked.

"What?"

"I just love that kid!"

Nancy finished cleaning up the kitchen, put the leftovers in the refrigerator, and came back into the living room.

"I'm finished, Joe. I'm going to go home and make sure Cindy gets to bed."

He got up, went to her, and put his arms around her.

"Thanks for dinner, Nancy. It was great, as always."

"Walk me to the door?"

"Sure."

As they started toward the door, they put their arms around each other's waists. It was a nice feeling, for both of them.

"You know," she said as they turned to face each

other at the door, "I'd almost like to insist on coming back later, but I won't."

"Why not?"

"Because you promised me that everything would be resolved in a little while, and I want you to keep working hard toward that goal."

"I intend to."

She took hold of his shirtfront and pulled him to her so she could plant a long, delicious kiss on him.

"That's just to keep you motivated."

"Oh," he said as she released him, "I'm motivated."

"Good night."

"Good night, Nancy."

As Nancy turned to leave, they were both able to see into the other apartment, where Cindy was watching them, a big smile on her face.

A few hours after Nancy left, the phone rang. Keough jumped at it and answered on the first ring.

"You're anxious," the Lover said.

"Yes, I am."

"That's good. It didn't take me long to find an attorney who would take my case."

"I didn't think it would."

"That means the, uh, ball is in your court, if I may use a sports idiom. When can you make the arrangements with Mr. O'Donnell and the television-news media?"

"I don't think that will take too long, either," Keough said, and suggested a time and place for the meeting.

"Detective, you amaze me."

"Why is that?"

"Another policeman might have tapped his own phone in an attempt to find me."

"That would have been useless."

"No, it wouldn't have," the Lover said, chuckling. "You see, I have been using my own phone to call you."

"Well, I guess it really doesn't matter, does it, now that you're giving yourself up?"

"No, it doesn't matter. I just wanted to tell you that, not to try to make you feel foolish, but to illustrate to you how much faith I have in you."

"I'm touched."

"You think me mad, don't you, for the things I've done?"

"What are the chances that my answer will fuck up our bargain."

The man chuckled again.

"No chance. Our bargain is set."

"Well, then, yeah, I think you're one sick son of a bitch."

There was a long moment of silence, during which Keough became afraid that he had indeed blown the deal.

"Have you intentions of trying to capture the man who killed those little girls in Brooklyn?" the Lover asked when he spoke again.

"Oh, yes."

"Then I suggest you take a good look at him when you do catch him. That will be a sick son of a bitch."

"So what does that make you?"

The chuckle came again, and Keough hoped he wouldn't ever have to hear it again.

"Read my book when it comes out."

Chapter Thirty-nine

Keough appeared at the office of the chief of detectives at One Police Plaza at 9:00 A.M. sharp the next morning. He already had his deal with the Lover in his pocket; now he had to make one with the C of D.

Last night, after talking with the serial killer on the phone, he'd had a quick beer to calm himself and then called Mike O'Donnell at home. He'd relayed his conversation with the Lover, his voice still shaking, while O'Donnell listened anxiously.

"Then we're in," O'Donnell said when he was done. "I'll call the TV people tomorrow. All we need to do is pick a place to do this."

"I've already picked one."

"Where?"

He told him.

"That's brilliant. How about the when?"

Keough told him that, too.

"That's cruel."

"Maybe I'm in a cruel mood, but I can't change it now. The Lover will be there with his attorney."

"Did you get his real name?"

"No," Keough said, "we'll get that when he surrenders."

"Jesus, Joe, this is big."

"I know, Mike."

"I can't thank you enough."

"We'll think of a way."

"I'm not gonna be able to sleep tonight."

"I don't think I will, either."

As it turned out, to his surprise, he slept like a baby and woke up feeling great. He felt so good about what was going to happen that day that he decided to drive into the city.

Now he was standing in the chief of detective's office, waiting for the secretary to get the word to take him into the inner sanctum. Under his arm, he held a file that had been put together by Len Swann but highlighted and edited by Keough. He didn't know if it would be concrete enough for the chief, but that didn't really matter, considering what the rest of the day had in store.

"Detective Keough?"

The voice came from his left, and when he turned, he saw a tall, elegant-looking man in his late forties coming toward him. The elegance was ruined, however, by dark circles under the man's eyes and the haggard look on his face. He looked like a man who was not eating and not sleeping well of late.

"I'm Inspector Paul Pollard."

"Oh, Inspector Pollard. I've heard of you."

"Have you?"

"Oh yes."

In the presence of bosses—captains and inspectors, mostly—Keough had always felt, well, inferior. That is, he was acutely aware of the distance between their respective ranks. He did not, however, get this feeling in the presence of Pollard. The man looked ill and worried, and he did not project a superior attitude.

He looked like a man on the block waiting for the ax to fall.

"We can go in now."

"Thanks."

Keough followed Pollard, who opened the door to the chief's office and then stepped aside to allow Keough to precede him.

"Chief, this is Detective Keough."

The chief's manner was brusque.

"Sit down, Keough."

"Yes, sir."

LaGrange was seated behind his desk. Keough had seen photos of the man, and had seen him once or twice at parade or funeral functions. He was quite a change from Pollard. The attitudes that were lacking in Pollard came off LaGrange in waves.

"I've got a memo here that you sent me some time ago." He passed it across to Keough. "You did write this, didn't you?"

"I sent it, yes, sir," Keough said, handing it back. "Mostly it was written by a detective named Len Swann."

"Swann," LaGrange repeated, looking at Pollard. "Where do I know that name from?"

Keough answered before Pollard could.

"He was recently murdered in his own home."

"Oh, yes, yes," LaGrange said, "I remember now. What did he have to do with this?"

"He was assigned to the Lover Task Force, sir. He shared my views on the case."

"That being that there were two killers and not one?"

"Yes, sir."

"Do you still feel that way?"

"Yes, sir."

"Detective, I first saw this memo yesterday. My secretary found it under her desk."

"Did she?"

"Yes. Apparently it had fallen there—"

"I don't think so."

"I beg your pardon?"

"That's not the memo I sent."

"I'm sorry," LaGrange said, frowning, "I don't understand. You just said—"

"That's a Xerox copy."

"Well, I can see that—"

"I sent the original memo. Someone made that copy from my original. If that was under your secretary's desk, where is the original?"

LaGrange stared at Keough for some time and then slowly moved his eyes over to Inspector Pollard.

"Paul, would you do me a favor?"

"Sir?"

"Would you get the fuck out of the building?"

Keough didn't turn to look at Pollard.

"Sir?"

"Get up off your ass and get out of the building."

"Where would you like me to go . . . sir?"

"I don't give a fuck, Paul. Go home. Go to a bar. Go and fuck that black whore you've been carrying on with. Get out of here!"

"Black—uh, sir, I don't understand."

"Pollard, you're suspended as of now. Leave your gun and shield on my desk and get out. Go home and wait for my call. Don't call anyone. You've done enough damage to yourself as it is."

"Sir, I don't understand," Pollard said, standing up. "How did you know about—"

"I know about the people who work for me, Pollard. Let's leave it at that."

"Chief—"

"Out."

"Chief, I'd Like to explain—"

"Don't make me have you removed, Inspector!"

Keough looked at Pollard now and the man seemed on the verge of fainting. Pollard saw Keough looking at him and suddenly turned and fled from the room.

"Why did you do that?"

"My correspondence goes through him," LaGrange said. "It's fairly obvious that he hid this from me. I don't know what he did with the original."

"He gave it to somebody."

"Who?"

Keough hesitated and then said, "I'd be speculating."

"Go ahead and speculate."

"There are other things I'd rather talk about right now, Chief."

LaGrange pushed his chair back from his desk and leaned back, eyeing Keough.

"You know, Detective, a friend of mine speaks very highly of you." As he said it, Keough noticed the chief put his hand on top of a personnel folder. He had no doubt that it was his.

"Does he?"

"Yes, Truxton Lewis. Do you know him?"

"We've met once or twice."

"Well, you've apparently made an impression on him. Now I'm going to give you the chance to make an impression on me . . . but I warn you."

"Sir?"

"I've been burned too many times during this serial killer thing. Don't try to pull the wool over my eyes. There are some things in your jacket that don't speak well of you."

"I tend to speak my mind, sir."

"I understand that. I also understand that you're on suspension, but I'm giving you a chance here to explain yourself."

Keough looked at his watch.

"That might take a while, sir."

"Do you have someplace else to be?"

"As a matter of fact," Keough said, "I do, but why don't I just start at the beginning. . . ."

LaGrange sat quietly and listened intently, interrupting only to ask a question and have something clarified. If ever a man had his day in court, Keough was having it now, and he was taking full advantage of it. From time to time, he'd glance at his watch, but he kept right on talking. His entire presentation had to do with the serial killings. He did not say anything at this time about Len Swann's murder.

When he was finished, he put the file he'd been holding in his lap on the desk.

LaGrange rubbed both hands over his face briskly—so much so that when he took his hands away, his face was red.

"Maybe I've been on this job too long."

"Sir?"

"I've made a lot of mistakes on this one, Keough. I see that now. I put too much faith in a man I knew was a fool."

"Uh, Pollard, sir?"

"That's right."

"What was that about a, uh, black whore."

"Oh, Pollard's got himself a little something going on the side with the daughter of a black minister and he thinks nobody knows about it."

"So somebody who had a knack for picking up dirt would certainly know about it."

LaGrange nodded.

"You're talking about Lieutenant Slovecky."

"Yes."

"And that explains to you why he got the assignment as CO of the task force?"

"Yes, sir."

"Another of my mistakes," LaGrange said. "I should have pulled Slovecky in here and interviewed him myself. I don't think I would have given him the job if I had."

Keough remained silent.

"It's decent of you not to ask why I didn't do that."

"It's not my business, sir."

"At the time, I was sitting in with the PC, trying to avert a strike."

Keough remembered when rumors of a strike were rampant. They disappeared just as quickly as they appeared, though.

"And I had a convention, and a . . . but you don't want to hear that."

No, Keough thought, I don't.

LaGrange leaned forward and with his right hand touched the file Keough had put on his desk. His left hand still rested on Keough's personnel file. For a moment, the man seemed to be weighing the two. Jesus, Keough thought, you urinate on one skell and people look at you funny for the rest of your life.

"Is there anything concrete in here, Detective?"

"I believe I have outlined the discrepancies between the Manhattan and Brooklyn murders in a concrete manner, sir."

Keough had explained everything to the chief, but he had not yet told the man that he was actually in contact with the Lover. He was close to letting the man in on it, though, as well as telling him about the arrangement to surrender. What happened over the next few minutes, though, changed his mind.

"Detective, I'm willing to admit that you got caught in some kind of a machine here. Everybody involved was willing to sluff those cases onto the task force rather than deal with them themselves. That's an attitude I intend to address myself to."

Keough remained quiet and waited for the other shoe to drop.

"I also intend to investigate further the possible connection between Inspector Pollard and Lieutenant

Slovecky. I'll probably be removing Slovecky as whip of the task force and assigning someone else. I'll probably suspend Slovecky until the investigation is complete. I will also be lifting your suspension.''

"I hear a *but* in here, sir."

"You've done a lot of work here, Keough, but I simply can't take your word for everything."

"There's the word of Len Swann."

"Who is dead and can't speak for himself."

"So what are you going to do?"

"I'm going to assign a new CO to the task force and have him look over this file."

"And if he disagrees?"

"It will be his job to proceed as he sees fit."

"Let me ask you something, Chief, in all candor."

"Go ahead."

"If I was a lieutenant, or even a sergeant, would you give my opinion more credence?"

"I sincerely hope that wouldn't be the case."

"That's my answer, then," Keough said. "Even with Tru Lewis's recommendation, I'm not a boss—"

"Don't become impudent, Detective. Truxton Lewis's intervention got you in to see me to tell your side, but I wouldn't push it—"

"Why not? What have I got to lose?"

"Your job, for one."

"That doesn't seem so important in the scheme of things, Chief, I have to tell you."

LaGrange frowned.

"Is there something else you're not telling me, Detective?"

"Not about the serial killings."

"Then what?"

"I'm not sure you'll want to hear what I have to say," Keough said. "It's my opinion, and after all, I am just a detective—"

"You're pushing it, Keough," LaGrange said. "You said that you speak your mind, so speak it."

"It's about Len Swann's murder."

"What about it?"

"I think Slovecky killed him."

"What?"

"Yes, sir, that's what I think."

"A cop killed a cop?"

"Yes, sir."

"Jesus," LaGrange said, looking ill, "if that gets out . . . Do you have any evidence?"

"No, sir, I don't . . . yet."

"Well, don't even bring it up to me again until you do. If this gets out . . ."

"Yes, sir," Keough said, standing, "I thought that would be your attitude."

"What are you saying?"

"Just that you're part of that machine you said I got caught in."

"Goddamn it, man, sit down!"

"I don't think so, Chief."

"Maybe I'll just leave you on suspension, Keough—how's that?"

"I tell you what, Chief. Let's make a deal."

"Now you're fucking Monty Hall?"

Keough remained standing and remained silent.

LaGrange sighed heavily and said, "Okay, what's your deal?"

"I'll deliver the Lover to you."

"That sounds like a tall order. In exchange for what?"

"When I do deliver him, I want the task force kept together, and I want the Brooklyn killings investigated separately."

"And?"

"And I want Slovecky looked at as a serious suspect in Len Swann's murder."

"That's all?"

"That's all."

"And in exchange for this, you say you'll deliver the serial killer?"

"Yes, sir."

"How will we know it's him?"

"Once I deliver him, you can have him examined. I think you'll be satisfied that it's him."

"And when would you be delivering him?"

"Soon," Keough said, straining to keep from looking at his watch, "very soon."

Chapter Forty

Keough was disappointed. Halfway into his audience with the chief of detectives, he had started to think that he and LaGrange were going to be able to work things out. LaGrange had started to sound like a reasonable man, but then he reverted back to what he really was—a boss.

In the police department, there were the cops and the bosses, and the bosses had a definite boss mentality. It started at the rank of sergeant, although the three-stripers were really straddling the line. When they got to lieutenant, that's when it really started, the conversion from cop to boss.

When LaGrange had started admitting his mistakes to Keough, Keough had been impressed with the man.

When the chief did his turnaround, Keough couldn't help but be disappointed.

There had been a point during his two hours in the chief's office where he was almost prepared to tell LaGrange about the Lover surrendering to him and Mike O'Donnell. Now, as he left the chief's office, he was ready to let the chips fall where they might. When he and O'Donnell met with the Lover and his attorney, it was going to be a slap in the face to the police department. If allowed, the department would claim that since Keough was a cop, the surrender of the Lover was a triumph. Keough, however, with the help of O'Donnell, did not intend to give the department that chance.

The meeting was to take place at noon, but O'Donnell was supposed to meet Keough at eleven. It was 11:15 when Keough came out the front door of One Police Plaza and saw O'Donnell standing there, waiting impatiently. In the distance, Keough saw a couple of TV vans, their crews milling about.

"They didn't waste any time," he said to O'Donnell.

"They'll keep their distance until we're ready."

"It's a good thing we arranged to meet in the back of the building," Keough said. "Come on."

They went around to the side of the building, where a stairway led to the back. They'd meet the Lover and his lawyer back there, then walk them around to the front, where the television press would be waiting.

"We've still got half an hour," Keough said. "There's usually a coffee and snack van under the bridge. How about some coffee?"

"What happened in the chief's office?"

"I'll tell you over coffee. Come on, my treat."

At 12:05 P.M. Chief LaGrange's secretary, Mary, came into his office.

"What is it, Mary?"

"Uh, you might want to turn on your television set, Chief."

"What for?"

Aware that in some ancient civilizations there was a custom of killing the bearer of bad news, she said, "You'll see."

LaGrange picked up the remote control from his desk and switched on the color TV in the corner.

"What station?"

"Any network."

He chose NBC. He liked looking at Michelle Marsh during the nightly news.

"... shock to the city, but a relief as well, to know that the Lover, the notorious serial killer who has been spreading a reign of terror for months, has surrendered today to Detective Joseph Keough of the New York City Police Department, and Michael O'Donnell, noted author and columnist for the *New York Post*."

"That son of a bitch!" LaGrange said. "That no-good son of a bitch." He looked at Mary. "Get me the PC."

"It was his secretary who called me about it," she said. "He's already watching."

"Great, that's just great."

"Once again, this is a live shot ..." the newsman continued.

"Oh fuck!" LaGrange said, staring intently at the

TV screen. He got up abruptly, went to his window, and looked outside. He could see down into the plaza, where a mob of television reporters was milling about.

"That son of a bitch! He's doing it right in front of Police Headquarters."

"Yes, sir."

LaGrange put his forehead against the cold glass and said, "Mary?"

"Yes?"

"Get your pad and take a letter . . ."

"Yes, sir."

". . . of resignation."

She stopped, halfway out the door, and asked, "Sir?"

Without turning, he said, "Never mind. Get me the PC on the phone."

"Yes, sir."

He breathed heavily on the glass until he had so fogged it that he couldn't see outside. It was going to take a lot more than that to make this nightmare go away.

Keough had been surprised when the two men first appeared. Neither of them fit his picture of a serial killer. Either of them could have passed for a professor or a lawyer, but neither looked like a killer.

He and O'Donnell had stood shoulder-to-shoulder as the two men approached through the drizzle that had started. Keough chose to think that the shorter, heavier man carrying the briefcase was the attorney. The other man was tall and slender, hair dark but graying at the temples. He wore wire-framed glasses and had the slight stoop of an academic who spent hours hovering over books. He did, however, appear to be in fairly good shape, and so he probably wouldn't have had any problem overpowering the women he had killed.

For just a moment, Keough was worried. What if this was just some psycho who wanted to confess to the murders? But that couldn't be. He had known about the note, and he had been able to find Keough's home phone number. This had to be the killer—the first killer.

He held his breath as the two men reached them. The man with the glasses smiled and asked, "Which of you is Detective Keough?"

That voice—it was the same voice as on the phone.

"I am," Keough said.

The man gave him his attention and asked, "Would I be correct in assuming that you would prefer not to shake hands?"

"You would."

"Mr. O'Donnell?"

"Yes."

"Excellent." The killer turned to the other man and said, "This is my attorney, Stuart Buckingham."

"Counselor," Keough said, "I've heard of you."

"Detective," Buckingham said. "For the record, my client's name is Professor Anthony Dunston."

"The Third," Dunston added.

"Yes," Buckingham said. "He wishes to surrender to you and confess to being the serial killer this city has come to call the Lover."

Dunston smiled at Keough, held out his wrists, and said, "I am all yours, Detective."

* * *

The press crowded around them when they appeared and, as Keough and O'Donnell had agreed, it was O'Donnell who made the statement to the press and introduced both Anthony Dunston III as the Lover, and Stuart Buckingham, his attorney.

"My client is here to surrender to Detective Keough and Michael O'Donnell of the *Post*."

"Surrender for what, counselor?" a man holding a microphone with the number on it asked.

"May I?" Dunston asked.

"Go ahead," Buckingham said, and under his breath he added, "but just what we agreed to."

Dunston smiled, spread his arms, and said, "Ladies and gentlemen . . . I am the Lover!"

The surrender made all the networks and also the local station's newscasts. There were special reports throughout the day, and then the regular newscasts at night.

O'Donnell was interviewed, as well as Keough, who kept his statements simple. He did not use the occasion to claim that there were two serial killers. He did not want to alarm the city, in the event that the second killer did indeed, as Nancy had suggested, cease his activities.

Keough was in the middle of an interview in the lobby of One Police Plaza, sometime after Professor Anthony Dunston III had been removed, when he saw a man hovering on the outskirts of the mob. The man had the look of a cop, not a reporter, even though he was dressed in a suit.

When the interview was over, the man approached.

"Detective Keough?"

"Yes?"

"The PC would like to talk to you."

Keough turned to O'Donnell and said, "I'll see you later."

Before O'Donnell could reply, the plainclothesman said, "You, too, Mr. O'Donnell . . . if you would."

"Is this an order?" O'Donnell asked.

"No, sir," the man said. "The PC requests your attendance at this meeting."

O'Donnell looked at Keough, who nodded.

"Lead the way," O'Donnell said.

Chapter Forty-one

When Keough and O'Donnell were shown into Police Commissioner Steiger's office, Keough was surprised to see no one else there. He'd felt sure the room would be full of people. The chief of detectives, people from Public Information, Community Service, press liaison people, and more. Instead, there was only the PC, a portly man in his sixties with a great shock of white hair.

"Sit down, gentlemen."

They sat, Keough on the left, O'Donnell on the right.

"It would seem that you gentlemen have done the city of New York a great service."

"It would seem," O'Donnell repeated.

"That is, if Anthony Dunston does turn out to be the Lover serial killer."

"The Third," O'Donnell said.

"I beg your pardon?"

"Anthony Dunston the Third," O'Donnell said. "He insists on that."

"I see."

"He's the serial killer, Commissioner," Keough said. "I have no doubt about that."

"I've just finished talking to Chief LaGrange, Detective Keough. He tells me that you and he made a little bargain."

"That's right."

"He seems to feel that the bargain was made under false pretenses."

Keough spread his hands.

"The bargain was a simple one, predicated on my delivering the Lover, which I did."

"Obviously," Steiger said, "your deal with the serial killer preceded your deal with the chief."

"I don't see where that matters."

"Semantics matter a great deal at this level of the game, Detective."

"I wasn't aware that we were playing a game, Commissioner," Keough said, "and even if we were, the chief made it very clear to me that I am not on the same level as you and he."

"Nevertheless, if indeed you have delivered the killer, then you've done us all—"

"A great service," Keough finished. "You said that. With all due respect, sir, is my bargain with the chief going to be upheld?"

"Uh, yes, of course it is."

"Fine." He started to rise. "I don't see what else there is to discuss."

"Please," Steiger said, holding out a hand, "indulge me a moment longer?"

Keough hesitated, then settled back into his seat.

"You accomplished what an entire task force could not," the commissioner said. "I'd like to know how."

"I approached the problem differently."

"How differently?"

"From an intelligent standpoint, rather than a political one."

Steiger frowned.

"I don't understand."

"Lieutenant Slovecky, the CO of the task force, was more concerned with becoming a deputy inspector than he was with catching the killers."

"Killers? Oh, yes, the chief mentioned something about a theory of yours that there were two killers."

"Mentioned it?" Keough looked at O'Donnell. The look on the newspaperman's face told Keough that they were thinking the same thing. "Commissioner, the chief did explain our bargain fully, didn't he?"

"Oh, yes, of course he did. You want the task force to continue to search for the, uh, second killer."

"That's right."

"And that's what they'll do."

"Under a new commander."

"Well, yes, that was part of the bargain, wasn't it?"

"Yes, it was."

"Then it will be done."

"When will the new CO take over?"

"I will consult with the chief. We hope to have someone in place as soon as possible. For now, we've assigned someone temporarily to oversee the interrogation of the man you brought it.''

"The Lover," O'Donnell said, "we brought in the Lover."

"With all due respect, Mr. O'Donnell," Steiger said, "we'll be more sure of that after the interrogation.''

"Sir, may I ask who is conducting the interrogation?" Keough asked.

"Of course. I've assigned Deputy Inspector Harold Orlick.''

"Inspector Orlick?"

"Do you know him?"

"I know of him," Keough said. He'd never met the man, but he'd heard good things about him. He was a young man, a Slovecky with a better education and a better understanding of how the game works, who had not gotten stuck on his way up.

"He'll be taking charge immediately."

"How nice for him," Keough said. He figured Orlick would also get the assignment to the task force.

"Mr. O'Donnell," the commissioner said, "we're a little concerned with how this is going to look in the newspapers.''

"How so, Commissioner?"

"Well," Steiger said with a phony laugh, "it is a potentially embarrassing situation, and we were hoping that you could work with someone from our Publicity—"

"I write my own story, Commissioner," O'Donnell said, without giving the man a chance to finish.

"Well, yes, of course—"

"You can't control the press."

"I know—"

"And even if you could, you wouldn't be able to control me."

Steiger matched stares with O'Donnell for a moment and then said, "Perhaps not."

"Commissioner," Keough said, standing, "I really don't see that this is getting us anywhere."

"Detective Keough," Steiger said, with more steel in his voice than he had used over the past few minutes, "it's my understanding that you tend to, uh, let's say not fully cooperate with your superiors."

"Commissioner," Keough said, "if I had gotten more cooperation from my superiors, Detective Len Swann might not be dead."

"Swann? How does he come into this?"

"I thought you said you were fully briefed by the chief?"

"Well, it was a rather . . . hurried briefing, having to do with the serial killer."

"Well, I suggest you have the chief come up and give you an indepth briefing. Also, I'd like to know where I am currently assigned. Am I still with the task force, am I back at the Six-Seven, or am I on suspension?"

Steiger stood up and looked at Keough.

"I think until all of this has been figured out, Detective, you should consider yourself on leave."

"With pay?"

Steiger gave him a brief smile, one that never touched any part of his face but his mouth.

"Of course."

*   *   *

"Son of a bitch!" Keough said in the elevator on the way down. "They're going to shitcan it."

"How can they?" O'Donnell said. "I'm going to write this up, Joe. Everything will come out.

"There's no way they can claim that Dunston is not the Lover—not once my piece comes out in tomorrow's paper."

"I've got a bad feeling, Mike," Keough said, "a real bad feeling about this."

As soon as Keough and O'Donnell left the commissioner's office, another door opened and Chief La-Grange stepped in.

"I think you're right, Robert," Steiger said. "He's not going to cooperate."

"What do you want to do, sir?"

"Even if this Dunston does turn out to be the serial killer—and I hope to God he is, so we can at least close the door on that mess—I think I want Detective Keough put on permanent leave."

"What about Slovecky?"

"I want him buried," the PC said. "Reassign him and don't let him talk to any reporters."

"Yes, sir. What about O'Donnell?"

"I'll be making a phone call that will take care of Mr. O'Donnell."

LaGrange approached the PC's desk.

"What if there's another murder, Ray?" he asked. "What if Keough turns out to be right?"

"If there's another murder, we'll make a statement that it's the work of a copycat killer. As far as we are concerned, all of the murders were committed by the same man. Understand?"

"Yes, sir."

"But there won't be any more murders," Steiger said unconvincingly. "We've got the son of a bitch. Where is he?"

"Inspector Orlick is interrogating him right now, sir."

"I want to know his findings immediately, understand? No delays on this, Robert."

"I understand, sir."

"This has the potential to be a big mess, Bob," Steiger said. "God forbid there were two killers and our task force whip was hiding it. This could blow up in our faces."

"Well, the mayor should be happy, anyway."

"He's called me already," Steiger said. "Wanted to know if we really had the bastard. That's why I need Orlick's findings as soon as possible."

"You'll have them."

LaGrange headed for the door, but Steiger stopped him.

"Bob?"

"Yes, sir."

"Don't fuck up from here on out."

LaGrange turned and looked at the PC over his shoulder.

"I won't, sir."

"We're too old to be looking for new jobs," Steiger said. "We've got to stay in control of this."

LaGrange turned to face Steiger.

"May I make a suggestion then, sir?"

"Go ahead."

"Putting Keough on leave doesn't accomplish much. If he talks, people will still listen."

"What do you suggest?"

"If we terminate him, then if he talks, people will just look at it as sour grapes."

"How the fuck do we terminate the man who caught the Lover?"

"The Department is a team, sir. Keough is not a team player. No matter what he did, in our eyes he did it the wrong way."

Steiger thought it over for a few moments, then looked at LaGrange and said, "All right, goddamn it. Do it!"

Chapter Forty-two

For the most part, it took a week for things to get sorted out.

The one thing that happened right away was that Mike O'Donnell lost his job at the *Post*.

The night of the surrender, he called Keough at home.

"I'm canned, Joe."

"What?" For a moment, Keough thought O'Donnell was telling him that he was drunk.

"I got fired."

"Fired? Why?"

"I think somebody made a phone call," O'Donnell said. "My editor said they don't like writers who make grandstand plays. I'm not gonna get a chance to write this up for tomorrow.''

"What about some of the other papers?"

"Whoever made the call has a long dialing finger," O'Donnell said. "Nobody would talk to me."

"Jesus, Mike, I'm sorry."

"That's okay," O'Donnell said, "I don't think they'll be able to get to my publisher, so I'll still get to write the book. People will just have to wait a little longer for the truth. You better watch your ass. If they dropped the ax on me, they can sure do it to you."

And they did.

Keough got a call several days later that he was being pensioned off. The call came from Robert LaGrange.

"There wasn't anything I could do, Keough," he said. "The PC was hot about the way you went about this."

Keough had tried for several days to get either the commissioner or the chief on the phone. Failing that, he had called the task force number, but it had been disconnected. That was when he was sure this call was going to come sooner or later.

"How do you explain to the press that the man who caught the Lover gets fired a few days later?" Keough asked.

"We don't have to justify our hiring and firing practices to anyone, Keough, but if they ask, we'll give them an answer, don't you worry."

"Well, I guess I'll be giving them an answer, too, won't I?"

"You won't be giving it to your friend O'Donnell, will you?" LaGrange asked nastily.

"This isn't over, Chief. You can't just push me out and shut me up."

"Your termination will be announced tomorrow. Whatever you say after that will be seen as sour grapes. You tried playing with the big boys, Keough, and you lost."

"You know what, Chief? This was all about stopping the killing, which I've done, even if it's just for a little while."

"That second-killer theory again? Forget that, Keough. Get on with your life."

"When the second killer hits, Chief," Keough said, "do me a favor . . . don't call me."

He broke the connection.

A full week later, Mike O'Donnell was over at Keough's for dinner. Nancy was cooking in the kitchen, and Cindy was doing her homework at the kitchen table. Keough and O'Donnell were sitting in the living room drinking John Courages. Earlier in the day, O'Donnell had called Keough's place and was surprised when Nancy Valentine answered. She said she was preparing dinner and that Keough was out flying a kite. O'Donnell knew of his friend's penchant for kites, and he asked Nancy where he could find him. She gave him directions to that area of the Belt Parkway where Keough would be.

Keough was surprised when O'Donnell appeared, and he promptly invited him to come home with him for dinner.

"So my publisher thinks this could be my biggest book," O'Donnell said.

"What do you think, Mike?"

"Well, considering the one best-seller I had just squeaked onto the list, it wouldn't take much, but yeah, I think so, too. Hell, just the extra publicity with me getting fired should help. Even without that, though, this is a good case. It ain't the Son of Sam, but it's a good one. And then I got you."

"Yeah, that'll help you a whole lot."

"It will. With all of your insights into the case, this book is a 'can't miss.'"

"Well, I hope so."

"And don't worry, I'm gonna take care of you, Joe. I ain't gonna forget that you came to me with this."

"I trust you, Mike."

There was a moment of silence, during which Keough could hear Cindy reciting something for her homework.

"*Rosa gallica officinalis, Rosa gallica versicolor . . .*"

"So my friends on the police beat tell me Dunston's the real McCoy."

"Is that a fact?"

"Yep, they're charging him with all of the murders, even the Brooklyn ones."

Keough blew air out of his mouth in disgust and shook his head.

"Been talkin' to anybody?" O'Donnell asked.

"Not about that. Talked to Clapton about Swann's murder. He said he's getting nowhere."

"Did you tell him about Slovecky?"

"Yes," Keough said sourly.

"What happened?"

"LaGrange was right. Clapton wanted to know if I was sure I wasn't just trying to get back at Slovecky because my 'downslide,' as he called it, started with him.''

"Sour grapes.''

"Just like the chief predicted.''

"Been approached for any interviews?''

"A TV station wanted me to go on. I said no.''

"Why?''

"What's the point, Mike?''

Silence again, and still he could hear Cindy.

''. . . Lincoln, Olympiad, Precious Platinum . . .''

"Looks like your Brooklyn killer went to ground.''

"It's only been a week.'' Keough took a long swig from his bottle, finishing it. "He'll surface again.''

"You don't think reading about his hero being caught will stop him?''

"No,'' Keough said, getting up from the sofa and walking toward the kitchen. "I think if anything, it will fuel him on. Now he'll want to prove that he's even better. Want another beer?''

"Sure.''

As Keough entered the kitchen, Cindy looked up and smiled at him.

"What's that you're reciting, honey?''

"We're studying roses in school,'' she said. "I have to memorize some of the varieties. Did you know there was a rose called Mr. Lincoln?''

Keough looked at Nancy and they exchanged a smile.

"Really?''

"Yes, it's a very red rose. Also Olympiad.''

Keough opened the refrigerator to get two more beers.

"Why are you studying roses?''

"It was the teacher's idea."

"What you study usually is, isn't it?"

"To tell you the truth," Nancy said, "I think the teacher was influenced by what was happening in the papers, you know, with roses."

"That's a little morbid, don't you think?" Keough asked.

"I thought so," Nancy agreed. "Cindy, recite the *gallica* roses again."

"Gallica?"

"French roses," Nancy translated for him.

"Oh."

As he headed back for the living room, Cindy began to recite.

"Rosa gallica officinalis, Rosa gallica versicolor—"

"What's another name for them?" Nancy asked.

"Here," Keough said, handing O'Donnell another John Courage while continuing to listen to Cindy with one ear.

"Apothecary's Rose," Cindy said, *"Rosa mundi—"*

"Whoa!" Keough said, straightening up.

"What is it?" O'Donnell asked, but Keough was heading back to the kitchen.

"What was that last one?" Keough demanded, startling both Nancy and Cindy.

"Which one?" Cindy asked, wide-eyed.

"Joe?" Nancy asked.

Keough reined himself in and knelt next to Cindy.

"I'm sorry, honey, I didn't mean to scare you, but that last rose you mentioned. What was it?"

"The *Rosa gallica versicolor—*"

O'Donnell came into the room and exchanged glances with Nancy, who shrugged.

"The other name, honey."

"Rosa mundi?"

"That's it." He stood up, then flopped into one of the other kitchen chairs and looked up at Nancy and O'Donnell.

"What is it, Joe?" Nancy asked.

"A rose," he said in triumph, "it's a rose."

"What is?" O'Donnell asked.

He ignored the question.

"Cindy, is there a picture of that rose in your book?"

"Sure, Joey."

She found it and showed it to him.

"That's it," he said again. "I thought it was a person, but it's a rose. And now I remember that the desk officer mentioned a garden."

"Joe," O'Donnell said, "you're losing us."

"It was weeks ago, when I was sending the memo out to the chief of detectives. I went downstairs to drop it into the precinct mail basket and there was a woman at the front desk. She wanted the police to stake out her garden."

"Her garden? Why?"

"She was complaining that something was happening to her 'Rosa Mundi.' I wasn't really giving it all my attention because I was talking to Sal Adamano, but I thought she was talking about a person."

"So?" O'Donnell said.

Keough grabbed Cindy's book and turned it around so Nancy and O'Donnell could see.

"See that rose? It's called *Rosa mundi*. It's supposed to be white, but it's got red stripes. Sometimes the stripes are so wide, the rose is more red than white. See it?''

"I see it," Nancy said.

"I repeat," O'Donnell said, "so?"

"This is the rose I found in—on Mindy Carradine, the first Brooklyn victim. This," he said, tapping the picture with a stiff forefinger, "is the whole reason I started thinking about a second killer."

"Keep walkin' me through this, Joe—"

"Don't you see, Mike?" Keough said. "The Lover, according to what I read in the newspapers these days, bought the roses that he used, and he always used the same red rose. The Brooklyn killer didn't buy his roses; he picked them. That's why they still had thorns on them."

"Oh boy," O'Donnell said.

"He picked them from this woman's garden, and that's what she was complaining about."

"Who was the woman, Joe?" O'Donnell asked. "What was her name?"

"I don't know," Keough said. "Like I said, I wasn't really listening."

"Then who was the desk officer?"

"I was talking to Sal," Keough said, closing his eyes and trying to remember, "and the cop on the desk was . . ." He opened his eyes. "Phil Greco."

"Okay," O'Donnell said, "now you got to hope that Greco remembers who the woman was."

"I've got to talk to him," Keough said, standing up.

"Joe," Nancy said, "dinner's almost ready, and it's getting late."

"When is he working?" O'Donnell asked.

"Wait," Keough said, "Nancy's right. It's getting late, and the day tour has gone home. I'll call tomorrow, talk to someone in the roll-call room and find out when he's working. What's another day going to hurt?"

"As a matter of fact," Nancy said, facing the stove, "dinner's ready right now. If we don't eat, it will be ruined."

"All right, Nancy," Keough said, "all right."

"So we eat," O'Donnell said. "Like you said, what's another day?"

Chapter Forty-three

Tonight was the night.

Kopykat had the girl all picked out. All he had to do was follow her. This would be the first one he killed since the Lover got caught. Ha! Some idol he was. He actually gave up, surrendered, walked right into the arms of the police and gave himself up. The newspapers and television were giving him credit for all the murders. Well, tonight they'd find out that he wasn't the man they should have been afraid of.

Tonight they would find out who the real killer was.

Chapter Forty-four

The next morning, there was a knock on Keough's door. He and O'Donnell had finished all the John Courage, plus the six pack of Budweiser Ice beer that O'Donnell had brought with him. Even after Nancy and Cindy went home to bed, they had gone out to a 7-Eleven to get some more.

His head was pounding, and so was somebody's fist on the door. He staggered out of bed and almost blindly felt his way to the door. When he swung it open, he looked into Nancy's tearful face.

"Oh, Joe."

"What is it?"

She handed him the morning edition of the *Daily News*.

"And I was worried about dinner."

Keough looked at the headline: GIRL KILLED, ROSE FOUND ON BODY.

In smaller print it said, "City asks, What's Going On?"

"Jesus," he said, remembering that both he and O'Donnell had said, "What's another day?"

Nancy had her face pressed to his shoulder and he put one arm around her.

"Take it easy," he said. "It's okay, take it easy."

He was trying to soothe her while his own head was reeling.

Could he have avoided this?

He had just gotten Nancy calmed down enough to go back to her own apartment when the phone rang.

"Keough."

"Did you see it?" O'Donnell asked.

"I saw it. Nancy was just here, all upset. She thinks it's her fault because she made me stay here and eat dinner last night rather than go out to find Phil Greco."

"You couldn't have stopped it last night, you know. It's not her fault, or your fault. He was already in motion."

"I know."

"What are you going to do now?"

"I'm going to read this story, then get dressed and go looking for Phil Greco."

"It happened in the Seven-Oh. Isn't that the precinct that borders the Six-Seven?"

"Yeah."

"He's working that same area. The Six-Seven, the Six-Three—"

"I know, Mike."

"Don't you think you should talk to the detective who caught last night's case?"

"Why? Is he going to listen to me?"

"So what are you going to do, Joe? Bring this one in on your own?"

"I don't know, Mike," Keough said. "I just know that I can't stand by and do nothing. I've got to stop him before he strikes again."

"Think they'll call you?"

"Fuck 'em if they do. I'll talk to you later."

He hung up and sat down to read the story. It actually led off with a quote from Chief of Detectives LaGrange, who said, "There is absolutely no connection between this murder and the murders of the now-incarcerated Lover serial killer. We are convinced that this is the work of a copycat killer."

Asshole.

He read on. The girl was found in a Dumpster behind a bowling alley, lying on top of the garbage. There was a rose on the body, the story said, but Keough knew without being told that it was a rose inserted in the girl's vagina, with the thorns still attached. He didn't know if it was a *Rosa mundi*, but he knew it'd be a picked rose—a fresh-picked rose.

Jesus, if it was a fresh-picked rose, maybe the woman would show up at the Six-Seven again to complain. It had been Keough's experience that people like her, who believed that picking a flower was as big a crime as murder, never gave up.

He dropped the paper on the floor, dressed quickly, and left.

*   *   *

"Orlick?"

"Yes, sir."

"Where are those reports on this new murder?"

"We're processing them now, sir."

"I want them on my desk within the hour. Goddamn it, I don't believe this. We did get the right guy, didn't we, Inspector?"

"I'm convinced, from all of my interrogations, that Anthony Dunston is the Lover serial killer, sir." Privately, he thought, *We* didn't get anybody; Joe Keough got him. "This has got to be somebody else."

"A copycat."

"Yes, sir. Sir?"

"Yes?"

"Perhaps we should call Joe Keough in on this."

"Joe Keough is no longer a member of this department, Inspector."

"I know, sir, but his theory about a second killer seems to be—"

"Did you read the papers, Inspector?"

"I did, sir."

"Did you read my statement?"

"Yes, sir."

"That is the official standing of the department, Inspector. There is no connection between this crime and others. Got it?"

"Yes, sir."

"Then hang up the goddamned phone and get me those reports!"

Orlick hung up but kept his hand on the receiver. He wondered why LaGrange had bothered keeping the Lover Task Force together if he hadn't expected another killing.

How long would it take some smart newspaperman to ask the same question?

When Keough walked out the front door of his building, he was surprised to find Arthur Dolan standing off to one side, waiting. He was slouched against a big flowerpot, and when he saw Keough, he straightened up.

"Sarge, what are you doing here?"

"We've got to talk, Keough."

"About what?"

Dolan looked nervous.

"About a lot of things."

"Look, Sarge, I don't have time. I'm on my way to the Six-Seven. If you want to ride along—"

"No!" Dolan said. "We have to go someplace . . . quiet."

Now the man seemed agitated.

"Sarge, look, I'd like to help you, but—"

"Damn it, Keough." Dolan looked around quickly and then pulled his gun and pointed it at Keough.

"What the hell—" Keough said.

"Quiet, just keep quiet. Hold your arms away from your body. Are you carrying? Yeah, you are. You're not supposed to be carrying, Keough. You're off the job."

Dolan was speaking quickly, nervously.

"What's going on, Artie?"

"I knew it," Dolan said, putting Keough's gun in his pocket. "I knew when you got canned, you wouldn't stop looking for Swann's killer."

"You got that right."

"Sure, what do you have to lose now, huh? Your

job's already gone. Well, mine ain't. I still got my job, and I'm still on the task force, but I coulda been sent to Staten Island, like Slovecky. I could still get sent there, if you keep poking around."

"Artie . . . tell me what you're talking about." But Keough thought he knew. There was a cold rock in the pit of his stomach. He'd thought all along that Slovecky had killed Swann. Had he been wrong?

"You know what I'm talkin' about, Keough."

"You did Swann? You?"

"I know, you thought it was Slovecky. The lieutenant is real loud about what he wants, but me, I'm quiet."

Keough remembered now the day he'd gotten suspended how Dolan complained that he was tired of being a sergeant.

"Aw, Sarge—"

"I didn't mean to," Dolan said, "but he wouldn't give up the file, you know? He had a bug up his ass, like you, about making things right."

"That's our job, Dolan."

"Our job sucks, Keough!" Dolan hissed. "Long hours, short pay, mixing with shit that walks—"

"Artie," Keough said, "we all knew that when we got into it."

"I didn't know," Dolan said, looking around. They were closer to the front door than the street. No one would know what was happening unless they took a good look. Of course, it was early; somebody could still come out of the building to go to work . . . or school. . . .

"Come on," Dolan said, "we've got to go."

"Give yourself up, Artie. Come on—"

"I can't! Damn it, Keough, I'm a cop killer. You know what that means."

"You're also a cop."

"It ain't gonna matter. It ain't," Dolan said, almost in tears.

Keough took a deep breath and said, "Artie, I'm not going with you."

"What?"

"If I let you take me somewhere, you're going to kill me. I'm not going. You're going to have to kill me right here."

Dolan looked around again, fearful that someone would be coming.

"I can't do it here!" he almost whispered.

"Then either give me the gun or get moving."

Dolan stared at him.

"You won't let me go, not now that you know I killed Swann."

"You're right, I won't let you go. I'll come after you, so you're better off giving me the gun and giving up now."

"I can't do that. I can't. I've got to do it this way."

"Then pull the trigger, Artie. Go ahead, pull it now."

If killing Swann was an accident, then Dolan might not be willing to pull the trigger—at least not until he was ready. His plan was to take Keough someplace quiet, and by that time, he might have been ready to do it. By insisting that he do it now, Keough was taking him out of his game plan, and Dolan was starting to look confused.

"Damn it, Keough—"

At that moment, though, the situation changed. The

front door of the building opened and both Nancy and Cindy stepped out.

"Joey!" Cindy shouted happily, waving. She came running over to him. Behind her, Nancy was smiling, then frowning as she saw the two men standing close together.

"Cindy, stop there!" Keough snapped.

Dolan immediately read the situation correctly.

"Hi, Cindy," he called out.

"Hello." The girl had stopped running, but she was only about six feet away. "Are you a friend of Joey's?"

"I am. Are you?"

"Oh yes," Cindy said. "Joey and my mom are boyfriend and girlfriend."

"Is that right?" Dolan asked, looking at Keough.

"Joe?" Nancy called. "Is everything all right?"

"Everything is fine, Nancy," he said, keeping his eye on Dolan. The man was holding the gun closer to his body, so neither Nancy nor Cindy could see it. "Why don't you just take Cindy to school."

"Joe and I have to get going, too," Dolan said, "to someplace quiet."

"Dolan—"

"Joe, you don't want one of these young ladies to get hurt, do you?" Dolan said, low enough for Keough to hear.

Keough had a choice. He could agree to go with Dolan to make sure that Nancy and Cindy weren't hurt, but if he went with him, he was sure to be killed.

"Artie, you can't do this—"

"Watch me," Dolan said, and he moved the gun

away from him so both Nancy and Cindy could see it.

"Is that a gun?" Cindy asked.

"Cindy!" Nancy called, her eyes wide with fear. "Come here!"

"Artie, don't—" Keough said, holding his hand out to stop Nancy from moving.

"Which one do you love more, Joe, the girl or the woman?"

"I love them both, Artie. Which one are you going to shoot? The girl? A little girl, Artie? I thought you said killing Swann was an accident?"

"It was."

"Killing this little girl won't be an accident, will it? Or her mother?"

"That would be your fault."

"That's bullshit, Artie," Keough said. "You've got the gun; you'd be pulling the trigger."

"It doesn't have to be this way," Dolan said. "All you have to do is come with me."

"No, that's not the case anymore," Keough said. "What happens when I go with you and you kill me? When my body is found, Nancy and Cindy will remember this. They'll go to the police. No, Artie, now you've got to kill me, and them, and you're going to have to do it right here."

Keough kept watching Dolan carefully, waiting for just the right split second.

"Shit!" Dolan snapped. "Shit, shit, shit!" On the last one, he closed his eyes tightly, just for a second, and that's when Keough moved.

He grabbed Dolan's gun hand by the wrist and twisted it away from Nancy and Cindy. Nancy moved

Robert J. Randisi

in that moment also, rushing forward, wrapping her arms around Cindy and turning so that her body was between the two men and her little girl.

Dolan struggled, but his heart wasn't in it. When Keough hit him in the stomach, the man sat down on the ground hard. Keough twisted the gun from his hand, then leaned over and took his own gun out of Dolan's pocket. That done, he backed away from the man until he was standing near Nancy and Cindy. He wanted to hug them both, but he kept the gun pointed at Dolan in case the man had a sudden burst of energy.

"Are you all right?" he asked.

"Yes," she said, "are you?"

"I'm fine. Why don't you take Cindy inside and call nine-one-one."

"A—all right." He could see that she was visibly shaken by what had happened, but she was keeping it together.

"Come on, honey."

As they walked back to the front door, Keough heard Cindy ask, "Does this mean I don't have to go to school today?"

Chapter Forty-five

When Keough walked into the Six-Seven, it marked the first time he'd been there since his transfer. He didn't bother stopping at the front desk, but walked directly to the roll-call room.

A radio car had responded pretty quickly to Nancy's 911 call, and luckily Keough knew one of the cops. He had them take Dolan—who did not resist—to the precinct and told them to have the detectives call Det. Keith Clapton, who was working the Swann case, and also Insp. Orlick at the task force.

"Joe, you got to come, too," the cop said.

"I will," Keough said, "but I've got something I have to do first. It can't wait."

"Joe—" the cop called, but Keough was already moving. He felt an urgency to act on his hunch now.

A pretty, heavyset civilian woman named Peggy sat behind a desk and spotted him as soon as he came in.

"Joe Keough! How are you?"

"I'm okay, Peggy."

"Gee, Joe, I'm really sorry about what happened to you."

"Thanks, Peg. Listen, I really need to talk to Phil Greco. When is he scheduled to work again?"

"I'll check." She looked through her paperwork and said, "Not for two days, Joe. He's on his swing."

That meant he might have been in yesterday—but he couldn't think like that. Even if he had spoken to Greco yesterday, there was no guarantee that he would have remembered the woman's name. Like O'Donnell said, he couldn't have stopped last night's killing.

"Peg, do you have Greco's phone number there?"

"Gee, Joe, I'm not supposed to give out addresses or phone numbers . . . and since you're not on the job anymore . . ."

"Never mind."

"Well . . . maybe I could give it to you—"

"No, never mind. I don't want to get you in trouble. Are either Sal Adamano or . . ." He searched his brain for another cop he knew who hung out with Greco.

"Adamano's working today," Peggy said while he was still groping around.

"On the desk?"

"Yup."

"Thanks, Peg."

He'd have known that if he had stopped at the desk first, but no harm done. He left the roll-call office and went to the front desk. Sure enough, there was Adamano.

"Keough! Jesus, did they fuck you over or what? After the collar you made?"

The master of understatement, Sal Adamano.

"They fucked me over."

"You gonna fight it, Joe?"

"I don't know, Sal. I haven't decided."

"Talk to the PBA?"

"Not yet."

"Geez, Joe, you oughta—"

"Sal, do you have Phil Greco's address and phone number?"

"Philly? Sure I do. Whataya want Philly for?"

"I've got to ask him something."

Adamano hesitated now. He knew Keough from the squad, and that was it. Phil Greco, however, was his friend and had been for a long time.

"Uh, Joe, I can't give you Philly's address."

"How about his phone number?"

"Ah, I dunno—"

"How about you call him for me and hand me the phone?"

Adamano smiled and said, "That I can do. Just hang on a minute."

Keough waited while Adamano dialed the phone. He recognized that a lot of the guys down here had worked together for a long time and that he was just another in a long line of detectives moved in and out of the squad. He took no offense at Adamano's refusal to give out his friend's address and number.

"Joe?"

He looked up at Adamano.

"Philly's not home. His old lady says he went fishing."

335

"Would you have any idea where?"

Adamano looked around, then leaned on the desk to get closer to Keough.

"Just between me and you, Joe, if Philly ain't home with his old lady, he ain't fishin'—if you know what I mean."

Keough knew.

"You don't have a number where I can reach him, do you, Sal? It's real important."

"If he's with his *goomada*, I think I can get him, Joe. If he's got somethin' else goin' on the side, it might be hard. Either way, though, he'll be pissed. Is it real important?"

"I wouldn't ask if it wasn't, Sal."

"Okay," Adamano said, "I'll try."

He picked up the phone, dialed another number, spoke briefly, and then handed the phone to Keough.

"What's up, Joe? I'm kinda busy, you know?" Phil Greco said.

"I'm sorry to bother you on your RDO, Phil, but this is important. Some time back, there was a woman here complaining to you about somebody picking her flowers." RDO was a cop's regular day off.

"Wha'?"

"She wanted you to stake out her garden."

"Is that what you called me for?"

"Come on, Phil, this is important."

"Excuse me, Keough, but you ain't even on the job no more. Whataya doin', workin' private?"

"Phil, I just need to know her name."

"I don' know her name, Joe. She's just a crazy broad complains about somebody pickin' her flowers."

336

"Roses, right?"

"Huh?"

"She complains about somebody picking her roses?"

"Yeah, roses. So?"

"Phil, if you don't remember her name, do you remember where she lives?"

"How the hell should I know where she lives. I never sent a car there."

"I saw her at the station house twice. Did she usually come in?"

"No, she usually calls for a car, but we never send one."

If they never sent a car, then there wouldn't be any sort of a log entry for the call.

"Phil, I need some way to find this woman. Got any ideas?"

"Geez, I'm gonna kill Sal for even makin' this call. Look, ask the TS operators. They've talked to her a lot more than I have. Maybe they know."

"Okay, thanks, Phil."

"Hey, no offense, Joe, but fuck off, huh?"

Keough handed Adamano back the phone.

"Is he mad?"

"Naw, he's not mad. Thanks, Sal."

"Sure. Take it easy, Joe. Talk to the PBA, huh? What they done to you sucks."

"Yeah, right."

Keough went over to where the civilian telephone-switchboard operator sat. They weren't really switchboards anymore, just push-button phones to relay calls, but they still call them TS operators.

This particular operator, he knew by sight but not

by name. She was a skinny black girl with a nose that had sort of a bulbous tip. He had heard rumors that she had something going with one of the cops in the precinct.

He stood by while she finished a call, and then she turned to look at him.

"Help ya?"

"Yeah. I'm Joe Keough."

"I know who you are."

"I need to ask you something."

"Go ahead."

"Have you ever gotten a call from a woman about somebody picking her roses?"

"Oh sure, the rose lady."

"You remember her?"

"Who could forget her. I was working one day—I think it was a couple of weeks ago—when she actually came in here to complain. I sent her over to Sergeant Greco. He loved me for that."

"Okay, this is important. Do you remember where she lives?"

"I don't know the address, but I know the corner."

He couldn't believe his luck.

"Where is it?"

"Corner of New York Avenue and Snyder Avenue. I passed that way once to take a look. You can't miss it. She's got roses all over her yard."

"Look, thanks a lot. I really appreciate it."

"Forget it. Bring me a coffee and a doughnut one morning. A little milk, no sugar, and anything gooey."

"You got it."

Keough's heart was racing as he hurried out the front door to his car.

Chapter Forty-six

On the way out, Keough caught two cops he knew and asked them to drive him to within two blocks of New York Avenue and Snyder Avenue. He could have walked it, since the precinct itself was on Snyder Avenue, or driven himself, but since they were there, he hitched a ride.

"What the hell are you doin' in this neighborhood, Keough?" one of them asked.

"I just have to meet somebody."

"Heard you got canned," the other one said. "What are you doin', workin' private?"

"Something like that."

"If you ever need some help, you know, with any of your cases, we could always use some extra cash."

"I'll keep that in mind, guys. Thanks for the ride."

Keough didn't want the sector car to drop him too close to his destination. If the killer lived around there, he didn't want to spook him.

He walked the rest of the two blocks, and before he even reached the house, he could see the garden. When he came within view of the house, he saw what the TS operator meant. The entire yard was filled with flowers, and not only roses. The woman probably had the greenest thumb in creation.

As he started up the front walk, there was a little sign in the dirt that said THE HALL's. He assumed that was the name of the residents.

The house was a large wood-frame structure with white shingles that had long since turned gray. It was not nearly as well kept up as the garden. It also didn't seem to belong in this neighborhood, because to the right and left of it stretched brick two-family homes, and within easy walking distance, more than one set of projects. The neighborhood—and, in fact, the entire precinct—was more than 80 percent black, Haitian and Jamaican, and if Keough remembered correctly, the woman complaining about her plants was white.

He mounted the front porch and pressed the doorbell. After a few moments, he pressed it again, but there was no answer. Rather than accept that she wasn't home, he decided to walk around the house and see if she was outside, possibly tending her flowers.

He walked around the side, which was also lined with plants and flowers. There was a lot of land around the house, making this one of the biggest lots Keough had seen during his stay in Brooklyn. The house and land, in a different neighborhood, would have commanded a lot of money.

When he came to the back of the house, he found the roses. Almost the entire backyard was filled with them, and the scent was thick in the air, almost sickly sweet. Keough enjoyed the fragrance of a rose under normal circumstances, but he supposed too much of anything was too much.

He almost didn't see the woman who was working the garden. She was wearing an outfit that pretty much had all of the colors of the spectrum in it, with mostly greens, yellows, and red, so that she almost blended in with the landscape.

"Mrs. Hall?"

She turned quickly, and he inspected what he could see of her face beneath the straw hat she was wearing.

"What do you want? What are you doing on my property?" she demanded peevishly. Why was it, he wondered, that people who spent most of their time with plants had little or no patience for other people?

"Mrs. Hall, are you the woman who has complained to the precinct about your roses being picked?"

"Not picked, young man," the woman said, "Cut! Snipped! Hacked! It's a sin, I tell you."

"I'm sure it is."

"Are you from the precinct?"

Keough lied—sort of.

"Yes, ma'am, I just came from there."

"Well, it's about time."

She moved away from the bush she'd been pruning, putting down a pair of pruning shears and removing heavy gloves from her hands.

"Are you going to stake out my garden?" she asked as she approached him.

341

Robert J. Randisi

She could have been in her sixties or seventies; he
couldn't be sure. Her face was a mass of wrinkles and
loose skin hung around her neck. She had deep lines
running from her top lip up to her nose.

"Well, first, ma'am, I'd like you to show me where
the roses have been cut from."

"Come this way, then, young man." She started
walking, with him trailing behind. She was still talking, and he was only catching snatches of what she
said. "... can't believe it ... about time ... never
happened on *Kojak*. . . ."

She led him to a row of rosebushes that sat against
a wooden fence. The fence was not high, and the roses
were easily accessible to anyone walking by on the
sidewalk. He was surprised she didn't complain even
more than she did.

"I would think you'd be losing a lot more roses
than you are, Mrs. Hall. Don't people just pick them
as they go by?"

"I don't mind people picking them, Detective. You
are a detective, aren't you?"

"Uh, yes."

"If a young man walking by wants to pick one of
my roses to give to his girlfriend, I don't mind that so
much. It is to be expected. But this," she said, pointing, "this is a sin."

Keough looked at the bush she was pointing to and
it was covered with the striped roses, one of which he
had seen on Mindy Carradine's body.

"*Rosa mundi*," he said.

She whirled on him in surprise.

"You know roses?"

"I know this one."

He moved closer so he could take a better look. Some of the roses had wider stripes than others, and they were mostly a dark pink rather than red. It had been dark that night when he saw it on—in—Mindy Carradine.

"See there?" she said, moving closer to him. She smelled of some sort of flowered scent—unless it was just the smell of all the flowers sticking to her. "Right there."

She was pointing to a stem from which a rose had obviously been cut, not picked. The cut had left a clean break, while a picked flower would have left behind a ragged end.

"I see."

He put his hand out to touch it and promptly jabbed himself with a thorn.

"Ouch!"

"Careful," she said. "That's my only consolation, you know."

"What is?"

"The animal who cut my roses probably has his fingers all cut up."

"He's taken others?"

"Oh my, yes."

"This is important, Mrs. Hall. How many roses has he taken?"

"That's easy," she said, "Four—the most recent one being yesterday. In fact, I was going to go to the precinct today as soon as I finished my pruning."

"Mrs. Hall, when do these roses bloom?"

"This particular one blooms only once, in the early summer, but they stay in bloom for some time."

She was answering all his questions perfectly. She

had lost one rose for every dead girl, and the *Rosa mundi* that had been on Mindy Carradine would have bloomed early enough to come from here.

"Were all the roses from this bush?"

"No, there were two of these taken—the last one yesterday—and two from my Mr. Lincoln bush down there."

The Lincoln was just a bit farther down, and the roses were blood-red. While the *Rosa mundi* were on a compact bush, the Lincoln bush was vigorous with red stems and dark green foliage. Keough wondered why the killer would pick two of one and two of the other rather than taking them from the same bush.

It didn't seem likely now that the killer would be back for some time to pick another. Keough figured that if he intended to stake out Mrs. Hall's garden, he'd need help to do it.

"Well, Mrs. Hall, I've seen what I have to see."

"Are you leaving?"

"Yes, but I'll be back. Can you tell me approximately when the culprit picks—"

"Cuts!"

"Cuts your roses?"

"All hours," she said. "At night, and in broad daylight."

"I see. Well, I'll have to start staking out the garden. . . ." He was looking around for a likely place to watch from, either from a car or someplace inside the yard.

"Well, it's about time that Dexter boy got what's coming to him."

Keough froze.

"Dexter boy?"

"Of course."

"Mrs. Hall . . . you know who's been picking—uh, cutting—your flowers?"

"Of course I do, young man. I've seen him."

Keough's heart began to race.

"I just couldn't prove it, because it's my word against his. I see that on *Law and Order*. I figured you were going to have to stake out the garden and catch him in the act."

"Well, that is one way to do it, ma'am. Um, do you know where he lives?"

"Well, of course I do. Right over there."

She pointed right across the street at a run-down one-family house that was set back from the street. Her address was a Snyder Avenue address, while this little house had a New York Avenue address.

"He can see my garden right from his window. That front one on the right, see?"

Jesus, she was handing him the killer's name, address, and even pointing out his window.

"I see it. Ma'am, can you tell me what the boy looks like?"

"Well, he doesn't look like a boy, I can tell you."

"Is he black or white?"

"He's white, about nineteen years old, but he is very big."

"How big?"

"A giant, actually. He is probably six and a half feet tall."

That would explain the damage to the dead girls' necks.

"He's kind of funny-looking, you know?"

"Funny-looking how?"

"Well . . . I don't like to say things like this, but he sort of looks like his mother and father might have been . . . you know, related."

"You mean he looks . . . Mongoloid?"

"More like . . . retarded. I know his mind isn't as old as he is."

"So then he is retarded?"

"I believe so, but he does have a job."

"What does he do?"

"He delivers groceries for the Met Foods on Nostrand Avenue. The one near Brooklyn Avenue."

"Where does he deliver to?"

"Oh, all over, and he does it on a bicycle."

That would explain why his victims came from different precincts around Brooklyn. He could have seen them while delivering groceries and picked them out.

"That lad rides that bike all over Brooklyn. I've seen him."

"Just a few more questions, Mrs. Hall. Does he live alone?"

"No, he lives with his mother. What a slut! She brings men home from bars." She leaned closer to Keough and said, "Just between you and me, I think she abused the boy when he was young."

"Have they lived there long?"

"Long as I can remember."

While she was talking to him, she was fingering some of the petals, pruning some of the bushes by hand, and suddenly she stopped.

"That's odd."

"What is?"

"Look here. This is a Ferdinand Pichard."

Keough looked at the rose in question and at first

346

thought it was red, but it was actually a combination of red and pink stripes.

"What about it?"

"Look closer."

He looked where she was pointing and saw that a stem had been cut.

"He's taken another one."

Jesus, Keough thought, he's going to hit again so soon.

"Mrs. Hall, do you know if either Dexter or his mother are home?"

"Dexter is their last name," she corrected him, "and I haven't seen either of them today."

"Are you sure this rose was here yesterday?"

"Young man, I tend to my roses every day. I know that rose was not missing yesterday. In fact, I could swear that it was here earlier this morning." She whirled on him and asked, "He's gone too far, two in as many days, don't you think?"

"Yes, ma'am, I do. I'm going to go right over there and talk to him about it."

"Well, it's about time somebody did something."

"What's the boy's name, ma'am?"

"Arnold," she said. "Arnold Dexter. His mother's name is Gloria—although she calls herself 'Glory.' Imagine a grown woman calling herself that?"

"Thank you for your time, ma'am."

"That's all right. It's just nice to know something is going to be done."

Keough nodded and left her standing by her rose-bushes. He was able to go around the other side of the house this time, to the front gate and out. When he was out of sight of Mrs. Hall, he pulled up his pants leg and removed a small automatic from his ankle hol-ster. He'd turned in his .38 with his shield, and this was his off-duty gun. He should have turned it in, as well, but he decided to wait until they came to get it. It was small enough to fit in his jacket pocket, and that's where he put it.

With the gun comfortably within reach, he started across the street to the Dexter house.

Chapter Forty-seven

Aware that Mrs. Hall was watching, Keough approached the house as nonchalantly as he could. He decided to play it straight and go right to the front door. Maybe the mother would be home and he could talk to her. If the boy, Arnold, was home, there was no way he could arrest him. He had no proof, and he wasn't a cop anymore. All he really wanted to do was take a look at him. He didn't know what he would do after that. It certainly would have helped if he'd been able to get the task force on the phone again—not that he'd tried that hard. He probably could have made some calls, found out if the task force was still in existence, and then found out the new number, but at the time he had just figured, Fuck them.

He could have simply left and tried to talk to someone in the department about this Arnold Dexter, but the fact that the boy had cut another rose so soon had him worried.

He mounted the rickety porch and looked for a doorbell. There was a hole where the bell button should have been. He opened the screen door then and knocked on the peeling paint of the wooden door. He waited several moments, listening for movement inside. When there was none, he knocked again. Still no answer.

He figured he'd walk around the house and look in the windows, but before doing that, he decided to turn the doorknob once, just to try it. He turned it, and kept turning it, and the door opened. Considering the bad neighborhood, this surprised him.

He took the gun out of his pocket, pushed the door open all the way, and entered the house.

The air inside was musty, as if the windows hadn't been open for years. Stale odors assailed his nose: beer, booze, food, sweat, and sex. He was in a hallway and stopped to listen. He thought he heard a voice.

He followed the hallway along, past a kitchen and a bedroom, both of which were empty. These rooms were on his left. One look inside the bedroom told him it was a woman's. The sheets on the bed were soiled and wrinkled, there was flowered wallpaper— and there was a pair of panties on the floor. On his right was another bedroom, this obviously belonging to a male. The bed was neatly made, the walls were blue, covered with sports and girlie pictures.

He stopped suddenly as he heard a male voice, talking softly, an almost singsong quality to it. It was coming from just ahead. He moved along the hallway and saw a sofa, a coffee table . . . and a woman's legs.

Holding the gun ready, he stepped into the living room.

"See? This was my first one, Mama. I did this, not him. See? They wrote about me, even if they didn't know it."

The woman was lying on the floor, naked. She was on her back, her neck at an unnatural angle. Between her legs, protruding from her vagina, was Mrs. Hall's Ferdinand Pichard.

Sitting on the floor, cross-legged, was a large young man who could only be Arnold Dexter. Keough could see over the boy's shoulder that he had a photo album. It seemed to be filled with newspaper clippings. He was talking to his mother very gently, turning the pages. What was eerie and gave Keough the chills was that the woman's eyes were open and he was actually holding the album, showing it to her as if she could see.

"See here? That was my second one. They all thought the Lover was killing girls in Brooklyn, but that was me."

Jesus, Keough thought, he's confessing.

"And see here . . ."

"Arnold."

". . . on this page? This was my third. She was pretty, Mama. . . ."

"Arnold!" Keough said louder.

The boy stopped what he was doing. His shoulders hunched, and then he turned his head quickly to look at Keough. The detective could see what Mrs. Hall had meant about the boy's appearance. There was a great ridge of forehead overhanging two deep-set eyes,

351

and his jaw was like an anvil. His cheekbones seemed swollen to the point of bursting through his skin.

"Who are you? What do you want?" he demanded. Now his voice was deep, menacing, not the little boy's voice he'd been using to talk to his mother.

"I just want to talk, Arnold."

"I can't talk. I'm reading to Mother."

"Arnold . . . your mother is dead."

"Dead?" Arnold turned and looked at his mother, and then suddenly he skittered away from her, the album falling to the floor. It fell open and Keough could see one of the Lover headlines.

Arnold Dexter stopped when his back banged into the wall, and he stared at his mother's body. He was wearing jeans and a torn T-shirt. His body was huge, brutish rather than muscle-bound.

"Did you kill her, Arnold?"

Arnold looked at Keough, then at his mother again, and then Keough. His menacing demeanor was gone, and once again he was a little boy.

"Yes, I killed her."

"Why?"

"She . . . she came home without a man, and she . . . she wanted me to do things," he complained. "I didn't want to . . . to do those things no more. She used to make me do them all the time." He looked at Keough, his eyes pleading. "It's not right for a son to do that with his mother, is it?"

"No, Arnold," Keough said, feeling sick to his stomach, "it isn't."

"So . . . so I told her no and she . . . she slapped me."

"And you killed her?"

"No. First . . . first I wanted to show her what I did, so I . . . I told her about the girls."

"The girls you killed here in Brooklyn?"

"Yes," he said, nodding. "Yes. I told her, but she . . . she didn't believe me." He looked at Keough, hurt now. "She said I was crazy! She shouldn't have oughta said that."

"No, Arnold, she shouldn't."

"I wanted to show her my scrapbook, but she wouldn't look at it. First . . . first I just put in clipping of his murders."

"The Lover."

The boy nodded.

"He was great—he was better than a . . . a baseball player. He was my idol."

"So you started copying him."

"You ever watch Krazy Kat?"

"What?"

Arnold looked at Keough, his mouth agape in a grin, revealing gaps and yellow teeth.

"Krazy Kat? She used to get hit with a brick. You ever see it?"

"Uh, yeah, I saw it years ago." Keough also remembered it as a comic strip.

"They show reruns on TV. I like Krazy Kat, so I started my own part of the scrapbook. See?"

He crawled across the floor and began to turn pages of the book. When he got to the page he wanted, he turned the book around to show Keough. He'd written on the black page with a white marker the word *Kopykat*.

"That's me."

"Kopykat," Keough said.

Robert J. Randisi

"That's my part of the book. I took my clippings and put them in there." He turned the pages so Keough could see the clippings.

"Arnold . . . when did you kill your mother?"

The boy frowned and stuck out his lower lip.

"I don't wanna talk about that."

"Come on, Arnold. I need to know."

Suddenly, a crafty look came into Arnold's eyes and he wasn't a little boy anymore.

"Are you a policeman?"

"Yes, I am."

"The Lover gave up to the police," Arnold said, "but not me. I'm gonna be better than he was."

"Arnold, when did you kill your mother?"

"I killed her this morning!" he shouted suddenly, spraying spittle on his scrapbook. "She wouldn't listen, so I . . . I grabbed her by the neck and she . . . she broke."

"What about the rose?"

Arnold looked at his mother and then reached out and touched the rose. The petals were flush with the woman's vagina, the entire stem pushed up inside of her.

"A rose for Mama," he said, stroking it. "The other girls got roses, so why not Mama?"

Sure, Keough thought, why not?

He looked around the room for a phone and saw it on a table by the window. Slowly, while Arnold was engrossed with his mother, he moved to it and picked up the receiver. He dialed 911 left-handed, holding the gun in his right hand, and took his eyes off Arnold only long enough to pick out the numbers on the old rotary phone.

That was all Arnold needed.

Suddenly, the huge body was hurtling toward Keough and Arnold was screaming something unintelligible. Keough turned, trying to bring the gun up, but Arnold hit him right in the midsection with a tackle that sent both of them through the window.

Glass showered down on them as they fell to the porch outside. Keough managed to hang on to the gun, but there was no breath in his body. It was hard to think or move when you couldn't take a breath. It's like everything in your body stops until you can get another breath, only the breath won't come. In addition, he couldn't see that well, although he had no idea that a shard of glass had cut his forehead and blood was streaming into his eyes.

Arnold got to his feet and looked down at Keough.

"You wanna take me to jail. I can't go to jail. I'm better than him!"

Keough struggled to say something, to move, but he was helpless as Arnold bent over and took hold of him. The boy's strength was immense and he lifted Keough over his head and threw him off the porch.

Keough felt himself twirling through the air, and as he hit the ground, the gun was jarred from his grasp. It kept going as he hit the lawn and landed some twenty feet away from him.

The odd thing was that landing on the lawn seemed to jar some air into his lungs, and suddenly he could breathe again. He took a shuddering breath and fought to get to his feet. He saw Arnold come down the steps from the porch and start across the lawn toward him.

"Arn—Arn—Arn—" was all he could say, holding his arms out to try to keep the giant at bay.

"I have to kill you, too," Arnold said to him. "You're a bad man. You came to fuck my mother, didn't you? And to arrest me?"

"Arnold—" Keough finally managed to squeeze the name out. "Don't—"

"No," Arnold said, shaking his head, "I have to."

Keough, who was only halfway to his feet, anyway, sank back onto the lawn in a seated position. As Arnold advanced on him, he put his hands down on either side of him and suddenly lashed out with both feet. One foot caught the boy on his huge left thigh, doing no damage, but the other caught his right knee. Arnold shouted in pain and reached down to grasp the knee.

Keough started to skitter back on his butt, much the way Arnold had done inside the house. When he was out of reach, he turned and started looking for the gun. He was on his hands and knees, feeling around the unkempt lawn for the gun, when suddenly he was grabbed from behind and lifted into the air.

Arnold was shouting something in Keough's ear, squeezing Keough around the midsection. Once again, the detective couldn't breathe.

"You hurt me!" he heard the giant shout, but then he couldn't hear anymore. Arnold squeezed tighter and tighter and Keough thought he felt something pop, like a rib.

Arnold was going to kill him and there was nothing he could do about it. He felt the way he had when Slovecky had been squeezing his neck. Everything started to go fuzzy around the edges, and there was a loud roaring in his ears. . . . No, not a roaring, a ringing . . . more like a siren . . . lots of sirens.

Suddenly, he was on the grass, gasping for breath, clutching at the pain that was lancing through his ribs.

"Just hold it right there!" he heard somebody shout.

Abruptly, it became quiet, and for a moment he thought he had lost his hearing. He looked up and saw four uniformed police officers standing with their revolvers pointed. He turned his head and saw Arnold standing above him, staring at the officers.

No, he thought, but the word wouldn't come out. He wanted Arnold alive; he wanted him to confess to the Brooklyn killings.

"Go away!" he heard Arnold shout. "Go away or I'll kill all of you."

"Just stay there, fella," an officer called. "Lie down on the grass with your hands behind your back."

"... kill you all," Keough heard. His hearing seemed to be coming and going.

In fact, he must have gone deaf there for a minute, because as the officers started to fire their guns, he couldn't even hear the shots.

Suddenly, a great weight fell on him . . . as did total darkness. . . .

Chapter Forty-eight

The kite soared and dove at the whim of the winds. All Keough could do was work the string out so the kite would get high enough that there was no danger of it crashing back down. Flying it here by the highway assured the fliers that there would be no trees to snag either the kites or the strings.

"Okay," he said to Cindy, "it's high enough now for you to hold it."

"Oh good, give it to me," she said, slapping her hands together.

"Please?" Nancy said firmly.

"Please," Cindy said.

She snatched the spool of string from Keough's hand and said, "Mommy, look, I'm flyin' it."

"Yes, you are, honey."

Keough stood next to Nancy and watched Cindy happily hold the string. He was happy to do it. Even the light tugging of the kite made his broken rib hurt. He turned his head and looked at Nancy's profile. This was the first time he had ever taken anyone with him to fly a kite. He liked it.

"Joe, are you all right?"

He looked at her and said, "I'm fine."

He had the one cracked rib from having the killer fall on him, and he had a bandage over a scalp wound that had not required stitches.

"It's all over, isn't it?" she asked.

"It's over . . . in a way."

"What's that mean?"

"Well, both killers are caught, and Dolan will go down for Swann's murder."

"Will he?"

He nodded.

"We've got a witness that puts him at the house that night."

"Who?"

"Slovecky. Apparently he was going to go to the house to talk to Swann, but when he got there, he saw Dolan leaving. Something told him not to go to the house then."

"So he knew all along that Dolan killed Swann?"

"Maybe," Keough said. "He won't admit that. That would mean he kept evidence to himself, and he's in enough trouble."

It was funny, but Keough felt sorry for Dolan. The man had expected to do his job quietly at the task force and then, when they caught the killer, follow Slovecky up the ladder. Maybe the man hadn't even known how badly he wanted it until it looked like Swann was going to ruin it for everyone. He went to talk to Swann and accidently killed him. He wondered, If Dolan hadn't been coming out of the house when Slovecky got there, would the same thing have happened to Slovecky?

And what about Swann? He was the one to feel sorry for. All he ever wanted to be was a real detective.

"And the Lover and his, uh—" Nancy said.

"Copycat," Keough said. "We found a scrapbook inside the house. Apparently, this kid idolized the Lover, tried to emulate him, and then got upset when the man gave himself up. After that, he was going to be better than his idol."

"And you caught him because he was picking roses instead of buying them," she said, shaking her head.

"That's the way a lot of police work gets done, Nancy," Keough said. "Accidents, coincidences, chance."

"Will you get your job back?" she asked.

"If I want it."

"Why wouldn't you?"

He smiled at her.

"I just have to think it over."

"Come on," she said, "tell me what happened."

He told her then what was really bothering him, that the chief of detectives had called him and offered him his job back if he kept his mouth shut about the Brooklyn killer. LaGrange said that the boy—if he survived the four bullets that had been put in him—would go up for his mother's murder. All of the rose killings would continue to be attributed to the Lover.

"And the department gets away clean," Keough said. "Nobody ever finds out how badly everybody fucked up."

"Everybody except you," Nancy said.

"That's what LaGrange said."

"He was being nice to you?"

"No," Keough said, "he was trying to buy me."

"How?"

"He called me Sergeant."

"But you're not a sergeant."

He smiled at her and said, "I know."

"Oh," she said, understanding that the chief of detectives had been trying to bribe him.

"What are you going to do?"

"I like being a cop, Nancy, but I don't want the job under those conditions. I have one other option."

"What's that?"

"I can tell everything to Mike O'Donnell so he could put all of it into his book. When it's published, everybody will know the truth. Oh, the department would deny it all, but lots of people believe what they read—especially when it's in a book."

"If you do that," she said, touching him lightly, "you won't ever be able to be a cop again."

"Well," he said, smiling at her, "not here. . . ."

FOUR ORIGINAL NOVELLAS BY

BENTLEY LITTLE
DOUGLAS CLEGG
CHRISTOPHER GOLDEN
TOM PICCIRILLI

FOUR DARK NIGHTS

The most horrifying things take place at night, when the moon rises and darkness descends, when fear takes control and terror grips the heart. The four original novellas in this hardcover collection each take place during one chilling night, a night of shadows, a night of mystery—a night of horror. Each is a blood-curdling vision of what waits in the darkness, told by one of horror's modern masters. But as the sun sets and night falls, prepare yourself. Dawn will be a long time coming, and you may not live to see it!

- -

Elizabeth Massie

Sineater

According to legend, the sineater is a dark and mysterious figure of the night, condemned to live alone in the woods, who devours food from the chests of the dead to absorb their sins into his own soul. To look upon the face of the sineater is to see the face of all the evil he has eaten. But in a small Virginia town, the order is broken. With the violated taboo comes a rash of horrifying events. But does the evil emanate from the sineater...or from an even darker force?

___4407-2 $5.99 US/$6.99 CAN

HUNGRY EYES

BARRY HOFFMAN

The eyes are always watching. She can feel them as she huddles there, naked, vulnerable, in an iron cage in a twisted man's basement. Someday she will be the one with the power, the need to close the eyes. And she'll close them all.

___4449-8 $4.99 US/$5.99 CAN

Dorchester Publishing Co., Inc.
P.O. Box 6640
Wayne, PA 19087-8640

Please add $1.75 for shipping and handling for the first book and $.50 for each book thereafter. NY, NYC, and PA residents, please add appropriate sales tax. No cash, stamps, or C.O.D.s. All orders shipped within 6 weeks via postal service book rate. Canadian orders require $2.00 extra postage and must be paid in U.S. dollars through a U.S. banking facility.

Name_____
Address_____
City_____ State_____ Zip_____
I have enclosed $_____ in payment for the checked book(s).
Payment <u>must</u> accompany all orders. ❏ Please send a free catalog.

BRASS

ROBERT J. CONLEY

The ancient Cherokees know him as *Untsaiyi,* or Brass,
because of his metallic skin. He is one of the old ones, the
original beings who lived long before man walked the earth.
And he will live forever. He cares nothing for humans,
though he can take their form—or virtually any form—at
will. For untold centuries the world has been free of his
deadly games, but now Brass is back among us and no one
who sees him will ever be the same . . . if they survive at all.

___4505-2 $5.50 US/$6.50 CAN

B|TE RICHARD LAYMON

"No one writes like Laymon, and you're going to have a good time with anything he writes."
—Dean Koontz

It's almost midnight. Cat's on the bed, facedown and naked. She's Sam's former girlfriend, the only woman he's ever loved. Sam's in the closet, with a hammer in one hand and a wooden stake in the other. Together they wait as the clock ticks down because . . . the vampire is coming. When Cat first appears at Sam's door he can't believe his eyes. He hasn't seen her in ten years, but he's never forgotten her. Not for a second. But before this night is through, Sam will enter a nightmare of blood and fear that he'll never be able to forget—no matter how hard he tries.

"Laymon is one of the best writers in the genre today."
—Cemetery Dance

___4550-8 $5.50 US/$6.50 CAN
Dorchester Publishing Co., Inc.
P.O. Box 6640
Wayne, PA 19087-8640

Please add $1.75 for shipping and handling for the first book and $.50 for each book thereafter. NY, NYC, and PA residents, please add appropriate sales tax. No cash, stamps, or C.O.D.s. All orders shipped within 6 weeks via postal service book rate. Canadian orders require $2.00 extra postage and must be paid in U.S. dollars through a U.S. banking facility.

Name_____
Address_____
City_____State_____Zip_____
I have enclosed $_____ in payment for the checked book(s).
Payment <u>must</u> accompany all orders. ☐ Please send a free catalog.
CHECK OUT OUR WEBSITE! www.dorchesterpub.com

DOUGLAS

HALLOWEEN
THE
MAN
CLEGG

The New England coastal town of Stonehaven has a history of nightmares—and dark secrets. When Stony Crawford becomes a pawn in a game of horror and darkness, he finds that he alone holds the key to the mystery of Stonehaven, and to the power of the unspeakable creature trapped within a summer mansion.

___4439-0 $5.50 US/$6.50 CAN

Dorchester Publishing Co., Inc.
P.O. Box 6640
Wayne, PA 19087-8640

Please add $1.75 for shipping and handling for the first book and $.50 for each book thereafter. NY, NYC, and PA residents, please add appropriate sales tax. No cash, stamps, or C.O.D.s. All orders shipped within 6 weeks via postal service book rate. Canadian orders require $2.00 extra postage and must be paid in U.S. dollars through a U.S. banking facility.

Name_____
Address_____
City_____State_____Zip_____
I have enclosed $_____ in payment for the checked book(s).
Payment <u>must</u> accompany all orders. ❑ Please send a free catalog.
      CHECK OUT OUR WEBSITE! www.dorchesterpub.com